Parties & Potions

have you read all of the

Magic in Manhattan

novels?

Bras & Broomsticks

Frogs & French Kisses

Spells & Sleeping Bags

Parties & Potions

Parties & Potions

sarah
mlynowski

EMBER

 Published in the United States by Ember, an imprint of Random House Children's Books, a division of Random House, Inc., New York. Originally published in hardcover in the United States by Delacorte Press, an imprint of Random House Children's Books, New York, in 2007.

Ember and the E colophon are registered trademarks of Random House, Inc.

randomhouse.com/teens

Educators and librarians, for a variety of teaching tools, visit us at randomhouse.com/teachers

The Library of Congress has cataloged the hardcover edition of this work as follows:
Parties & potions / Sarah Mlynowski. — 1st ed.
p. cm.
Summary: High school sophomore Rachel and her younger sister Miri, both witches, are introduced to a wider community of witches while grappling with the problem of whether or not to reveal their powers to their school friends, father, and step-mother.
ISBN 978-0-385-73645-9 (hc) — ISBN 978-0-385-90610-4 (lib. bdg.) —
ISBN 978-0-375-89206-6 (ebook) — ISBN 978-0-385-73646-6 (trade)
[1. Witches—Fiction. 2. Magic—Fiction. 3. Dating (Social customs)—Fiction. 4. High schools—Fiction. 5. Schools—Fiction. 6. New York (N.Y.)—Fiction. 7. Humorous stories.]
I. Title. II. Title: Parties and potions.
PZ7.M7135Par2008
[Fic]—dc22
2008010020

RL: 5.0

Printed in the United States of America

12 11 10 9 8 7 6 5 4

First Ember Edition 2012

For Wendy Loggia,
the editor with the magic touch

Acknowledgments

Thanks to the power of a gazillion to:

Laura Dail, my superstar agent, and Tamar Rydzinski, the queen of foreign rights.

All the hardworking Random House Children's Books people: Wendy Loggia, Beverly Horowitz, Elizabeth Mackey, Chip Gibson, Joan DeMayo, Rachel Feld, Kenny Holcomb, Wendy Louie, Tamar Schwartz, Tim Terhune, Krista Vitola, Adrienne Waintraub, Isabel Warren-Lynch, and Jennifer Black.

Robin Zingone, who makes Rachel look adorable every time.

Aviva Mlynowski, my Miri—love you, Squirt!

To my four reader goddesses, I would be lost without you. Seriously. Lost and unemployed. Thank you thank you thank you thank you to:

Lauren Myracle, the goddess of motivation (she gave up her weekend to help me!),

E. Lockhart, the goddess of language (and telling me when I can do better),

Jess Braun, the goddess of honest reactions (yup, she made me take out a line by telling me it made her puke),

And my mom, Elissa Ambrose, the goddess of always-knowing-what-I-meant-to-say (and reading every book chapter by chapter!).

Also love and thanks to my family and friends: Larry Mlynowski, Louisa Weiss, John and Vickie Swidler, Robert Ambrose, Jen Dalven, Gary Swidler, Darren Swidler, Shari Endleman, Heather Endleman, Lori Finkelstein, Gary Mitchell, Leslie Margolis, Ally Carter, Bennett Madison, Alison Pace, Lynda Curnyn, Farrin Jacobs, Kristin Harmel, David Levithan, Bonnie Altro, Robin Glube, Jess Davidman, Avery Carmichael, and Renee and Jeremy Cammie (who should have been listed last time!), and BOB.

And Todd Swidler, my amazing husband! I love you!

Parties & Potions

1 So Many Outfits . . . Only One First Day

Do I like red?

I pirouette before the mirror. Yes, the red shirt could work. Red makes my hair look super-glossy and glamorous and goes great with my favorite jeans.

If I do say so myself.

The shirt has a scooped neckline and adorable bubble sleeves. It's my back-to-school top for the big, BIG day tomorrow—the very first day of sophomore year! My BFF, Tammy, and I went shopping last week for the occasion. I know I could have just zapped something up, but the first rule of witchcraft is that everything comes from something. I didn't want to accidentally shoplift a new shirt from Bloomingdale's.

I like the red. It works with my complexion. But I don't know if it *truly* shows off my fabulous tan. Hmm. I touch the material grazing my collarbone and chant:

"Like new becomes old,
Like day becomes night,
Pretty back-to-school top,
Please become white!"

I've found that adding "please" to my spells really helps. The Powers That Be seem to appreciate it when I'm polite.

A chill spreads through the room, sending goose bumps down my back, and then—zap!—the spell takes effect. The red of my top quickly drains from the material, which turns fuchsia, dark pink, pale pink, and finally as white as Liquid Paper.

Now we're talking! Yes. It should be white. White shows off my awesome summer tan.

My awesome *fake* summer tan. Obviously. It's not like I have a pool in downtown Manhattan to lounge by, and anyway it's been way too muggy and humid in this city to stay outside for more than twenty seconds, so how could I get naturally sun-kissed? Unfortunately, my camp tan is long gone. But is my fake tan a spray-on? Nope. Is it from one of those tanning booths that could pass for a medieval torture chamber? Again, nope.

How did I get it, then? Why, I call it the Perfect Golden Tan That Makes Me Look Like I Live in California spell. (Patent pending.)

I made it up last week and it worked immediately. True, at first I looked like I had a rash, or perhaps a severe case of the measles, but by the following afternoon, the color had settled into a golden glow. A golden glow that makes me look like a native San Franciscan. Or is it Francistite? Francissian?

Anyway, I am very in control of my powers these days.

Ever since Miri taught me megel exercises (you control the flow of your raw will by lifting and lowering inanimate objects such as books and pillows. Not glasses. Don't try glasses. Trust me on this), my magic muscles have gotten much stronger.

I finally got my very own copy of A^2 (otherwise known as *The Authorized and Absolute Reference Handbook to Astonishing Spells, Astounding Potions, and History of Witchcraft Since the Beginning of Time*), but since I'm so good at making up my own spells, it's not like I need it. If you know how to cook, do you need a recipe? I think not.

Yes, my top has to be white. Everyone knows white is the best color to wear when tanned. Tomorrow, when I glide into JFK High School, they will say, "Who is that perfectly bronzed girl? Could that be Rachel Weinstein?" And "Did you hear? She's going out with the wonderful and gorgeous A-lister Raf Kosravi! Isn't she amazing?"

Yes, it's going to be a great year. The best year ever. I'm calling it *The Sophomore Spectacular*! My very own Broadway show. And tomorrow is opening day.

Nothing can go wrong, because:

I am healthily tan, I have a boyfriend, and I have a groovalicious new haircut with lots of fabo layers. And I am a witch.

Yup, I'm a witch. Obviously. How else would I be able to change the color of my shirt over and over again? My mom and sister are witches too. We're chanting, broom-riding, love-spell-casting magic machines. Well, Miri and I are magic machines. Mom is a mostly nonpracticing witch.

Luckily, I did not need a love spell to make Raf fall in love with me. Nope, he loves me all on his own. Not that he's said those three magic words. But he will eventually. Am I not lovable? I think I'm pretty lovable. He's definitely lovable.

He's my honey-bunny.

Okay, I haven't actually called him that to his face. But I am auditioning potential terms of endearment in my head. Other options are sweet pea and shmoopie.

Shmoopster?

Just shmoo?

Even without the names, we make everyone sick. Not throwing-up sick, but yay-for-them sick. I think. Since we became a couple at camp, we've spent practically every day together. We hung in the park. We watched TV. We shopped. (He bought this awesome-looking brown waffle shirt that brings out his brown eyes, olive skin, and broad shoulders, and every time he wears it, I tell him how hot he is.) We kissed. (There was a lot of kissing. A ginormous amount of kissing. So much kissing I had to buy an extra-strength Chap Stick. But it tasted like wax paper, so I switched to extra-shiny cherry lip gloss. Yum. The problem is I love it so much I keep licking it off. Which just increases the chappedness of my lips. It's a vicious cycle.)

As I was saying, I don't need to use spells around Raf. Okay, you got me; that's a bit of a lie. Last week I poofed up fresh breath after gorging on too many pieces of garlic bread. I didn't want him to have to hold his nose while playing tongue gymnastics. But that's it. I would never cast a love spell on him. Okay, that's another lie. When Miri first got her powers, we zapped him with one. (Miri, my two-years-younger sister, discovered she was a witch before I found out that I was.

How unfair is that?) But we accidentally cast the spell on Raf's older brother, Will, instead, so no harm done. Well, not too much. Will and I dated but broke up at the prom when I realized he was really truly in love with my friend Kat.

Now, what was I doing? Oh, right. White!

I pretend that my room is a catwalk and sashay away from the mirror and then back toward it. Here's the prob: wearing white might be mega-obvious, since everyone *knows* that you wear white when you're trying to show off a tan. Also, for some reason, white is making my head look big. Do I have a big head? Is having a big head bad? Or does it mean I'm smarter?

Perhaps I should try blue. Blue looks good on me. It brings out my brown eyes. Yes! I must bring out my eyes! I clear my throat and say:

"Like night becomes day,
Like calm seas become wavy,
Pretty back-to-school top,
Please become navy!"

Cold! Zap! Poof!

Interesting. I twist for a side view. Not bad. But is it better than red? I mean, I could always wear blue eye shadow. Maybe my shirt *should* be red. Or white. Or maybe something shimmery? Gold?

"Like night becomes day,
Like new becomes old,
Pretty back-to-school top,
Please become gold!"

The top starts pulsating with color. It's yellow! It's red! It's blue! It's a rainbow of cloth!

"Rachel!" Miri bellows, throwing my door open and wagging her finger at me in the mirror. "Enough! You've been at it for forty-five minutes! Just choose a stupid color, and get ready for tonight!"

Ah. The one annoying part of the day. My thirteen-year-old sister is insisting that instead of going out with sweet shmoopie tonight, I accompany her to some weirdo Full Moon dinner. "I'm almost ready," I say. "But I want to lay out the perfect outfit for tomorrow. It's so hard! Do you think I have a big head?"

She laughs. "You? Full of yourself? Never!"

I cluck my tongue. "I mean, does my head look *physically* big?"

She plops down cross-legged on my pink carpet. It used to be orange, but when Tigger, our cat, had fleas, the exterminator's chemicals somehow turned it pink. Oh well. At least I like pink.

Maybe I should make my shirt pink?

"Your head is bigger than mine," she says. "But only slightly."

"Huh." My big head is my second major physical imperfection. The first is my uneven boobs. The left one is larger than the right. It's not ideal. "Do you think there's a color I could wear that would make my head look smaller?" I would use a body-morphing spell, but my mom claims they can do serious damage. Like accidentally shrink my brain or give me a mustache.

Miri sighs. "Do you know that every time you choose a new shade, my bedspread changes color?"

"Really? Cool!" Like I said, in magic, everything comes

from something. If I zap myself new sandals, the shoes have to come from somewhere. If I zap myself up twenty bucks, someone's wallet just found itself twenty short. If my top turns navy, some piece of fabric just had its blue pigments zapped right out of it.

"Not cool!" she wails. "My bedspread is currently a hideous shade of pale puke."

I straighten the shirt and square my shoulders. "Miri, take one for the team."

"I'm *always* taking one for the team. Team Rachel. You better turn your shirt back to its original shade before bedtime."

Original shade? Like I can remember. "Or what?"

"Or . . ." She eyes my purse, focuses on it, and makes it slowly rise off its spot on my desk. "Or I'll spill your stuff all over the floor."

"Oooh, now I'm scared. Anyway, whose house are we going to for dinner tonight? Huh, huh?" She can't argue with me, because I am ridiculously in the right. "Wendaline is your fake friend, is she not? I would much rather be going out with *my* friends, thank you very much." Unfortunately, I agreed to this dinner before Raf invited me to a pre-back-to-school bash at Mick Lloyd's. I claimed I had a family function I couldn't get out of. Which is kind of true. I just didn't give the witchy specifics.

"She is. You're right." Miri met Wendaline on Mywitchbook.com. It's a social network, kind of like Facebook or Myspace, but just for witches. It's enchanted so that no one else can access it. Liana, our cousin, my mom's sister's daughter, sent us both friend requests. I declined. Ever since she tried to steal my body at camp, I'm wary of all things Liana-related. Anyway, it's not like I have the time to friend surf. I'm way too busy with shmoo pea. And Tammy. And my other good friend, Alison, who does not go to my school but does go to my camp. I am way too busy for witch friends. Especially ones you meet over the Internet. Everyone knows that a cyber friend counts as only a fourth of a real friend.

Miri, on the other hand, loves online friendship. She made three friends on her first day and is desperate to make more. Last week, on her thirteenth birthday, they all sent her e-brooms. Ha-ha. In real life she got a cell. We've been bugging Mom for practically the last decade to get us phones, so I'm ecstatic she finally caved. I'm not complaining about the fact that Miri got one and I didn't—yet—because my birthday is on Thursday (four days away! Wahoo! I'm having a little get-together to celebrate. Yay!), and I'm assuming I'll be receiving mine then. Although it's kind of annoying that my little sister, who is still in middle school, got a cell, like magical powers and boobs, before I did. (And unlike mine, her boobs are a matching set.)

Anyway, one of Miri's e-broom-sending Mywitchbook .com friends—Wendaline—lives right here in Manhattan and goes to JFK with me. Wendaline's the one who invited us to the Full Moon dinner at her house tonight. Whatever that is.

Miri is psyched.

I'm concerned Wendaline might be a *psycho*.

"What are you gonna wear?" Miri asks me now.

"Black pants and a T-shirt. And ruby slippers in case I have to urgently tap my heels to go home."

"Rachel, she is not a psycho! She's a witch!"

"Exactly. What if she's a bad witch? Like the one in *Hansel and Gretel* who lures unsuspecting children with promises of food and then eats them?"

"She's not a cannibal. She's super-nice."

"Sure she is." When Miri woke me earlier this week with the groundbreaking news that there was another witch at JFK, I feared the worst.

"Tell me who it is," I demanded, imagining the most evil person in my class. "Is it Melissa?" Melissa is my archenemy and Raf's ex-girlfriend, who constantly tries to steal him away. Obviously she wasn't a witch last year, because then I would so be a frog by now. At the very least, she would have turned the whole school—no, the whole world—no, the whole universe—against me.

"My life is over!" I wailed, pulling the covers over my head.

"Why are you such a nut?" Miri asked. "It's not Melissa."

"Oh. Good." I removed the covers.

"She's a freshman. Her name is Wendaline."

"Seriously?"

Miri's brow wrinkled in confusion. "Why not?"

"Wendy the Witch? Does that not sound familiar? From *Casper the Friendly Ghost?*"

"It's Wendaline. Not Wendy."

"She still sounds like a made-up character. Like Hannah Montana. Or Nate the Great. It's too much rhyming."

" 'Wendaline the Witch' doesn't rhyme. It has alliteration."

"It still sounds made-up."

"I'll make sure to tell her that."

Anyway, I'm meeting Wendaline tonight, at her Full Moon dinner. I still have no idea what "Full Moon" means. I am hoping it does not involve any kind of nudity. Mom seemed to think it was kind of like the Jewish Shabbat, or Friday-night dinner, but for witches. And monthly instead of weekly, 'cause of the full moon part.

"What's her last name?" Mom asked.

"Peaner."

"Hmm," Mom said, deep in thought. "Okay. You can go if you want to. It might be healthy for you to meet some nice"—read: non-body-snatching—"witches."

Yeah, I can't believe she's letting us go either. I mean, Internet witches? How much sketchier can you get?

"Are you ready?" Miri asks me impatiently, my purse still hovering above her head. "I don't want to be late. And your bag is getting heavy. Why do you have to carry so much stuff around with you?"

"I just do," I say, opening my closet. "I'll be two secs. I need to change."

"Why can't you just wear what you have on?"

"It's my back-to-school top! It needs to be fresh."

"Just zap it fresh tomorrow."

"Just hold your horses." I slip it over my head, hang it up, and put on a V-neck purple shirt. Then I change out of my jeans and into black pants. More appropriate for a family dinner, no? I check myself out in the mirror. Not bad. Good enough to meet She Whose Name Sounds Like a TV Character and her family.

Imagine if *I* were a TV character! My life is pretty fascinating. It would make a killer TV show. A comedy about two sister witches in NYC? Who wouldn't watch? That's good television. The premise could also work well for a reality show.

Omigod! I'd be famous! I'd get to go on all the talk shows! People would stop me in the street and ask to take my picture, and I would smile modestly and murmur, "Anything for my fans."

Except then everyone would know I was a witch. Awkward.

Maybe I can still do it. In disguise. I'll wear a blond wig. Although then I'd be covering up my awesome new layers that make me look like I have real cheekbones. Not that I don't have cheekbones. Obviously I do. But I never noticed them before Este the hairstylist got her expert hands on me. Alison recommended her after I showed up at her apartment with a bald spot. I had attempted to zap my own hair.

I'm trying to convince Miri to pay Este a visit. She could use some cheekbones.

What was I thinking about? Right. Wigs. I'd have to wear one if I were on a reality show. Although technically, viewers would probably be able to figure out my identity from my Greenwich Village apartment, my high school, and my friends.

My friends, who would wonder why I was always being trailed by a TV camera. I'd have to tell them the truth. About the show . . . about my double life.

Imagine. If everyone knew.

In a way it would be a relief. I wouldn't have to keep my big secret squished down inside me like dirty clothes in the laundry hamper.

Looking in the mirror, I watch as my still-airborne purse quivers and then lands with a thud on Miri's face. "Ouch," she whines.

Or maybe they'd think I was a freak. Or worry that I'd cast love spells on them that accidentally bewitch their older brothers.

No, my secret must stay squashed. I shiver and sling my purse over my shoulder. "Let's get this show"—my secret reality freak show—"on the road."

2 Moon over Manhattan

"Do we have to stay long?" I whine while pressing the front bell of a building at Thirteenth Street and Broadway. "How long do these Full Moon thingies last, anyway?"

"A few hours." Miri shushes me, clutching a candle—our gift—to her chest. It was the witchiest thing we could think of. Besides a cat. But bringing an animal as a dinner gift might be weird. Maybe a stuffed animal? Also weird.

"Stop being such a baby," she continues. "This is exciting! Our first real witch experience! I just wish you hadn't made us ten minutes late."

The truth is I *am* a little excited. Miri and I have never been invited to anything witchy before. Since Mom only just this year told us about our powers (she had to after Miri accidentally brought a lobster back to life at a formal dinner), we haven't had any exposure to the witchcraft community. In fact, until Miri discovered Mywitchbook.com, we weren't even sure there *was* a witchcraft community.

It would be great to have people I could talk to about all this magic stuff. Then the secret wouldn't always be bubbling inside me, threatening to overflow.

I buzz a second time. The early-September breeze blows through my shirt. "No one's home. Are you sure this is the right place?"

Miri sighs. "Ring again."

"You ring, if you're so sure."

She buzzes and we both wait. And wait. We can practically hear the chirping cicadas. Not that there are cicadas in New York City. But that's what the sound effects would be on my TV show.

"Maybe they're already on the roof," Miri says.

"It's kind of rude of them not to answer the bell, don't you think?"

"It's kind of rude to be ten minutes late," Miri counters.

"Ten minutes isn't late. Everyone knows you have a fifteen-minute grace period."

"You'd think that, since you're always late. Let's call her. Do you have your cell? Oh right, you don't have a cell. I do." She whips out her phone, wiggles it under my nose, and then punches in the number.

"Hi, Wendaline? It's Miri. We're downstairs. We tried buzzing but—"

I feel a burst of air, and a witch appears beside me. And I mean, a witch. On a broomstick. The girl is wearing a black witch hat and a matching robe. I leap back.

"Great! You're here!" the witch says, wrapping Miri and

me in a tight hug. "So nice to finally meet you in person, Miri! You're even prettier than your picture! And you must be Rachel!"

I can't believe she just "Appeared" on Broadway, one of the busiest streets in the city. I anxiously study the passersby. Did anybody see? Are they going to call the police? Is there a law against Appearing? Luckily, no one seems to be gaping at us. Hey, it's New York. Weird things happen hourly. Yesterday a man on a unicycle almost pedaled over my foot. "Nice to meet you too," I tell Wendaline.

"This is for you," Miri says shyly, handing over the candle.

"You are so sweet! But you didn't have to bring anything." She looks around. "Where are your brooms?"

"We walked," I say, appraising her. She's taller than we are, about five foot five, and pretty. Clear, smooth skin; big doelike green eyes outlined in dark charcoal. Although a doe probably has brown eyes. Whatever. Her lips are coated with a pretty purplish gloss. The hair pouring from under her pointy hat is long, dark, and curly. Nice, but a bit Rapunzelish.

On closer inspection, I notice that her robe is embroidered. And satiny. Like the kimonos my dad brought us back from a business trip in Tokyo, except black. She's wearing tight black leggings and three-inch-heeled black patent leather Mary Janes. Very witch-chic.

"I love your cloak," Miri gushes.

"Thank you!" Wendaline says. "Shall we zoom up to the roof? Oh, wait, no brooms. It's all good. We can take the elevator. Are you guys gray?"

"Gray what?" I ask. I didn't zap my skin color along with my back-to-school shirt, did I?

"Gray witches," Wendaline clarifies. "Is that why you walked all the way?"

Miri shakes her head. "What's a gray witch?"

"You know, someone who tries to use less magic in everyday life. Environmagically conscious. Keep the black and white balance in the universe and all that."

She obviously has not seen the state of Miri's comforter.

Wendaline unlocks the door. "I try to be less wasteful, but my parents are so old-school, you know?"

"I'm definitely gray," my sister the suck-up says as we follow our new friend inside. If I know Miri, she'll now be dressing in all gray for the rest of her life just to make a point.

We pass a mirrored hallway, where I check myself out to ensure I am not in fact gray, and then we zoom up twenty flights to the roof. "Zoom" in the mere mortal sense, aka taking the elevator.

About twenty-five people, sitting around a ginormous, beautifully set oval table under the dark sky, are waiting for us. Who are all these guys? For some reason I thought it would just be us and Wendaline's family. And omigod—they're all wearing black robes and witch hats. Are they all witches? It's like I just stepped into a haunted house. I peer at their faces. They look normal. No pasty white skin or bloodshot eyes. No serial killers. Hopefully.

"It's all good," Wendaline tells us. "They don't bite."

Guess they're not vampires, either. Ha-ha.

"Hello, hello!" exclaims a woman at the head of the table. She looks like an older version of Wendaline. Same long hair, only streaked with silver. She's also wearing a black satin robe. "Happy Full Moon! You arrived just in time. We're about to start!"

Wendaline ushers us to the only three empty chairs. *Gorgeous* chairs. They're gold and sparkly and each one is covered with an embroidered supersoft duvet-like cushion. Miri sits down in the middle one, and Wendaline and I take our places beside her. Ah. It's like a massage for my butt.

Wow. I haven't seen such a beautifully set table since my dad's wedding. There are fancy bowls and serving plates, many sizes of glasses, and at least five different forks per person. In the center of the table are what feel like hundreds of candles of various shapes, ranging from the size of a dinner plate to the size of my pinkie. Guess she didn't need another one. Oh well. We tried. Next time we'll bring a stuffed cat. I mean, a stuffed animal! Yikes, what kind of evil witch am I?

When I'm done ogling the table, I notice the moon.

The full, round, luminous moon hanging above our heads.

Sure, I've seen a full moon before, but never in the city. Once in a while you can catch a sliver of the moon peeping up from behind a skyscraper, but usually it's a pretty moonless town. From Wendaline's roof it's incredible.

Next I study the man with the salt-and-pepper beard on my right. He too is wearing a black robe and a witch hat. So that means . . . he's a witch! A wizard? A warlock? I've never met a boy witch before. I knew they existed. I've heard of them. But here they are! Right next to me! I look around and count ten—yes, ten!—men at the table.

Unfortunately, none are my age. Not that I'm looking

for a potential crush. I have a boyfriend already, thank you very much. A perfectly good boyfriend too. Shmooperou! Or shmoopster. Or whatever. But still, it would be cool to meet a teen witch-boy.

"Everyone," Wendaline says. "This is Rachel and Miri."

"Hello, Rachel and Miri," everyone says.

"Hi," we say a little shyly.

I put my napkin on my lap and nudge Miri to do the same. These people seem formal.

"This is my mom, Mariana," Wendaline says, pointing around the table, "my dad, Trenton; my little brother, Jeremiah." He's maybe six. "My mom's sister Rhonda; my uncle Alexander; their daughters, Edith and Loraine; my dad's brother Thomas and my aunt Francesca, my cousins Nadine and Ursula, my Moga Pearl . . ." I have no idea what a *moga* is, but since she's pointing to the oldest witch at the table, I'm thinking it's a grandmother. Or maybe just an old person. Either way I can't help admiring Wendaline's funky black nail polish. "My dad's sister Alana; my uncle Burgess; my other moga, Moga Gisela; my Mogi Thompson"—Grandma and Grandpa?—"my parents' friends Brenna and Stephen; their kids, Coral and Kendra; and their other friends Doreen, Jerry, Brandon, Nicola, Dana, and Arthur."

Yowza. That's a lot of names. Most of which just sped through my head faster than a cabbie trying to make a yellow light.

"There will be a quiz after dessert," says Arthur, the salt-and-pepper guy sitting next to me. The rest of the table laughs.

"Time to begin," Wendaline's mom says, hushing the

table with her long hand. Wow, those are some pointy black nails. Guess I know where Wendaline gets her fashion tips. Her mom turns to me and my sister. "Would you two like to say the *Votra*?"

Huh? "Um . . ."

"It's all good," Wendaline says, sensing my discomfort. "I'll do it." She rises, wiggles her fingers in the air, and says,

"Ishta bilonk higyg
So ghet hequi bilobski.
Bi redical vilion!"

Or something like that. I actually have no idea what she said. None. Zilch. Zip. Zero. I turn to Miri and give my best "Did you understand what just came out of her mouth?" look, but she's too busy staring at Wendaline in awe. I need a dictionary at this thing. Although it might help if I knew what language she was speaking.

When Wendaline is done, she tilts her head way back so that her face is directed to the sky, and chants, *"Kamoosh! Kamoosh! Kamoosh!"*

All the candles on the table instantly light up.

Omigod! I push my seat back to avoid catching on fire. Unfortunately, my chair falls backward and I land with a crash on my back. Oops.

Half the table rushes to pick me up.

"I'm fine, I'm fine," I murmur. "I hope I haven't broken the fancy chair. Or my head."

Wendaline laughs. Miri is scowling and looking like she wants to crawl under the table. Apparently, I have embarrassed her in front of her sophisticated Internet friends.

When I'm back upright and everyone has returned to

their seats, Wendaline's mom snaps three times and says, "*Ganolio!*"

All our bowls fill with red soup. Coolio. It must be tomato soup, right? It has to be. I think back to my *Hansel and Gretel* crack. It's not blood soup. It can't be. I lean in to take a sniff. Tomato. Definitely tomato.

I think.

I wait for Miri to taste it just in case.

Wendaline's mom takes a spoonful. "So, tell me, girls, let's play witch genealogy. What are your parents' names? Do we know them?"

"You don't know my dad," I say quickly. "He's not a witch. Or a wizard. Warlock?"

"Warlock," Arthur says, sipping his wine.

"And your mother?" her mom asks.

"Carol," Miri says. "Carol Graff."

"Carol Graff, Carol Graff . . . no, I don't know that name." She dips a piece of bread in her soup and chews off the end.

Aunt Rhonda leans directly across the table toward us, and I get a whiff of her strong sugary perfume. "Do you mean Carolanga Graff?"

I shake my head. Is that actually a name? It sounds like a disease. Poor kid. "Her name is Carol."

"Does she have a sister Sasha?" Aunt Rhonda asks.

Huh. That's strange. "Carol Graff has a sister Sasha," I say.

"It must be her," Aunt Rhonda says. "We used to run in the same circles. Years ago. Maybe she changed her name?"

"I guess," Miri says, tensing.

Could our mom have had another name and never bothered to tell us? How could she do that? Why would she do that? Does she have another identity? A secret family? Or is it some sort of witness protection thing? Have we just blown her cover? Maybe we'll have to move somewhere random, like Wisconsin.

Witches in Wisconsin is not a bad name for a TV show. It even has alliteration.

"I wonder why she'd change it. Carolanga is such a beautiful name," Aunt Rhonda says. "*Langa* means *light* in Brixta, you know."

I have no idea what she just said.

"Sorry, but what's Brixta?" Miri asks.

Aunt Rhonda drops her spoon in surprise. "The ancient witch language! You girls don't speak it?"

Miri shrugs helplessly. "I didn't even know there *was* an ancient witch language."

Our mother of light sure kept us in the dark.

"Wendaline is fluent, you know," her mother brags.

"So, what is your mom up to?" Aunt Rhonda asks. "I haven't seen her in ages."

Miri hesitates. "She kind of went off the witch grid for a while."

"Please give her our regards."

"Oh, we will," I say, finishing my soup. Secret name? Secret language? I'm going to give her more than regards. I'm going to give her a piece of my mind.

When we're done with the soup, Wendaline's mom snaps her fingers and says, "*Moosa!*" The bowls disappear.

I'm so going to have to try that at home. Perhaps the

next time Mom makes her chickpea curry. Only I'll do it before I have to eat it.

When she yells "*Ganolio*" again, a pear, pine nut, and goat cheese salad appears on a fresh plate. My favorite kind of salad—no vegetables.

Miri and I don't talk much while we eat it; we have too much listening to do.

They gossip about people they know.

"Did you know that Mitchell Harrison got married last week?" Aunt Rhonda says, and then whispers, "To a *notch*."

"No!" the table cries.

I don't know who the notches are, but to fit in I put on my "That's unbelievable!" face. I'm not sure if it's unbelievably good or bad, but clearly it's unbelievable.

"Yes," her husband says. "Last week."

"That is so sad for his parents," Wendaline's mom says with a loud sigh.

Unbelievably sad, apparently. I shake my head to commiserate.

"It's his life, and he can do what he wants," Wendaline says indignantly. "If he's happy, you should be happy for him."

I stop the shaking and start nodding and then decide just to keep my head still and focus on my salad before I accidentally bite off my tongue.

They talk about politics.

"The witch union is just so useless these days," Aunt Rhonda says.

"Seriously," says one of the relatives. "Is there anyone in charge over there?"

Miri squeezes my knee under the table. She is soaking it all up, enjoying every second. At least until Wendaline's mom *ganolios* up the main course, veal Parmesan. I look worriedly at my vegetarian sister. "What are you going to eat?"

She prods her main course with her fork.

"If you zap your meal back into a cow, no one here would be too surprised."

"Ha-ha."

"Yours is tofu, Miri," Wendaline tells her. "It's all good. I know you don't eat meat. It's on your Mywitchbook profile."

The happy look returns to Miri's eyes. These witches sure know how to throw a dinner party.

We both dig in.

"Will you girls be doing your Samsortas this year?" Wendaline's mom asks us between bites.

"Sorry?" Miri squeaks. "What's a Samsorta?"

Mrs. Peaner's eyes bulge.

"Your coming out!" Aunt Rhonda cries. "You've never heard of Samsortas?"

We shake our heads.

"It's only the biggest social event of the calendar year," Cousin Ursula says. "You've never been?"

We shake again.

"It's on October thirty-first," Aunt Rhonda explains. "New witches from around the world are announced to witchcraft society. It's a tradition."

"It's pretty cool," Wendaline says. "It's like a debutante ball for witches."

"It's gone on since the Middle Ages," her mom adds.

"I know," Aunt Rhonda says. "I was there."

A "huh" escapes my lips.

She nods. "It was six lives ago, but I have an excellent memory."

Um . . .

"That's where Halloween comes from," Wendaline explains. "That's why notches and norlocks dress up. They come out like witches, and they don't even know why!"

Okay, I have to ask. "What are notches and norlocks?"

"Oh! Nonwitches and nonwarlocks," she says.

If only I had a laptop to take notes on. Maybe my dad will get me one for my birthday? That would be so cool. "So what happens on October thirty-first?"

"All the new witches gather in Zandalusha, the old witch burial grounds, and perform the Samsorta ceremony."

A cemetery? On Halloween? Sounds creepy. "Is it in New York?"

They all chuckle.

"Here in the New World? Hardly," Aunt Rhonda says, turning up her nose. "Zandalusha is on a small island in the Black Sea, off Romania. It's where all our foremothers are buried."

A witch cemetery in Romania. Creepy to the power of a gazillion.

Wendaline must see my "ick" expression, because she hurries to say, "It's really beautiful. I went to Ursula's Sam a few years ago and it was the most amazing thing. Really spiritual. You're given away by an older witch who was already Samsorted, and you add a lock of hair to the Holy Cauldron, and there's a candle ceremony, and you perform a spell that came from the original spell book in Brixta."

Is the original spell book A^2? It comes in Brixta, too? It's tough enough to read in English, never mind Brixta. There are way too many sections.

"I am so excited for mine," Wendaline continues. "I started training last month. Oh, you guys should do it too!"

"Um . . ." A cemetery on Halloween with a bunch of witches? Thanks, but no thanks. "We'll see," I say. But what I really mean is "no way."

During dessert (Chocolate cake! Mini crème brûlées! Fancy exotic fruit tarts!) Wendaline asks me lots of questions about JFK.

"Is it huge?"

"Not too big."

"I'm so afraid I'll get lost."

"Don't worry. Lots of people get lost on their first day." Not me. But lots of other people. Fine, I got a little lost. How was I supposed to know that room 302 was on the second floor? Does that make any sense? No, it does not.

"I'm sure I'll get lost. I've never been to school before."

"You mean, you've never been to *high school* before."

"No." She bites the corner of her bottom lip. "I've never been to school. I was homeschooled."

What? "Seriously?"

She laughs nervously. "Yeah. A lot of witches are homeschooled. So our parents can balance our witchcraft studies with our notch studies."

Poor girl! "But . . . where do you meet boys?"

"Oh, you know. Mixers. Parties. Teen tours."

Is she kidding me? Teen tours for witches? Where do they go, from cemetery to cemetery?

"But you've never been to any type of organized school before?" Miri asks.

Her eyes are rimmed with worry. "No."

"Don't worry," I say, taking another bite of cake. "I'll show you around. Why don't you meet me at the opening assembly? I'll walk you to your homeroom class."

"Really?" Her eyes shine. "Thanks, Rachel. You're the best!"

Why, yes, I am. I can be, like, her mentor. Follow me, little one. Just call me Obi-Wan. I'll take her under my wing. Show her how to use a lightsaber.

Or at least the school ropes.

"How cool is Wendaline!" Miri exclaims. Our arms are linked and we're kind of half walking, half skipping home. Sure, we could have zapped up our brooms, but we'd rather walk, gray-style. What can I say? That's how we roll.

"So cool," I say.

"I like how she says 'It's all good.' You forgot to take your broom? It's all good. You brought us a candle even though we already have four thousand? It's all good."

"You don't remember your past lives?" I say. "It's all good."

We giggle and I squeeze her arm against me.

"Are you glad you came?" she asks.

"I am one hundred percent glad. It's like a whole different world over there, huh?"

"I know! They're so sophisticated and witchy!"

"I can't believe that's where Halloween comes from!" I love Halloween. It's my absolute favorite holiday. And I inspired it! Well, not me exactly, but my kind.

"I know!" She stops in her tracks. "Maybe we should do it."

"Do what?"

"The Samsorta!"

"Seriously, Mir? Why would you want to do that?"

"Because! Why wouldn't you?"

"First of all, because it's creepy. Second, because we don't speak any gibberish."

"You mean Brixta," she corrects, poking me.

"Whatev. And third, because Wendaline said you need someone to give you away. And unfortunately, Mom didn't have a Sam—"

Wait a samsecond! She lied about her name. She never mentioned Brixta. Or notches. Or norlocks. Or anything at all. I turn to Miri. "Do you think Mom had a Samsorta?"

We run the rest of the way home.

3 The Way We Were

We face my mom on the couch. Glaring. My sister and I have matching crossed arms.

"Mom!" I begin. "We are very disappointed in you. You never told us you knew Wendaline's aunt. You never told us you had a Samsorta. You never even told us your real name!"

Now I understand why she let us go to some stranger's house for a Full Moon dinner in the first place. They weren't strangers; they were childhood friends.

"Are you even our real mother?" Miri asks, raising an eyebrow suspiciously.

Mom squirms in her seat. "I'm sorry, I'm sorry. You know I don't like to talk about all that. It's in the past."

"You better start spilling in the present!" I order, slamming my fists into the pillows.

She sighs. "Hold on. I have something to show you."

She disappears around the corner. I check my watch. It's already quarter after ten. I have to get to sleep soon so I can look my best for day one of *The Sophomore Spectacular*! Under-eye circles are not part of the plan.

Mom returns with a small black leather book. "Do you want to see my Samsorta album?"

Is that a rhetorical question? "Yes! Why have we never seen this before? Where was it? Do you have some sort of invisible bookshelf in your room?"

She squeezes in between us on the couch. "It was in the one place where you two never dare go. The cleaning supplies closet. Behind the Windex."

"We have a cleaning supplies closet?" I ask.

"Exactly."

She turns over the black front cover, and Miri and I gasp at the close-up of my mom's adolescent face. It looks just like Miri's! But it's my mom's! It's my mom with a totally unwrinkled forehead! And dark black eyeliner! And an updo! "It's Teen Mom! And your hair is brown!"

"Of course it's brown."

"Well, I've never seen your natural color before. You know, I don't think I've ever seen any kid photos of you. I've seen college photos and wedding pictures, but no kid photos. Let me guess: you had to hide them from Dad and then you forget all about them?"

"Exactly," she says.

How sad—she had to bury her entire childhood in the back of a closet so the man she was married to would never see it.

"But witches don't take too many pictures anyway," she

adds. "It's not part of the culture. There's a superstition that getting photographed steals part of your soul."

"Gee, thanks, Mom," I say. "There are only like a gazillion photos of me out there. Way to warn me."

"I don't believe it, obviously. I had these taken, didn't I?"

My mom, the rebel.

It's super-weird to see my mom as a young girl. I can't picture her as a teen. I can't imagine her as a real person without kids. Isn't she on this planet to be my mom?

"You were pretty," I say.

" 'Were'? Gee, thanks."

"*Are* pretty," Miri says. "That's what she meant."

"Totally. That's what I meant."

In the next photo, I get a better look at the outfit. Mom's wearing a long-sleeved purply satin dress. The neck is low and shows off her—

"Mom! You had boobs! How old were you when you had your Samsorta?"

"Thirteen. Miri's age."

"But you're huge. Did you pad? You so padded."

She giggles. "I may have padded a *little* bit."

The bodice of the dress is tight, and the skirt flares into ruffles. She's looking off into the distance. Behind her is the Eiffel Tower.

"You had your Samsorta in Paris?" I ask. "I thought they held it in Romania."

"No, it was in Romania. We just popped by Paris for pictures."

Popped by. La, la, la, I think I'll pop by Paris on my way to school. Pick up a baguette. *Merci beaucoup*.

She flips over to a two-page spread. On the left is Teen Mom with Today Mom. No, that makes zero sense. Unless she's Time-Traveling Mom.

"Is that Grandma?" Miri asks.

Ah. So clever, that little one.

"It sure is."

"She looks just like you do now," I say. "Except for the black hair."

"Yeah, she had gorgeous thick black hair. I got mine from my father."

"Is he in any of the photos?" I ask.

"No." Sadness creeps into her voice. "He stayed out of the witch stuff. Didn't want to get in the way."

At least he had the opportunity to get in the way. Unlike Dad.

Imagine if Mom had told him—had told all of us—about her Samsorta years ago, when we were still one family. The four of us, cuddled together on the couch, flipping through the pictures, teasing, laughing, sipping hot chocolate by the fireplace—

"Hey, Mom," Miri says, interrupting my trip down Alternate-Reality Lane. "Does *mogul* mean 'grandma'?"

"It's *moga,*" she answers.

"That's what I said."

"You said 'mogul.' " I snicker.

"Did not. Next picture, please."

The next page is Teen Mom . . . with a boy. A boy who's looking at her adoringly.

She gets a girlish smile on her face. "That's Jefferson Tyler."

Reeeeeally. "And *who* is Jefferson Tyler?"

"My very first boyfriend," she says.

No way. "You had a boyfriend before Dad?" I squeal.

"Yes, dear."

Miri and I study the picture. He has short, curly dark hair and a big smile. "He's cute," I say.

Miri asks, "Is he a warlock?"

"Yup."

This is all too much. "Other men, other name. . . . Who *are* you?"

Mom clucks her tongue. "I did have a life before you were born, you know."

Apparently! "How long did you go out with him exactly?"

"I don't know . . . about five years?"

"What?" I shriek.

"We met a few months before my Sam, and we stayed together until I was about eighteen."

"That's forever," Miri says, folding her legs underneath her. "I can't believe you never told us about him!"

"Have you seen him since? Did you love him? Did you guys—" I'm about to say "make out," but I decide I don't want to know the answer to that. At all. Yuck. So instead, I say, "Break up?" which makes no sense. Obviously they broke up.

Miri snorts. "No, they got married."

"He wanted to get married," Mom says. "But I wanted to go to college."

"No way," I say. "I can't believe another guy proposed to you before Dad. At eighteen. Yikes."

"Things were different back then. Witches got married

young. I wanted to excommunicate myself from the world of witchcraft; he wanted to get more involved. . . . My mother wanted me to marry him, of course."

"Why?" Miri's eyes are wide.

"She wanted me to avoid the problems she'd had by marrying a norlock. That's a—"

"We got it," Miri says with a nod. "Nonwarlock."

"Right. But I wanted to explore my options."

"Then you met Dad," I say.

"Then I met your dad."

None of us speaks. We're all thinking, And look how well that turned out. At least, that's what I'm thinking. For all I know, they're thinking about padded bras. Or about what ever happened to Jefferson Tyler, because how cool would it be if after all these years they met up, fell back in love, and got married?

So cool.

Yeah, yeah, I know she's had a serious boyfriend for five months now—so serious she even told him our witchy secret—but still. It's soooo romantic.

Must find Jefferson Tyler! Maybe he's on Mywitchbook.

"Back to the Samsortas," Miri says. "How did you know what to do? Did you have a tutor?"

Mom groans. "I had to take these horrible lessons. At Charm School."

I laugh. "It was actually called Charm School?"

"No, the official name was Charmori, but everyone called it that."

"Wow," says Miri wistfully. "Where is the Charmori? In New York?"

"In Switzerland."

"You never told us you've been to Switzerland," Miri grumbles.

"Miri, she never told us anything. She was a witch! Of course she's been to Switzerland. She's probably been to every country on the planet." I refocus on the subject at hand. "Did you do any skiing?"

Mom laughs. "I wasn't there to ski; I was there to learn."

What a nerd. "Was there chocolate? I bet there was really good chocolate."

"Do you speak Brixta?" Miri asks. "Say something in Brixta."

"I doubt I remember anything," she says.

"Oh, come on," I tell her. "Say 'hello.' You can say 'hello.' "

She closes her eyes. "*Kelli. Fro ki fuma imbo oza ge kiro?*"

Shut up! I squeeze her arm. "What does that mean?"

"Hello. Can I have another piece of chocolate?"

See? I knew it.

"Cool," Miri says.

"A waste of time, actually. I spent over a year learning Brixta. I've never used it again. In my opinion, the entire Samsorta ceremony is pretty useless. You don't get any more powers or rights. It's not like getting a driver's license. You're not any more of a witch. It's just a public spectacle."

"So why do people do it?" I ask.

She shrugs. "It's a way to make yourself known in the witch world. To network with other witches."

We silently flip through the rest of the pictures. It might

be a big waste, but she sure looks glamorous. The gorgeous dress, the thick black eyeliner, the fancy updo.

I want to look that glamorous.

Do I want a Samsorta?

I want to get dressed up. I want to get my makeup and hair done and have a boy look at me adoringly. But the boy I want to look at me adoringly is Raf. And how can he possibly come to my witch party if he doesn't know I'm a witch?

He can't. So really, what's the point?

Anyway, do I want to learn a new language and then have a weird candle zombie ritual at a cemetery on Halloween?

Not so much.

I look at my watch again. It's almost twelve! If I don't get to bed soon, I'm going to *look* like a zombie tomorrow. "Don't hide these away in your secret closet," I tell Mom, motioning to the albums. "I want to check them out again. But I need sleep. Miri, have you prepared *your* first-day-of-school outfit?"

She rolls her eyes. "Unlike you, I am not obsessed with how I look. Speaking of which, did you change my comforter back to its original color?"

"What? Gotta go!"

"Rachel! It's hideous!"

What a whiner. "You won't be able to see it in the dark."

"You have until tomorrow," Miri says.

"Or what?"

"Or I'll zap your shirt off and you'll be wearing a comforter."

"Oooh, big talker."

Mom stretches her arms above her head. "Why exactly is your comforter a different color? What did your sister do?"

"Shhh." I kiss Miri on the forehead and my mom on the cheek. "It's all good."

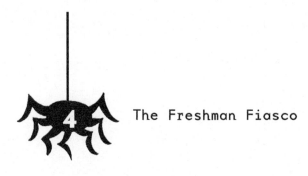

4 The Freshman Fiasco

"I love your new shirt," my BFF, Tammy, tells me as we walk into the JFK auditorium for the welcome assembly. "When did you get it?"

"Hello! Last week. I was with you!"

Her face squishes with confusion. "That's not the shirt you bought with me. That one was red. Yours is blue."

Whoops. "Oh, yeah, I, uh, forgot. I exchanged it for another color."

"I like it," she says.

"Are you sure? 'Cause it looked pretty funky in white, too. And red. And gold."

"Too late now."

Or not. I could always slip into the bathroom before the bell. Although Tammy might worry she was having some sort of color-activated stroke.

The second we enter the auditorium, my Raf-radar goes

on. Where is he? Where is that Shmoopie? Shmoopoo? Poo poo?

Tee hee, I said "poo."

Must get a grip! I have to act mature now that I have a boyfriend.

How I love to say that. A boyfriend. Or as they say in French, which, according to my schedule, I have second period, *mon amour*. My love. Are you supposed to tell your boyfriend you love him after only a month? Or should you wait for him to say it first? I wish there were a high school boyfriend manual I could check. I bet that would be covered in chapter one.

Is that him? Nope. There? Nope. Wait, there he is, there he is! He's sitting in the right-hand corner of the auditorium with a group of his friends.

Yes!

Why doesn't he look up? Shouldn't he have Rachel-radar? I should zap up a spell for that. Meanwhile, should I go up to him? Is that stalkerish? I mean, we've seen each other practically every day since camp ended. But does that mean we're supposed to sit side by side for orientation? Do boyfriends and girlfriends have to sit together?

That would be covered in chapter two.

What do I do, what do I do? Sit with him or no? I look down at my shoes. I look up at the ceiling. Hello, halogen lights. I look back down. My neck hurts. What if the transition from summer boyfriend to school boyfriend is too weird for him? I've seen *Grease*. I don't want to have to ask him what happened to the Danny Zuko I met at the beach. Not that I met Raf at the beach.

A Pink Ladies jacket would be cool, though.

"There's Raf," Tammy says, opening her hand and pointing, which is the scuba signal for "let's go that way." Tammy learned to scuba dive last year and occasionally likes to communicate by underwater mime. I don't mind. If I ever fell into the ocean, at least I'd know how to tell people I was drowning.

"Really?" I say, feigning ignorance. "Where?"

"You're such a liar. You spotted him the second you walked in."

I laugh. She totally knows me. Except for the witch part. "Should we go over? I don't want to be a stalker."

"He's your *boyfriend*. You can't stalk your boyfriend. I'm sure he wants to sit with you."

Tammy has a very mature outlook on boyfriends, mostly because hers, Bosh, is very mature. He's a college freshman. He's off at Penn, but they talk and text like ten times a day.

Tammy is pretty mature about everything. Not much fazes her. Her relationships. Her friendships. Her two stepmoms. Yup, she has two. Her dad is remarried, and her mom is remarried—to another woman. And they all get along. They went on a joint vacation over the summer. A cruise. How crazy is that? My parents would never go on a joint summer vacation. I mean, they did when they were married, obviously, but they wouldn't now.

We used to drive to Stowe for the weekend to go skiing. Those car rides were insanely long, but fun in a singing-along-to-Broadway-show-tunes-and-playing-geography kind of way.

And then we would all share a hotel room, and we'd laugh at my dad 'cause he slept with socks on.

Imagine the four of us—no, make that seven (the four of us plus Lex, my mom's boyfriend; Prissy, my stepsister; and my pregnant stepmom)—going on a cruise together now. Not. I can't even picture the seven and a half of us being in the same room for more than four and a half seconds. Never mind a week on a boat.

Raf looks up at me and smiles.

Swoon.

I could definitely imagine spending a week on a cruise ship with Raf. I could imagine spending a week in a canoe with Raf.

Yay! He's wearing the brown shirt! The one we bought together! He must want me to think he looks hot. And he does. That smile! Those eyes! Those lips!

Seriously, he has great lips. Soft and sweet and perfect. He's the best kisser in the entire universe. Not that I've kissed that many other guys. Only one. Raf's brother. During the whole magic-love-spell-fiasco thingy. But anyway. Raf is an amazing kisser, even though he's younger than Will and has had less experience.

The only other person he's ever kissed is Melissa Davis.

I grimace. Speak of the devil. I spot her flaming-red hair only a few rows away from Raf. I should totally put a border spell on her so she can't get within twenty feet of him.

She is sitting with my Ex-Bee-Bee (Ex Best Bud), Jewel. Jewel, who dumped me last year and replaced me with Melissa.

Melissa's giving me dirty looks. Rolled-in-mud-and-sautéed-in-garbage dirty looks.

She turns around and says something to the group of

girls sitting in front of her. A group of seniors. I recognize Cassandra Morganstein from last year's fashion show—really a dance show with a catwalk and designer outfits. Last year I used Miri's magic to give myself mad dancing skills and get a part. Unfortunately, I kind of ruined the show when I tripped and decapitated the Eiffel Tower. It's a long story. On the plus side, that's where Raf and I got to know each other. Anyway, two seniors run it every year, and this year Cassandra is one of them. Cassandra has this insanely curly blond hair. It's gorgeous from afar, but terrifying up close: she sculpts it with so much product each curl looks like a spiral weapon. I try to avoid her in the hallway so I won't lose an eye. Today she's wearing all red—red top, red jeans, red boots—apparently adopting the trademarked mono-color look of London Zeal, the awful head of last year's ruined fashion show. Thank God *she* graduated in June.

Tammy notices too. "Look at Cassandra," she says. "Guess she's declaring herself top dog."

Top dog, female dog, top . . .

Well, you know.

I keep my head down. This year I am going to stay out of the fashion show people's way. They are all very attractive, extremely intimidating meanies. All except Raf. He's just very attractive. Maybe he won't want to be in the show this year.

As we make our way through the auditorium, I feel like I'm being watched. Or maybe that's my big head talking. I wonder if having an actual big head correlates in any way to having a big ego. Worth a scientific study, maybe. I'll suggest it in chemistry, which I have right after lunch. Is it weird that I'm excited about taking chemistry? It sounds kind of exciting. You know, bubbling potions and exploding test tubes and all that.

I breathe deeply and take a moment to pump myself up. You are fabulous! You look fabulous! Your new shirt is amazing! You have Raf! You have Tammy! Life is good.

Twenty feet until I reach Raf. Fifteen feet. Ten feet! Now what am I supposed to do? Should I kiss him hello? On the lips? On the cheek? Things to be covered in chapter three!

In preparation, I reach into my bag and oh-so-subtly dab on my cherry lip gloss. Yum.

Five feet.

But what if I try to kiss him hello and he isn't expecting it and then I end up kissing the air and everyone laughs? Or what if he doesn't want to kiss me in front of his friends? What if I kiss him and he's horrified and then he hates me and then breaks up with me tonight on the phone? Or right now? Oh God, what if he breaks up with me right here in the auditorium? And Melissa laughs and laughs and then I have to run out of the room because large tears are rolling down my face and snot is coming out of my nose and I run from the room but I can barely see so I trip and then the room is silent and then I have to kill myself? What then?

One foot.

Here he is. And . . .

Raf kisses me. On the lips.

Not a hard-core kiss, but a kiss. A hard-core tongue kiss would be inappropriate in these circumstances. I don't need a handbook to know that. Anyway, his kiss announces to everyone that I am his girlfriend.

"Hi," he says, post–lip action. "You look great."

I. Look. Great. Blue was the right choice.

"Thanks," I say, sitting beside him. "You too."

He winks. "I wore the shirt just for you."

How perfect is he? So perfect!

I wonder if we get to kiss hello every time we meet. Let's see. That means at least one kiss a day every morning. Plus whenever we bump into each other in the hallway. Plus at lunch. So say, five times a day? Are we going to kiss hello five times a day? Wait, we'd kiss hello and good-bye. Not just hello. That's what couples do, right? If we stay together for all of high school, that's three more years. So say ten months of school over three years is thirty months, twenty days a month, which is six thousand kisses. Plus say at least two kisses per weekend, totals six thousand two hundred and forty kisses! And I still haven't factored in summers. And extra kisses for birthdays (three days till mine, wahoo!), Valentine's Day, and anniversaries.

That's a lot of kisses. I'm going to need more lip gloss.

Tammy is in advanced math too. I make up crazy formulas for her when she's bored. She's going to love this one.

"Rachel!"

I look up at the sound of someone calling my name. But I can't tell where it's coming from.

"Rachel!" I hear again. "Rachel Weinstein!"

Oh no.

Oh no.

Oh no, oh no, oh please no.

Wendaline is in the center of the auditorium, waving at me. She's wearing her outfit from yesterday. Black tights. Black kimono. Black hat. Omigod.

"What, is it Halloween?" someone hisses. I turn around to see who. Cassandra. Terrific.

What is Wendaline doing? Is she insane? Is she trying to be ironic? Is she trying to ruin me?

"Who is that?" Raf asks.

"I'll be right back," I mutter, my cheeks aflame. I hurry over, grab her by the arm, and am about to pull her outside when Mrs. Konch, the principal, taps her microphone.

"Can everyone please sit down?"

What do I do? Should I zap her into a new outfit? No. People will see. And what if her clothing is enchanted or something? And then it explodes?

I pull her hat off, hand it to her, and whisper, "Put this in your schoolbag and do not take it out. Do you understand? Do *not* take it out." I'm tempted to make her sit by herself so no one will associate her with me, but unlike the fashion show people, I am not that mean.

"Wait, but . . . do I have hat hair?" She shakes out her long locks.

That's what she's worried about? Exasperated, I lead my startled new friend toward my group.

"Sit," I instruct.

She does. I do not look at her. How does she not know that her clothing is completely unacceptable? How is that possible? And while I thought her charcoal-lined eyes looked nice yesterday, today they just look . . . wrong.

Cassandra and company are snickering behind us. I'd turn around to glare at her, but I don't want to garner any extra attention.

"Hey, you," Cassandra jeers. "Girl in the black robe!"

Wendaline turns around. "Me?"

Oh great.

"Yeah. Where did you buy your outfit?" she asks. Her voice is syrupy sweet. "It's really something else."

"Thank you!" Wendaline chirps.

Cassandra licks her lips. "Are you going to a costume party?"

Wendaline looks confused. "No. Why?"

"Because you look like a witch."

"Well, that's because"—as Wendaline's voice carries, my heart sinks—"I *am* a witch."

5 The Fixer-Upper

She did not just say that. *She did not just say that!* She did not just tell the entire school she's a witch.

Maybe I imagined it.

Yes. I must have imagined it. My witchy brain is playing witchy tricks on me.

"Excuse me?" Cassandra asks, voice thick with repugnance.

"I said, I'm a witch. It's nice to meet you." She sticks out her hand. "I'm Wendaline. I'm new. I'm a freshman."

Cassandra just stares. She's obviously not sure if she's dealing with a freak or if she's being put on. "Whatever." She flicks a hard curl off her shoulder and turns away.

Her friends snicker.

This is not good. Not good at all. Wendaline just antagonized the new leader of the A-list. I've already experienced being hated by the leader of the A-list. It sucks.

Mrs. Konch walks across the stage. I sink into my seat and count the seconds until the assembly is over.

Throughout the welcome-back/greet-the-new-bio-teacher/please-keep-cows-out-of-the-refurbished-gym-this-year speech, my shoulders are so tense, they're practically in my ears. The second we're told to proceed to our respective homerooms, I mumble to Tammy and Raf that I'll see them later, and push Wendaline back in her seat.

I take a deep breath. "Please explain to me, why are you wearing what you're wearing?"

"What? The cloak?"

"Yes! The cloak! The witch cloak! To school! This isn't Hogwarts! It's JFK High! In New York City! Why are you wearing it?"

Her doe eyes are wide with bewilderment. "Because . . . because . . . Miri said it looked good!"

"Miri? My sister?"

"Yeah!"

My whole body shudders. "Never take fashion advice from my sister. Ever. And can you tell me why you thought you could wear the hat?"

She hugs her schoolbag. "I was having a bad hair day."

The homeroom bell rings and I shake my head. This girl is completely infuriating. "More importantly, why would you tell Cassandra what you told her?" I don't even want to say the word aloud. Not here. Too risky.

"What are you talking about?"

This girl needs a serious talking-to. "We have to get to class. Come find me at lunch, okay? I'll explain everything."

"Sure. Thanks, Rachel."

"No problem," I say magnanimously. "In the meantime, don't tell *anyone* else that you're"—I lower my voice—"a witch."

"But—"

"No buts. Oh, and you definitely need to change!" I hold on to her until we're the only ones left in the auditorium, focus on her, and chant:

"That outfit will not impress.
Please turn that cloak into a dress!"

A rush of cold and . . . zap! I know I'm messing with the rules of magic, but there's no other choice. All I can hope is that the dress she gets is off a hanger and not off some poor girl who's now wearing nothing but underwear.

The cloak morphs into a long black shirtdress. She looks great! She still has on her leggings, but her top has short bubble sleeves and a scooped neck. "You look great!"

"But, but—"

"What did I say about buts? We're going to be late!" I grab her arm and pull her through the swinging doors, down the now empty hallway, and up the stairs. "You're in there," I say, pointing to room 303. "I know it makes no sense that it's on the second floor, but that's JFK for you! I'll see you at lunch!"

"But, Rachel—"

"No buts!" I wave and hurry up the next flight of stairs, rush through the hall, and burst into my new room and the empty chair beside Tammy just before the second bell rings.

Phewf!

"Hey," Tammy says, eyeing me up and down. "Did you change?"

I look down. I'm wearing Wendaline's cloak over my jeans. Except in blue.

I sigh. At least I'm not in my underwear.

"Can I steal a fry?" Tammy asks me. It's eleven a.m., which, unfortunately for freshmen and sophomores, means lunch period. What normal people eat lunch at eleven? The school should at least call it brunch period. Tammy and I are sitting in the caf with the very serious Janice Cooper, the very chirpy Sherry Dolan, and the very big-breasted Annie Banks. Seriously, they're huge. They're like massive watermelons. And I'm massively jealous. Anyway, the five of us have been kind of a clique since last year. But not a mean clique. No way. We're nice, we're smart, and we're B-list and proud.

Although I'm kind of A-list—A-minus maybe—now that Raf and I are going out. 'Cause he's A-list. When you date an A-list boy, some of it automatically rubs off on you. Not that I care about stuff like that.

All right, I kind of do. But only a little.

"Have as many as you like," I say, pushing my plate toward her. "I'll warn you: they're not great. Kind of soggy."

I carefully pat my outfit to make sure it's still there. After homeroom, I managed to turn my cloak into a more appropriate minidress. Whoever ended up with the cloak isn't going to be happy (and will probably be seriously confused) but whatev. I had to do *something*.

"Do you need more ketchup?" asks a new voice.

Everyone at the table jumps. The voice belongs to Wendaline, who was not sitting at the table two seconds ago. But now is.

Is this chick trying to give me a heart attack?

"Holy crapola!" Sherry squeals. "Where did you come from? You just scared the heck*ie* out of me!" Sherry loves the sound of *ee*. She tends to use it often in conversation, even adding it to words where it doesn't belong. Kind of like pig Latin but less creative. I wouldn't be surprised if her name was originally *Cher* and she changed it to Sherry just to be annoying.

Tammy coughs and grabs her apple Snapple. "I think I swallowed a fry!"

This has got to stop. "Wendaline, can I talk to you for a second in private?"

"Sure," she says. "Where do you wanna go? Somewhere good? In the city? How private? I can poof us over to—"

Oh! My! God! "Wendaline. *No*. Let's just go to the other side of the cafeteria for a sec, 'kay?" I nod toward the window.

She follows my lead. "What's up?"

I angrily place my hands on my hips. "What are you trying to do?"

"What do you mean?"

"Dressing like that! Telling people you're a witch! Zapping yourself into the cafeteria! You can't do that kind of stuff in school!"

"Why not?"

Why? Why me? "Because! You don't want everyone to know you're a witch!"

She blinks. And blinks again. *No comprendo*. "But I *am* a witch."

"So am I," I say, enunciating. "But that doesn't mean I want to broadcast it to the entire world."

"Why not?"

"What do you mean 'why not'?"

"Well, why not?"

"Because . . . because . . . because . . ." Excellent question. Why not? "Because then everyone will know!"

She throws her arms into the air. "So?"

"So!" I feel like we're just repeating each other here.

"Why shouldn't everyone know?" she asks. "I *am* a witch."

"I know. I get it. But see, they don't. They've never heard of witches before."

"How is that possible?" she asks. "There are hundreds of TV shows and movies and books about witches! We're all over the media! You have to be pretty isolated to have never heard of a witch."

"Wendaline, just because they've watched *Wizards of Waverly Place* doesn't mean they *believe* in witchcraft. You've seen *A Christmas Carol*. Does that mean you believe in ghosts?"

She looks shocked. "You've never met a ghost?"

Is there a wall nearby? So I can bang my head against it? "Wendaline, before my sister got her powers, I did not know that witches were real. I had never met a real witch before."

She looks dubious. "Never? What about at the Hexaton?"

"The what?"

"You've never been to the Hexaton?"

"I've never even heard of the Hexaton."

"You're kidding. I have to take you! It's so much fun. All the old society witches have tea there. I've been going since I was six!"

"I didn't know I was a witch when I was six."

"Well, neither did I, but I still went. I mean, I knew I was going to be a witch. Didn't you?"

"No! I had no idea! I didn't know about Hexaton! I didn't know about Brixta! I didn't know about moguls! Or mogis. Whatever. That's what I'm trying to explain! My mom never told us anything about magic. I was clueless! The same as everyone here. If you tell them you're a witch, they're going to think you're a freak. Do you understand? A freak."

She looks around the room, then sighs. "Well, maybe I don't care what they think. I'm not going to hide who I am."

Something is seriously wrong with her. "Don't you want to have friends?"

"Of course."

"Well, you're not going to if people here know you're a witch."

"But why?" she asks, clearly exasperated.

"Because they'd either think you're insane and lock you in the nuthouse, or if they actually believed you, they would lock you up so they could study you! Dissect you, even! Or they'd lock you up because they were terrified of you!"

"That's silly. Why would they be afraid of me? I would never use my magic to hurt anyone. I'm a white witch."

Gray? White? Why is she so obsessed with color? "What does that even mean?"

"I use my magic for good. Or try to, anyway."

"Look, you can do what you want. It's your life." Or funeral. "But don't tell anyone the truth about me. No one here knows, and I like it that way." I glance back at my table and notice that they're all watching us, trying to figure out what's going on. "And I'd really appreciate it if you wouldn't tell my friends you're a witch either. Because if—and it's a big if—they believe you, then they might get suspicious about me. Got it?"

"Whatever you say. You're the expert. But I have to tell you, it's a little weird."

It's a little weird?

Talk about the pot calling the cauldron black.

After an exhausting first day, all I want to do is fall onto my bed. Unfortunately, Miri is lying on said bed, *my* bed, her legs against the wall in a perpendicular position. This is how she thinks.

I approach her, hands on hips. "What?"

"What what?"

"What do you want from me?"

"Can't I just want to hang out with you?"

"Speak truthfully or leave. I'm tired."

"Well . . ." She hesitates. "I want to do the Samsorta. I want us both to do it!"

I groan. "Really? Why?"

"It'll be fun! We'll get dressed up and get our hair and makeup done! We'll be debutantes! We'll be the center of attention! You love being the center of attention!"

I do love being the center of attention. But what has this stranger done with my sister? "But you don't. So why do *you* want to do it?"

"Hmm?"

"You hate looking like a princess. You hate being über-girly. You take Tae Kwon Do. Explain."

"Having a Samsorta puts you on the map."

I climb under my covers and wedge Miri closer to the wall. "What map? No map that I've ever heard of."

"The *witch* map. And I want to be on that map. I want the people in the witchcraft world to know who I am."

"Your map sounds a lot like my A-list."

"It's not about being popular, Rachel. It's about mattering. I want to belong to this witch world. And for the first time in my life—"

"All thirteen years of it."

"For the first time ever, I think I could really fit in."

I want that for my sister. Of course I do. "So do it. You don't need me."

She pales. "Of course I do! I'm not doing it by myself! Are you crazy?"

"Why not? It'll be good for you."

She shakes her head. "I want us to do it together. Right

now it's like we're members of a club, but no one in the club even knows we're members."

"And no one outside the club knows the club exists."

"Exactly!" She smiles at me. "You get it! So will you do it?"

Cemetery . . . new language . . . more time with weird Wendaline . . . getting all prettied up with no one but witches to show off to . . . "I don't know, Mir. It sounds like a lot of work." A lot of work for nothing. "Can't you just meet people on Mywitchbook?"

"I'm trying to! But it's hard! Please? Pretty please?"

What if the witches talk to dead people? And zombies come out of the graves? And they all have headless torsos with blood pumping out of their necks? What if there really are vampires? "But it sounds so creepy—"

"It won't be! It'll be beautiful! We'll be beautiful!"

I close my eyes. "But what's the point in me being all beautiful if Raf won't even get to see?"

"Why won't Raf see you? He can be your date!"

If only. How hot would he look in a suit? So hot. And of course he wouldn't be able to take his eyes off me. But unfortunately, that just can't happen. "Miri, I can't invite Raf to my coming-out witch party."

"Why not?"

Hello? "Because then he'll know I'm a witch!"

"So then he'll know. Big deal."

I flip over my pillow. "I see you've been talking to Wendaline."

"She has a point," Miri says. "Witchcraft isn't something to be ashamed of."

"I'm not ashamed," I say. "I just don't want Raf to know. I don't want him thinking I'm a weirdo. Or being afraid of me. Or worrying that I zapped him with a love potion."

"You mean the love spell we put on Will by accident?"

Right. "I especially don't want him knowing about that."

"I bet he'd think it was cool," she says.

"Or he'd dump me and tell everyone I'm a freak."

Miri's quiet and I wonder if she's given up. But then she says, "You'll have to tell him eventually."

My stomach gets twisty. "No, I won't."

"Even if you get married?"

"Mom never told Dad."

"And look how well that turned out." She looks at me. "She told Lex. Doesn't that count? And shouldn't relationships be based on honesty?"

She does have a point. But who knows if Lex and Mom will last? They haven't even been together six months. What happens if their relationship cools off like an unused cauldron? What then? "Maybe, *maybe* I'd tell him if we got married. Or possibly engaged. But I'm not telling him now." No way. We haven't even said "I love you" yet. Saying those words would have to come before telling him I'm a witch. "No, there's no way I'm bringing him to my Samsorta."

She gives me a wide-eyed hopeful look. "Does that mean you'll do it? But just not invite Raf?"

"But what's the point, then?"

"Me!" she says. "I'm the point! Everything isn't always about Raf. I want us to do it together!"

Oy. She is obsessed.

Wait a sec. There's no way Mom's going to go for it. She said it was a huge waste of time and magic. And she wouldn't even let us *see* any of the *Halloween* movies. She's not going to let us *run around* with dead bodies.

"Well," I say, "if you really want to do it, I'll do it."

"You're in?" she says gleefully. "A hundred percent in?"

I nod. Good thing I'm two hundred percent sure Mom will say no.

6 Operation: Samsorta

We approach her in the kitchen.

"Mom," Miri begins. "We've been thinking."

"Yes, honey?" She's peeling an avocado for a salad.

Miri nudges me to continue.

"We want to participate in the Samsorta," I say, sliding into a kitchen chair.

Mom drops the avocado slicer. "Since when?"

"Since we heard about it," Miri says.

"Yeah," I say, trying to keep my voice flat and void of emotion. Hello, robo-Rachel. "It. Will. Be. Fun."

"Rachel, come on," Mom says, resuming the salad prep. "This is one of those things you say you want because it *sounds* like fun, and then you're sick of it within a week."

Just as I thought. No way.

"Remember the electronic piano?" she continues. "You

claimed you wanted to take lessons, we bought you the piano, and you only played it once."

I lean against the table. "I could never remember all those notes."

Mom rips open a bag of lettuce and dumps it into a large white bowl. A bowl that sometimes doubles as our cauldron. "And what about Tae Kwon Do? You wanted to take it, we bought you the outfit, and then you decided you wanted to be a ballerina instead. And we all remember what happened to you in ballet class."

I accidentally peed in my tutu during a plié. What can I say? Dancing just isn't my thing. Nice of her to bring it up, though. "What are you trying to say exactly? Are you calling me a flake?"

"If the ballet slipper fits . . . ," she says. "Remember Monopoly? It was all you could talk about. Monopoly this, Monopoly that, Jewel has Monopoly, I want Monopoly. And then we bought it for you and you've never even finished a game."

"But that's because only the first twenty minutes are fun and then you just go around and around and around!" Wait a sec. Why am I defending myself here? I don't even want to do the Samsorta! I'm just asking to be nice!

"All I'm saying is that I don't think the Samsorta is such a good idea. It's a big commitment."

I cheer. Silently, of course.

Miri's face falls. "But I didn't quit Tae Kwon Do! I still do it!"

Mom rummages in the fridge and pulls out a tomato and

a green pepper. "I know, honey, but still. It's a lot of work. And for what? Just to get the newsletter?"

Miri perks up. "What newsletter?"

"Oh, you know, what's happening in the witch world. You can't even unsubscribe. They find you anywhere. It's so irritating."

"Where are these newsletters?" I ask.

Mom shrugs. "In the cleaning closet."

I should really check out this closet. Who knows what else is in there? Diamonds? A new car? No skeletons, I hope.

"It's not just about the newsletter," Miri says. "Although I would like to see those. It's about being part of a community."

Mom turns on the faucet to rinse her vegetables and then shouts over the rushing water, "Exactly. That's the problem. It's so public. After your Samsorta, every witch knows who you are. You're *out*. Wouldn't you rather fly under the radar, so to speak?" She turns off the water, deposits her veggies on the cutting board, and starts chopping. "Miri, I'd think you of all people would be against it. It wastes a lot of magic. Didn't you just tell me last night you wanted to be a gray witch?"

"Yeah," she mumbles. "I guess."

"Well then, let's forget it." She dumps the veggies into the bowl. "Who's setting the table today?"

Way to go, Mom. I'd prefer to keep our skeletons securely in the closet.

And my salads veggie free.

"That sucked," Miri said, kicking my closet door.

"You can still meet people on Mywitchbook. More fun and less waste."

"It's not the same," she moans.

"I guess not. Sorry." I sit at my desk and open my chemistry textbook.

"Are you? You don't sound sorry." She gives me a dirty look. "You didn't try that hard to convince her."

" 'Cause I'm not dying to do it." Now, where was I? Right. Page one. The periodic table. "I'm a sophomore now. I have a lot of responsibilities. If I don't pay attention to this graph, I could blow up the school by accident."

"Yeah, whatever." She lies facedown on my bed.

I watch her out the corner of my eye. "What? No joke about how you're surprised I haven't blown up the school already?"

"Whatever."

I roll all the way over to her in my computer chair, which is not easy to do on carpet. "Miri! I can't stand you being so down! Smile!"

She flips her head over to face me. Her lower lip quivers.

Oh, no. "Miri, don't be upset."

"It's okay."

"Obviously it isn't."

"It's just that we've missed out on so much magic stuff already, I can't stand to miss out on this, too."

She does have a point, I guess. I lift my feet off the floor and balance my heels on the edge of my bed. "Miri, if you really want to do it, you can convince her."

She looks up at me. "Yeah?"

"I'll help you get her to agree, but I don't want to do it. You'll have to do it on your own. 'Kay?"

"You'll help me? Really?" she asks hopefully.

"Yes." What are big sisters for? "Let me tell you what you have to do."

It's Tuesday (aka two days to my birthday!) before school. We're lurking outside Mom's bedroom, about to embark on Operation Convince Mom to Let Miri Have a Samsorta.

I love operations. (Not real ones, obviously. No one likes being cut up. Except maybe the people on those Make Me Look Like a Celebrity plastic surgery shows.)

"Ready?" I mouth. "Set?" Pause for effect. "Go!" I open Mom's door and push Miri and her tray of goodies inside. It's breakfast-in-bed time, and we have the works: toast, jam, blueberry muffins, coffee, fresh OJ. Then I hit the floor so Mom can't see me. As I explained to Miri, a good puppet master never shows her strings.

I inhale a clump of dust. When was the last time Mom vacuumed in here?

"Good morning," Miri sings, placing the tray at the foot of the bed. "I made you breakfast! You're my favorite mother in the entire world!"

As I told Miri last night, there are five techniques by which to best manipulate your parents: sucking up, presenting an intellectual argument, staging an emotional ambush, promising to spend more time with them, and annoying them. The best attacks combine at least three of the above.

So far she's not bad at the sucking-up part. I sneak my head up to watch the action unfold.

Mom opens one eye. "I'm your only mother in the entire world."

"Not true. I have a stepmother. She counts. But you're the best."

"She kind of counts. What's all this?" Mom props herself up against her headboard and bites into a muffin.

"A token of my appreciation."

"Appreciation for what?"

"For being so wonderful. And for taking the time to consider what I'm about to say."

Mom cocks an eyebrow. "Yes?"

"I want you to reconsider your Samsorta decision. I've spent all night thinking about it, and it's something I really want to do. Last night you somehow got the impression that this is all Rachel's idea, but it isn't. Rachel doesn't even want to do it. I'm the one who wants a Samsorta."

"Oh," Mom says between chews. "I didn't realize."

Miri oh-so-casually looks at me for her next move.

I mouth, "Intellectual argument!"

She nonchalantly turns back. "I know you don't want to be involved in the witchcraft community, and I respect that. But as a maturing witch, I need to make that decision for myself. And before I make a decision, I need to be educated." Go, intellectual Miri, go! "You've always taught us to gather the facts first, and that's what I'm trying to do. Learn. The Samsorta experience would be an excellent opportunity for learning."

Mom puts down the muffin. "I see."

Miri leans in, extra-eager. "So can I do it?"

"Let me think about it. I'm not saying no. But I'm not saying yes."

Miri nods solemnly. "I understand. Have a good day. I love you."

She steps on me on her way out.

I yelp. Silently.

Mom sips her coffee. "And tell your sister to get off the floor."

Operation Convince Mom to Let Miri Have a Samsorta, take two!

I borrow Tammy's cell and head to the school stairwell. Luckily, the end of my lunch coincides with the beginning of Miri's. I make sure I am alone on the stairs before I call my sister's phone. "Are you ready?" I ask. "Are you pumped?"

"I can't believe what I'm about to do."

"Do you want to have a Samsorta or not?"

"I do, I do," she says.

"Then go ahead. Use conference."

" 'Kay, hold on."

She dials and then we hear Mom's cheerful "HoneySun, Carol speaking!" greeting.

"Mom?"

"Miri? Is everything okay? Where are you?" We never call her at work during the day and she sounds appropriately panicked.

"Everything is fine. I was just wondering if you've given the Samsorta any more thought. I really want to do it. I'd love to meet other witches my age—"

"Miri, no cell phones during school! It'll be confiscated!"

"Oh, don't worry. I'm in my special spot."

"What special spot? You haven't left school grounds, have you?"

"Of course not! I'm in the second-floor bathroom. In the back stall? I have lunch here sometimes. You know, when no one wants to sit with me?"

Kabang! Emotional ambush! Just like we planned. Bring on the waterworks.

My mom gasps. "Oh, Miri."

"Don't worry. I don't mind. Sure, the toilet isn't the best table—my milk carton sometimes falls inside—but it's only a few times a week. Four max." We didn't even practice this stuff! She is ad-libbing! "Anyway, I'll let you get back to work," Miri concludes. "Love you!" We hang up, and she calls me right back. "How'd I do?"

"You're a natural."

"I know, huh? Think she'll let me do it?"

"Definitely. After school, tell her again how important it is to you. How isolated you feel, and how you think this would be really good for you."

Something flashes at the bottom of the stairs. Wendaline. "I have to go," I mutter. "Your witch friend is zapping herself all over town. Tell Mom I'm going to Tammy's after school but I'll be home for dinner."

"Will do. Love you."

"You too. Wait—Mir?"

"Yeah?"

"Um, you don't really eat on the toilet bowl, do you?"

She laughs. "No. Don't be disgusting."

I end the call and stick the phone in my back pocket. "Wendaline, you have to stop doing that in public!"

She slams her palm against her forehead. "Whoops. Sorry! I keep forgetting. I've been flying around the school, trying to find you. I checked the cafeteria first, but you weren't there."

Great. What if somebody saw her? "I was until about five minutes ago."

"It's all good. I had to pop home for my gym clothes. I forgot to bring them."

By *pop*, I'm assuming she means *zap*.

"So, how's my outfit today?" she asks, twirling. She's wearing a black mesh skirt with a velvet turtleneck, fishnets, and black boots. "Better?"

"Better," I say. Not by much. "Very Goth."

"I know! Fun, huh?"

"Where do you get your clothes, anyway? Some witch catalog?"

"No, silly, on Eighth Street. At my cousin Ursula's. Didn't she mention it? She has a store that sells clothes and jewelry. She went to FET and everything. It's all good."

"Don't you mean FIT? Fashion Institute of Technology?"

"No! FET. Familiars, Enchantments, and Talismans. A postsecondary witch course that you can take in Paris during the summer." She pulls on her necklace. "She made this. You like?"

"Is that a silver broom?"

"Yeah! A broom charm! Fun, huh? You can add as many charms as you want. Spell books, wands, cats . . ."

"Cute." If you want people to think you're a weirdo.

"She sells a ton of them. They've gotten really popular."

The first bell rings.

"I'm going up," I tell her as a rush of students rams its way into the stairwell. "You?"

"I'm going down. I have to go to the bathroom before class. I didn't realize that you have to *ask* to use it. Isn't that ridiculous?"

I laugh. "That you have to ask or that you didn't know?"

"I have so much to remember!"

A wave of cool air blows through the hall and Wendaline vanishes.

If only she could remember to use the stairs.

"She said yes!" Miri screams when I get home from Tammy's. She throws her arms around my neck.

"Yay, yay, yay!" We do a victory dance in front of the door.

"You're brilliant!" she cheers. "It was the bonding plea that finally did it. I told her that having a Samsorta would make me feel so much closer to her! I am *so* happy," she says. "You are the best sister in the whole world!"

"I know." I kick off my shoes. "Is Mom home?"

"No, she went to dinner with Lex. She left us pizza money. Oh, and I got you black-and-white cookies. Your favorite. Do you want one?"

"Thank you!" Boy, it's nice to be appreciated. I dump my bag on the floor near the closet and head into the kitchen.

"I am just so excited. It's going to be so much fun! I'll meet so many people! I'll get a great overview of magic! It'll perfectly top off my training." She carries over a plate of cookies and a steaming cup of cocoa. It's always fun when Mom goes out with Lex. Miri and I get to have dessert before dinner. "Hey," Miri says. "I've been meaning to ask you. How's your training going?"

"My what?"

"Your witch training? With Mom? You know how she made me do it last year, and how I'm almost done with it? You didn't think she'd let you get away without it, did you?"

"Oh. Right. Training. Well, we haven't started it exactly." I bite into the deliciousness. Yum. I can't imagine what my mom could possibly teach me; I feel like I know more about magic than she does. "Maybe soon."

"I think she mentioned something about starting next week."

"Seriously?" I take a sip of the hot chocolate. Yum! Miri added mini-marshmallows!

"Yup. Lots of bonding with Mom."

I roll my eyes.

"It doesn't take too much time," Miri says. "Only like three hours."

I dig in to cookie number two. "Three hours a week isn't bad."

"No," she says forcefully. "Three hours a day."

Eeks. Did Miri spend that much time on her training last year? That doesn't sound like fun. "I'm sure she'll do an accelerated version with me." I am smarter. Or at least older.

"Maybe. Hey! You know what?"

I take another bite of cookie. "What?"

"Samsorta training is only once a week. If you did it, I bet Mom would consider it good enough."

"But then wouldn't I have to have a Samsorta?"

"Well, once you were doing the training . . ."

Wait a sec! The cookies, the you're-the-best-sister routine, the clever intellectual reasoning, the threat of parental bonding . . . I thump my fists on the kitchen table. "You're using my manipulation techniques! On me!"

She covers her face with her arm. "Mom said I could only do it if you do too!"

"Miri!"

"Please, Rachel? Pretty please? She said she doesn't want to worry about me going on my own. She thinks you'll keep an eye on me, and keep me from getting mixed up with the wrong crowd. Apparently, I'm not always the best judge of character."

She did get me body-snatched over the summer. But still. "I don't know, Miri. . . ."

"Puh-lease?" She opens her eyes all wide and sad-looking.

"I just want to have people to hang out with. You went to Tammy's after school. Mom went out with Lex. I stayed home by myself and watched television. Alone. Again."

"Gimme a break."

"I just wish I had people to talk to," she says in her extra-squeaky voice, "when you go out with your friends and desert me."

I groan. "If you don't stop, I'm going to make you eat this cookie in the bathroom."

"Please? How can you say no to me after all the stuff I did for you? The megels, the dancing spell, the love potion spell, the—"

"Guilt trip?"

"Puh-lease? Puh-leeeease?"

I know I'm going to regret this, but . . . I guess I do owe her. "*Fiiiiine*, Miri. If it's that important to you, we'll have a Samsorta."

"Yes!" She pumps the air in victory. "It's going to be so much fun!"

Wild and crazy Rafless cemetery fun. Wahoo. "What do I have to do?"

"Nothing," she says happily. "Mom is calling Charm School tomorrow and signing us both up. That's where Wendaline's going too."

"You just knew I'd say yes, huh?"

She blows me a kiss. "I learned from the master."

7 Watch Your Back

It's Wednesday (otherwise known as one day before my birthday), between second and third periods, when I know we're going to have a problem.

I spot Wendaline in the hallway, in a black and red polka-dot monstrosity, and wave.

She waves back.

At least she's not in her cloak. Not that this getup is much better. But at least there's no popping or zapping anywhere. All good, right? Normal. Until I watch, horror-stricken, as a random junior boy sticks his Converse-clad foot out in front of her, sending her toppling to the floor. A spiral notebook and a pencil case veer in different directions.

The junior smirks. His friends laugh.

I hurry to the disaster site and help her up. "Are you okay?"

"It's all good. I'm fine. So weird. I've been falling all over the place today. Something must be wrong with my equilibrium."

She's so clueless. "Wendaline! There's nothing wrong with you! That jerk tripped you!"

"He did not!"

"He so did. I saw him."

She shakes her head. "It must have been an accident, right? It was an accident?"

"Um . . ."

She flinches. "You don't think it was an accident?"

"No," I say. "I don't."

"But why would anyone trip me on purpose?" She bends over to pick up her now many-times-stepped-on notebook.

I spot a yellow paper taped to her behind. *Trip me* is scrawled in black marker. I pluck it off and silently hand it over.

Her jaw drops. "Why would someone do that?"

Sigh. "Because they're mean."

"But why? That is so awful! It's been happening all day! My elbows are all bruised!" She rubs her arm, punctuating her point.

I pick up her equally bruised pencil case from the floor and pull her into an empty classroom. I take a deep breath. "Wendaline, it's because of the way you dress."

She looks at me with dismay. "Because I'm not wearing the same jeans and a shirt like everyone else?"

"Yeah."

She throws her arms into the air. "That's ridiculous! I have the right to dress however I want!"

"Of course you have the *right*. But maybe you shouldn't." I point to my own outfit—of jeans and a shirt. "Sometimes it's better to blend in."

"But this is my style!" she cries. "I don't want to blend in. I want to be *me*."

I wave the yellow paper. "*Being you* is getting you tripped."

She snatches the note from my hand and crunches it into a ball. "Now it won't."

"Be careful," I say uneasily. "You have to watch your back."

"Literally, apparently." Her shoulders slouched, she hurries down the hall.

The cafeteria is extra-crowded because of the torrential rain outside. When it rains in Manhattan, it rains hard. It rains cats and dogs.

Cats and dogs. What kind of creepo expression is that? Why would it rain animals? If I were going to make up an expression about it raining animals, I would at least use airborne animals like pigeons or mosquitoes.

From our table, I watch a tiny freshman girl accidentally bump into Wendaline in the lunch line.

"How do you know Wendaline?" Tammy asks, following my gaze.

I fidget with my brown paper bag as Wendaline spins around, eyeing the other freshman suspiciously. Uh-oh.

Now she thinks everyone is out to get her. "Wendaline's an old friend of the family," I mumble. I'm afraid my family friend Wendaline is about to crack and turn the innocent freshman into a pigeon in about a millisecond.

Tammy sips her juice. "Right. Is she really a witch?"

I almost spit up my sandwich. Cough, cough! Choking, here!

"I know the Heimlich and I'm not afraid to use it," says a familiar voice behind me. Raf.

"I'm fine," I say quickly, and chug my water. "All clear. Hi. No tray?"

He gives me a quick kiss, takes a seat beside me, and drops a rumpled paper bag on the table. "I brought my lunch today. Leftover lemon chicken. Hey, Tam."

"Yum, I love Chinese food." I also love talking about Chinese food, if it keeps the conversation off Wendaline. "My favorite is General Tso. Delicious. I should have ordered that for dinner last night, instead of pizza." I look down at the two slices I brought from home. Keep talking, Rachel. Don't stop. "I eat way too much pizza. I'm going to turn into a pizza."

"You'd be an adorable pizza," Raf says. "Pepperoni eyes and tomato lips. I'll switch with you as a precaution."

"Really?" So romantic. He hands me his container of chicken and I hand him my pizza—as well as my heart.

Yeah, I know that was *cheesy* (wink, wink), and I don't care.

"Hey, Raf," Tammy says. "I was just asking Rachel for more info on her family friend. The one who says she's a witch?"

Tammy! Get over it already! "Wendaline is a big joker." I wave my hand. "Trust me. She was kidding. She kids around a lot." Ha-ha.

"She didn't sound like she was kidding," Raf says, unwrapping my pizza. "She sounded like she thought she was a witch."

"She was a hundred percent kidding." My heart pounds extra-loudly. If we weren't in the noisiest place in the world, they would one hundred percent hear it.

"Maybe she *is* a witch." Tammy shrugs, as though this entire discussion is no big deal, and not the scariest conversation of my existence.

Raf laughs. "Sure. And I'm a vampire."

Ha-ha. Ha.

"You don't believe in witches?" Tammy asks.

My heart fully stops. It is no longer beating. I'm pretty sure I am now dead, or at the very least, in a coma.

"Are you joking?" Raf asks, making a face. "You do?"

Stop, stop, this entire conversation must stop immediately. I'm going to pass out.

"I don't know," Tammy continues. "Maybe. Why not? Just because I don't know it's there doesn't mean it doesn't exist, right?"

Raf takes a whopping bite of the slice. "I'm more of a what-you-see-is-what-you-get type of person."

"Seriously?" Tammy asks. "Not me. I think there's lots going on that we just don't know about. Like in the water. When you go for a dive, you see an entire world that you had no idea existed from the surface. Sea horses! Cuttlefish!

Blue devils! Barracudas! It's overwhelming. One minute you're on the boat, and the next you're eye to eye with a hammerhead."

"Yeah, I think I'll stay above the surface," Raf says, laughing. "Not sure I'm ready to take on a shark."

Am I being compared to a shark? I'm mildly confused but relieved we've moved on to another subject. Kind of.

"They don't bite," Tammy says. "Not much. Anyway, my point is that you never know. If she says she's a witch—"

Oh, come on, Tammy! We've moved on! Hammerheads, give me more hammerheads!

"—then maybe she is."

Wendaline is now done with the line and moving

toward our table. She cannot sit here. No. It's too risky. Blood rushes to my head. What if she tells them again that she's a witch? No, what if she zaps something and *shows* them she's a witch? What if she tells them I'm a witch too? What if they're scared of me? What if they think *I'm* going to bite?

Wendaline needs to find her own friends and stay away from mine.

"Rachel," Raf says, patting my knee. "What do *you* think? Do you believe in magic?"

Blood. Rushing. "I—I—I—" I think I'd better cut Wendaline off before she catches the tail end of this conversation and ruins my life. I bolt out of my seat. "I'm going to buy a bag of chips."

I catch Wendaline and her lunch tray at the midway

point. I take a deep breath to calm myself down. "Hey. Wendaline."

"Hi, Rachel! Thanks so much for saving me. I haven't kissed the floor in the last hour, thanks to you."

"Oh, no problem," I say wearily.

"It's been the worst day ever. I forgot about that whole bathroom rule again, and Mr. Stein yelled at me!"

Great, now she has me feeling bad for her again. Telling her, *Please don't sit with me anymore*, is unlikely to cheer her up. "Oh! I have good news."

"I like good news."

"Miri and I are in. We're gonna do the Samsorta!"

"Really? Excellent! That *is* good news! We can celebrate together! Are they going to let you into Charm School?"

"My mom is calling them today."

She adjusts her hold on the tray. "Let's go sit down. I'm starved and this weighs a ton."

Here it comes. "Wait. There's something I want to talk to you about." Deep breath. "Don't you want to make friends with people in your own grade? You're still welcome to sit with me, of course." But please don't. Pretty please? Pretty please with a maraschino cherry on top?

She shrugs. "I haven't spoken much to anyone in my grade."

"Maybe you should try." I look around the room and scout out the cliques of freshmen. "Any girls you recognize from class?"

She points to a group of über-glossy-looking girls. I'm talking full-on highlights, designer jeans and tops, noses so upturned they're practically touching the clouds, or at least the ceiling. "They're in my homeroom."

Hmm. I don't know if they're the *best* place to start. "Anyone else?"

She glances around. "It's so tough to tell these people apart. They all wear the exact same thing. Oh, I think those girls are in my art class."

The girls she's pointing to look a little less snobby. One is wearing a purple peasant skirt and a matching off-the-shoulder blouse, and the other has a chunky pink streak in her hair and a silver nose ring. Peasant Skirt Girl is laughing heartily at whatever Pink Streak Girl is saying. Yes, they are a much better choice for potential friends. Since they are not wearing the traditional JFK uniform, they are obviously already a few degrees left of mainstream. "Perfect," I say. "Go say hi. Tell them you're in their class. Ask if you can join them for lunch. If they're rude, just pick up your tray and come sit with me. 'Kay?"

" 'Kay. Thanks, Rachel. Again. You're a lifesaver." She stands up straight and heads toward them.

"Wait!" I whisper. "Wendaline!"

She turns. "Yup?"

"Don't tell them. About . . . you know. Not right away. 'Kay?"

"But . . . Okay."

I watch her timidly approach them.

"Hi," she says. "I'm in your art class. Do you mind if I join you?"

"Sure," Pink Streak Girl says. "What's your name?"

Aw.

I *am* a lifesaver. Except it's not Wendaline's life I'm concerned with saving.

It's my own.

Miri accosts my mom the second she walks through the door. "So? So? What did they say? Are we in?"

"I have good news and bad news," my mom begins, leaning her dripping umbrella against the door. "Wow, it's really raining out there."

"Is it raining birds and mosquitoes?" I ask.

"Um, no." She looks at me quizzically. "Should it be? You didn't do a weather spell, did you?"

"Can we get back to the news, please?" Miri asks.

"Right." Mom slips out of her rain jacket and hangs it up. "I called the Charm School, but they started classes back in August. So it's too late for this fall, but they're happy to sign you up for next year."

Wahoo! A year's reprieve. I'm sure by then Miri will have forgotten about this crazy plan.

"Oh, no," Miri says, looking crestfallen. "I want to do it *this* year. Wendaline's doing it this year."

"It'll still be fun next year," I say. "More fun, even, 'cause we won't be rushed."

Instead of listening to my sage advice, my sister is babbling to herself. "There must be other places to train for this. I mean, witches from all over the world participate.

There can't be only one school. I'm going to ask around on Mywitchbook." She runs into her room.

Mom sighs. "She certainly has a bee in her bonnet, huh?"

"Seems that way." Am I a terrible sister if I'm hoping she loses her Internet connection because of a freak power failure?

For dinner, Mom serves a particularly vile vegetarian black bean burrito dish. I try to *moosa* it away like they did at the Full Moon dinner, but the plate just gets zapped from the table to the kitchen counter.

Mom snickers. "Nice try."

After helping with the dishes, I retreat to my room to read my American history assignment. Hello, Civil War. I'm daydreaming about Scarlett O'Hara's hoop dresses when Miri screams out, "Lozacea!"

"Bless you!" I call back.

"I found something! There's a place in Arizona that offers group lessons too! And they don't start until next week! I'm calling them right now!"

Mom and I both join Miri in her room as she's dialing.

I crawl onto her bed while she paces, the receiver pressed against her ear.

Mom leans against the doorframe. "Do you want me to talk to them?"

Miri shakes her head. My sister is not messing around. "I got it. Hello? My name is Miri Weinstein, and I'm calling because my sister and I want to find out more information about your Samsorta classes. . . . Really? You're not full?"

Terrific.

"Yes, we both have our powers. I'm thirteen and she's fourteen."

"Fifteen!" I correct. One more day! One more day!

"Sure," she continues. "That would be fine. We look forward to meeting you, Matilda." She hangs up the phone. "Wahoo! We're in!" She shimmies around the room.

"Um. Yay?"

"I'm so excited!" she shrieks, hugging me. "We're going to Lozacea!"

Mom crosses her arms. "Not until I check them out, you're not."

"They're very reputable," Miri assures her. "Here's their number."

Mom takes the phone, dials, and retreats into the hallway.

Meanwhile, Miri dances—if you can call it that—around her room. Clearly she didn't inherit dancing skills either. "We're in!" she shrieks. "All we have to do is pass the test!"

Er. I raise an eyebrow. "What test?"

"Matilda in admissions said she just has to make sure we actually have our powers. Apparently people have tried to fake it. She'll stop by sometime this week."

Pop quiz? Awesome. "Stop by where? Here? At school? Where?"

"It's all good!"

Yeah, right. I'm not just worried. I'm very worried. I'm actually feeling very queasy right now.

Of course, it's probably because of the un-moosa-able black bean burrito.

8 Birthday Lovin'

Happy birthday to me! I wake up singing to myself. It's my birthday and I'll sing if I want to!

I'm fifteen. Which is so old. I'm halfway through my teens! One year away from getting my driver's permit. Three years away from voting. Six years away from drinking. Twelve years away from getting married! (Yes, I've given it lots of thought, contemplated a few formulas, and I believe that twenty-seven is the ideal age to get married.)

After my birthday shower, I put on my birthday outfit (ha-ha, not really my birthday outfit, since I'm not naked), my favorite jeans and a cool magically altered top, and pad my way to the kitchen. "I'm fifteen!" I holler. "Hear me roar!"

My mom serves me a plate of banana pancakes, my favorite. "Happy birthday, honey! Do you want to open your present now or tonight?"

"Hmm, tonight is fine," I say with a straight face. Then I crack up. "I want to open it this very second, what do you think?" Gimme that cell phone, baby!

She hands me a small box wrapped in striped wrapping paper. I rip inside and it's a . . . pair of socks.

Just kidding! It's a cell phone! A beautiful silver pocket-sized cell phone! "Wahoo!" *Just call me on my cell. Excuse me, I think my cell is ringing. Nice to meet you; let me give you my cell number.*

"No surprises this year," Mom says. "Just don't go crazy with your calls and your texts. You and Miri are sharing minutes."

"Love you!" I kiss her cheek.

Miri hands me a wrapped rectangular box. "My turn!"

I tear the paper off in two seconds and uncover an adorable pink jeweled cell phone case. "Perfect! Thanks, Miri! Best presents ever!"

"You can return it if you don't like it," Miri tells me. "They have other colors."

"Miri, I love it!"

"It has extra padding for when you drop it," she says.

I slide the phone into the case right away. Gorgeous. I hug my new contraption to my chest. "I won't drop it! It's too precious!"

"Just in case," she says. "Get it? In case?"

"*Wakka, wakka.*"

She sits back and digs in to her pancakes. "So, who's coming tonight?"

My mom said I was allowed to invite a few people over for birthday cake even though it's a school night. I could have invited more people over on Saturday night, but we have to go to my dad's on Long Island this weekend. As we do every other weekend. Disadvantage number 107 of having divorced parents. I mean, I love my dad and all, but missing out on the social activities every other weekend sucks.

Other disadvantages include your parents no longer being married to each other, your father no longer sharing your house, lifetime relationship issues, and being forced to wear a puffy pink bridesmaid dress at your parent's second wedding, among other gems.

The advantage? You get two parental birthday gifts. The second of which I'll be getting on Saturday. Wahoo!

"Hello?" Miri says. "Rachel? Still with me? Who'd you invite?"

"Oh, sorry. Raf, Tammy, and Alison. And you, Lex, Mom. Obviously." Of course it would be nice if I could invite Dad, Jennifer, and Prissy, but that would make everyone uncomfy, particularly me.

She drags a piece of banana around her plate. "No Wendaline?"

"I think I'd rather it be just close friends. I like Wendaline, but she does weird witch things in public."

"Give her a break, Rachel. She's never been to a real school before."

"I know, I know, but I'd still rather keep some distance between her and my peeps." I wink. "Just in case."

I have a superb day. How could I not? It's *my* day!

Random people wish me happy birthday. Tammy brings me a cupcake during lunch. All my friends sing.

I drop my cell phone only twice.

"I didn't know it was your birthday!" Wendaline says, approaching our table for a quick visit. Luckily, her new friends seem to have stuck. Luckily she hasn't told them her witchy secret yet. "I would have sent you an e-broom!"

Everyone stares. I give her a look. "Don't you mean an e-*card*, Wendaline?"

"Right! An e-card! 'Cause why would I send an e-broom? That would be weird!"

And that's exactly why she's not invited over tonight. Hey, I'm not being mean. I've known her for only a week.

Fine, I'm being a little mean, but tough. It's my birthday and I can be mean if I want to.

"Happy birthday, dear Rachel. . . . Happy birthday to you! And many more!"

This song just never gets old, does it?

"Skip around the room, skip around the room," Alison sings.

What is she talking about? I don't skip.

"We won't shut up . . . ," Alison continues, *"till you skip around the room!* Come on, Rachel, it's a song I learned at camp."

"There's nowhere to skip; it's a New York kitchen!"

"Skip around the room! We won't shut up till you—"

I push back my chair and attempt to skip around the table while avoiding stepping on Tigger's tail.

Hmmm. Didn't Tigger used to be gray? When did he turn black? When did he gain twenty pounds? This cat needs some serious South Beaching. This cat looks like he swallowed Tigger.

Wait. This isn't my cat!

"What is that?" I shriek, pointing.

The fat black cat has big green eyes and velvety fur and is clutching something shiny between his teeth.

"How did a stray cat get into the apartment?" Tammy asks.

"It must belong to one of the neighbors," Mom says. "Go back outside, kitty! Miri, can you show him the way? Who wants cake?"

The cat nuzzles my leg. He's kind of cute. But what does he have between his teeth?

I squat to the ground. It's a pink gift bag. On the front, in black calligraphy, it says *Rachel Weinstein*.

Huh?

Who would send me a present via a cat?

A witch. The pop quiz? Tonight? Or . . . Wendaline! She sent me a present! Via a cat! "I got him," I say, gently scooping him up and carrying him into the hallway.

He snuggles into my boob. Smart animal: he went for the bigger one. I remove the bag from his mouth, place him on the floor, and check out his collar. *Tinkerbell*. Oh, it's a girl. On the flip side, it reads *Don't worry about me. I'm charmed and will find my way home!* This cat must belong to

Wendaline. Who else would announce her cat's charmed status to the world?

Do I need to be charming Tigger? It's not like he ever leaves the apartment. What a slacker. From now on, he's running all my errands.

When I open the tiny bag, a red balloon soars to the ceiling. Then a yellow one. And then more in silver, gold, white, and blue.

Next I pull out a card:

Happy birthday, Rachel!
Hope your day is magical!
Hugs & wishes, Wendaline

Finally, I pull out a small black jewelry box. I open it to find a delicate silver broom charm. Aw. How sweet. How thoughtful. I feel a ping in my chest for not inviting her.

How rude of her to make me feel bad on my birthday!

I must hide this charm before Tammy, Raf, or Alison sees it. Plus I must get rid of Tinkerbell. Except . . . where is Tinkerbell? She is no longer on the floor. Where is she hiding?

"Here, Tinkerbell," I whisper. "Where did you go?"

No Tinkerbell. I guess she disappeared. Why am I not surprised?

Tammy gives me a bunch of books (*Bliss*, *Fly on the Wall*, *A Great and Terrible Beauty*). "They're all a little paranormal," she says.

Er. 'Cause my life isn't paranormal enough.

Alison gets me adorable pink flannel pajama bottoms. "For camp," she says, although I'm pretty sure I'll be wearing them every night until camp, 'cause they're so cute and comfy.

I wait until only Raf is left before opening his gift. My mom and Lex are in the kitchen, cleaning up; Miri's in her room, trying to make more Mywitchbook friends; and we're cuddling on the couch. I open the card first.

> *Dear Rachel,*
> *Happy 15th. Hope it's a great one.*
> *Love, Raf*

Omigod. I reread the last line.

Love, Raf.

And again: *Love, Raf.*

He wrote *love*. Love! He loves me! He wouldn't have written it unless he loved me, right? I mean, I know it's a relatively common sign-off, but still. *Love*. Love! He said love! He loves me! I peek at him to see if he's waiting for a reaction. What am I supposed to do? Should I show happiness? Excitement? Should I throw down the card and shout "I love you too!"? Or maybe "I love you too and by the way I'm a witch."

No. No!

I'm not telling him. *Ever.*

At least until we're engaged.

Anyway, he didn't say "I love you." He just signed the card *love*. How do I know that this isn't standard practice for him? Maybe he signs all his cards *love*. Birthday cards. Anniversary cards. Mother's Day cards. Of course he signs Mother's Day cards *love*. What kind of son doesn't sign Mother's Day cards with *love*? Jerk sons. And Raf is no jerk. Maybe he signs Mother's Day cards *All My Love*. Or *Love Always*. Maybe *love* is a step down. A bad sign! Maybe he's breaking up with me. Maybe—

"Um, Rachel?" Raf asks, squeezing my shoulder. "Aren't you going to open the present?"

Right.

I delicately peel off the red paper. It's another jewelry box! Inside is a thin gold chain, and dangling on it, a small gold heart.

Omigod. He gave me his heart! Seriously! He totally loves me! I think I'm going to cry! "It's beautiful," I say, and blink the waterworks away.

"Really? You like it?"

"I love . . ." You! I love you! "It."

He helps me with the clasp.

And then . . . well, let's just say my calculations were right. Birthdays definitely include extra kissing.

9 A Pregnant Pause

"So, what are you going to do all weekend?" I ask Raf via my cell. Miri and I are on the train heading to Long Island.

"Talk on the phone with you?"

"Yes, besides that." Why is my knapsack rising off the floor? I glance at Miri and see her wiggling her fingers at my stuff. "Stop megeling my things!" I mouth.

She sticks out her tongue.

"My dad asked me if I could help out at the store tomorrow," Raf says, referring to Kosa Coats and Goods, their family's leather jacket factory store. They make their own jackets and sell them to department stores like Saks and Bloomingdale's. "And then I'm going to Dave Nephron's party tomorrow night. Wanna come?"

"Don't tease. You know I want to." Unfortunately, while I'll be stuck in the yellow meringue room that Miri and I share at my dad's, Raf will be surrounded by all the girls at JFK who wish he were their boyfriend. Like Melissa Davis. "You're not allowed to talk to any other girls, 'kay?" Omigod! I can't believe I said that! I didn't mean to! Miri's distracting me.

He laughs. "I'm not interested in any other girls, Rachel. I'm definitely not interested in the girls at the party."

My heart rate speeds up. "Melissa will be at the party. You used to be interested in her." I keep my voice light and playful, but of course I'm dying to hear what he's going to say. We've never really talked about why he chose me over her.

My knapsack starts rising again. I grab Miri's fingers and squeeze.

"Ouch!" she whines.

"Melissa isn't a bad person," Raf says. "She's just not the right person for me."

"And why not?" I hold my breath. And Miri's fingers.

"We just didn't connect, you know? I was with her because we thought we should make a good couple, not because we really were a good couple. It was superficial."

Wow. That's the most intense thing Raf has ever said to me. Unfortunately, I don't have brain power to process it, because Miri is wiggling her nose and making my knapsack smack me in the face.

"Rachel?" he says. "Are you still there?"

"One sec," I tell him. "What do you want?" I whisper.

"I'm bored."

"One minute," I whisper. "Then I'll get off. This is a really important conversation."

She crosses her arms and sinks back into her seat.

"Sorry about that," I say calmly. "Back to what you were saying. About Melissa being superficial?"

He laughs. "It's not that she's superficial. It's that we were a superficial couple. You and I have something more . . . real. Does that makes sense?"

"Absolutely," I say softly. "Something real. I like it, it being real and all."

"And I like you," he says.

I feel my face grow warm. Okay, it's not "I love you," but it's close. Just a half step away. "I like you, too," I say.

I hear him clear his throat. Aw, how adorable! He's embarrassed! "So, what time are you coming home on Sunday?" he asks.

"Eightish."

"Next weekend you're in town, though, right?"

"Yup."

"Should we do something on Saturday?"

"It's a date."

Miri pokes me in the side. "We have Samsorta classes next weekend."

I cover the mouth of the phone. "Miri! Are you listening to my conversation?" At least, I think it's the mouth. I don't totally understand how this thing works yet.

"Learn how to adjust the volume on your phone," she snaps. "Don't blame me."

"Samsorta class isn't all day, is it?" I whisper.

She shakes her head. "It's from one to four."

I roll my eyes. "Great. Only the entire afternoon."

"Can you please get off the phone already?" she begs. "I'm really bored."

"I'll be one more minute," I promise.

"You said that ten minutes ago! You've been talking with Raf for an hour!" she yells, not very discreetly. "Shared minutes!"

"It's not like you're going to use them," I mutter.

Her face crumples. Whoops. That was really mean. I'd better go. "Raf, can I call you later from my dad's?"

" 'Kay. Have a good night."

"You too. Enjoy the party. But not too much. Bye." Like you. Love you.

Not that I say that last bit out loud. 'Cause I've been thinking a lot about this whole love thing, about whether or not I should say it, and I've decided that gold hearts and birthday-card salutations are not the same as saying "I love you." I'm pretty sure. I don't know. How could I possibly know? I'm not a boy. I don't understand the workings of the boy brain.

I wish Miri were a boy. Then she'd—I mean he'd—be able to explain things to me. If Miri were a boy, she wouldn't be so sensitive. She wouldn't be ignoring me now and staring out the window.

I should really be careful about making strange wishes. What if when Miri turns around she has a beard?

"Sorry," I say. "That was a mean thing to say. About the minutes. And that I secretly wished you were a boy. But don't worry about that last part; I unwished it."

She shrugs, still refusing to turn around.

I drop my phone into her lap. "See? I'm off. I'm all yours. Talk to me."

Still nothing.

"Gimme a break. I said I was sorry."

"It's not you," she says. "You're right. What's the point of me having a cell phone? I haven't used it once!"

"Not true. I called you at school. And you conferenced in Mom. And you called Wendaline to tell her that we were downstairs at her place. That's three people."

She bites her lip. "My calls totaled three minutes."

"Wanna call me again now? I'm happy to chat. This train ride is totally boring."

Finally, she cracks a small smile.

"Miri," I say. "Your phone is going to ring off the hook beginning next week. That's why we're doing this Samsorta thing, right? So you can make friends!"

She looks into her lap. "It's not just about making friends. . . . Do you think I'll ever have a boyfriend?"

Omigod! Miri is asking me about boys! Abracazam! "Do you have a crush I should know about? Tell me absolutely everything!"

She turns bright red. "There's nothing to tell. It's not like there's anyone at school who *likes* me."

"Then they're stupid. Next! Or, we could always spike their drinks! We'll put a love potion in their water bottles. Huh, huh?" I wiggle my eyebrows extra-suggestively. "I know how much you love love potions. Or maybe we'll make you that love perfume that Mom used last year. Then you'll have a gazillion dates just like she did. Or we can—"

"I changed my mind," she says, interrupting.

"You want to try the love potion?" I ask.

"No." She hands my cell back. "I want you to call Raf again and stop harassing me."

When we arrive, Prissy, Dad, and a pregnant Jennifer are waiting at the station.

Not that she looks pregnant. She's only a couple of months in. But I can tell, I swear. Probably because she keeps rubbing her belly.

"You're here!" Prissy screams, jumping up and down like she's on a trampoline. "We've been waiting and I'm hungry and—"

"Hi, kids!" My dad throws his arms around us. "I missed you!"

"We just saw you two weeks ago," Miri says, giggling.

I pat the bald spot on his head. My special way of saying hello.

"Two weeks is too long to go without my girls," he says, and we pile into the car.

"How are you feeling?" I ask Jennifer.

She opens her window. "Oh, I'm fine. I have a little morning sickness, but it's not terrible."

"Is it a girl, Mommy?" Prissy asks.

She groans. "I told you, honey, I don't know."

"I want a girl."

"I know, honey, but it's not up to me."

"I don't want a boy. No brothers. No."

A brother, huh? Maybe he could help me understand boys better. Not right away, obviously. But in a few years.

Hopefully before I turn twenty-seven and get married.

The next two days go by at a broken broom's pace.

My dad and Jennifer got me a . . . bike.

"Oh!" This is not a laptop. Not that I really expected a laptop. They are super-expensive. But so are bikes! And I *need* a laptop. I don't need a bike. I don't even like biking that much. But I don't want to hurt their feelings, so I try to feign enthusiasm. "Great! Thanks!" Why would they get me a bike?

"I know how much you used to love riding," my dad says. "I thought you could take it out around here. I used to take you everywhere. . . ." He lets his voice trail off, remembering. "Miri, we can get you one for Hanukkah if you want. So you guys can go together."

Oh, sure, she gets a choice? Maybe she can get a new laptop and I'll trade her. I'm sounding ungrateful, aren't I? It's just that I haven't ridden a bike in a million years. (Besides when we flew our old canary bike into the city to magically turn it into a car. But that wasn't pleasure riding.) Doesn't my dad know me better than that?

Anyway. A new bike. Yay.

Instead of biking, I spend the weekend worrying about the upcoming magic pop quiz. When will it be? What if my dad is involved? What if they turn him into a frog and I have to reverse the spell? Surprise! You're a frog! Surprise! Your daughter's a witch! Yikes.

I also teach myself how to text on my cell. I find the letters a bit confusing, but if the rest of the world can do it, so can I.

But why can't I figure out how to make spaces or punctuation?

I also spend a lot of time thinking about what Raf said about us being "real." Are we real? How can we be real when he doesn't know my secret?

Should he know the real me?

Can I tell him the truth? After all, he did kind of tell me he loves me. Or at least, he used the word *love* in connection with me. That counts, right?

Almost. Fine, maybe he's not ready for the truth now, but maybe one day?

I text him Saturday night.

`Me: Howstheparty`

`Raf: Boring without you. Today was more interesting.`

`Me: aturdads`

`Raf: Yeah. I designed a jacket.`

I want to write *!!!!* but I don't know how, so I call him instead. "You what?"

He laughs. "I don't know, I was playing around with the sketches and one of the designers saw it and liked it."

"Seriously?"

"Yeah. Is that weird?"

"No! That's insanely cool."

How is it that Raf knows how to make a jacket, and I can barely figure out how to make an exclamation point?

When I dump my schoolbag in my locker on Monday morning, I can't help feeling uneasy. The whole idea of the pop magic quiz is still making me jumpy. I spend the entire morning looking over my shoulder. Will I be zapped away in midsentence? Will I need to be excused from school? Will I need props? A special witch outfit? Witch shoes?

Are there special witch shoes?

There are golf shoes and tennis shoes. There should probably be witch shoes.

Ruby slippers, maybe?

"You have no idea when she's going to show up?" I ask Miri that night.

"It's all good! Sometime this week."

"But when? During the day? In the evening?"

"It's all good!"

If I hear one more *It's all good,* I'm going to zap the expression into a paddle and bop my sister over the head.

Mom tells me not to worry so much. She popped over to Lozacea on Saturday to check it out, and she seemed happy with it.

But me? I remain a bundle of nerves for all of Tuesday and most of Wednesday. It doesn't help when, about four seconds after the Wednesday lunch bell rings, Wendaline accosts me in front of my locker.

"Rachel, I need to talk to you!"

She's wearing another long black velvet dress and—oh God—black satin gloves. I sigh and motion for her to follow me out of the caf and into the girls' bathroom. "What's wrong?"

She thrusts out her gloved palm. On it is a frog.

"What is that?" I scream.

"It's a frog."

"I got that, thanks. But *why* is it here?" Oh, no. "You didn't turn a teacher into a frog, did you?"

"No! I told you, I'm a white witch. I wouldn't do that." *Ribbit*. "Someone put it in my locker."

Ribbit.

"Someone put a frog in your locker?" I ask disbelievingly. "Who would do that?"

"I don't know!" Her face clouds over. "It could have been that senior girl. The one who always wears one color?"

My heart sinks. "Cassandra?"

"Yeah. We discussed frogs yesterday morning."

"Wendaline, why in the world would you discuss frogs with Cassandra?"

"I have to pass her locker on the way to bio. On Monday she told me I needed a haircut. Yesterday, she spit at me."

"No!"

She pets the animal's head. "I asked her to please leave me alone."

I groan.

"But then she said if I was really a witch, I'd stop her myself by turning her into a frog or something. Tell me, why are people so obsessed with witches turning people into frogs?"

I shrug. "So what did you do? Turn her into a frog?" I know that would break my no-magic-at-school rule, but that chick is begging for a frog-morphosis.

"Of course not! I told her I was a white witch."

Yeah, I'm sure that scared her mono-colored pants off. "And then?"

"I walked away. And now I just found this."

Ribbit.

"If you want her to leave you alone, you have to learn to blend in."

She looks down at her hand and sighs. "What do I do?"

"First of all, never tell anyone you're a witch. And remember: when you walk through those JFK doors, you're no longer a witch. You're a totally normal girl. Got it?"

She opens her mouth to say something, then closes it. Then opens it again. "Fine."

"Good. And we have to do something about your look." I appraise her outfit.

"Let me guess," she says. "I need a makeover."

I take it all in: the over-the-top dress, the over-the-top gloves. "No, my friend." I put my arm around her shoulder. "You need a make*under*."

I make plans with Wendaline to spend Sunday shopping. I'd zap her into shape, but after what happened last time, I'm afraid I'll somehow end up in polka-dot dresses and satin gloves.

By Friday, I'm hoping Matilda, whoever she is, has forgotten all about me and my pop quiz. Sorry, no Samsorta for me this year! I remain on Planet Denial through lunch and right into seventh-period math, when the recycling bin explodes into a pink puff of smoke.

I scream. Of course I do. Then I wonder, Why is no one else screaming?

I look around the room and discover that no one *can* scream. They're frozen. Like at camp, when the counselor calls "Freeze!" and everyone has to stay in the same position, and the first person who moves cleans the table.

When the cloud of pink clears, I spot a woman in the recycling bin, straightening her dress. She waves to me. "Hi, Rachel!"

"Matilda?"

"Yes, that's me. Are you ready for your test?"

Is she kidding? She doesn't appear to be. She appears to be stepping out of the recycling bin. I push back my chair and stand up. "Right now?"

"Why, are you busy?"

I look around at my frozen friends. "I was kind of in the middle of math."

"Don't worry. You won't miss anything. Your teacher will continue where she left off. She won't know she was paused."

Paused, huh? Cool! I didn't know we could pause time. I could pause time when I'm not done with an essay test question! I could pause time on my next birthday so it lasts even longer! I could pause time when I'm lip-locked with Raf, and then experiment with different kissing positions. I need to get myself some of that pink stuff. "I've never seen anyone pause time before."

"And you never will. It's impossible. I just paused the people in the room." She pulls on her earlobe. "Listen."

I hear the honks of the cabbies outside, as well as the sounds of the students on the other side of the wall. "Got it." So it won't work on essay questions or birthdays, but it would still work on kissing.

Matilda rolls up her dress sleeves. "This won't take long. I just need to make sure you qualify."

My heart speeds up. "Does anyone ever not qualify?" What if I don't qualify? What if I don't really have magical powers? What if everything that's happened in the last four months has been a figment of my imagination? What if I'm completely insane?

Do insane people know they're insane?

Do paused people know they're being paused?

Probably no on both. Omigod. Have I ever been paused?

She nods gravely. "You wouldn't be the first around here. Now, let's see. I usually try to use ingredients from around the room. Hmm." She scans the class. "I see chalk. Rulers. Calculators. Maybe your teacher has an apple. Don't kids bring their teachers apples?"

I shrug. "This is New York." Then I wonder who didn't qualify. Someone in this classroom? Someone at JFK? Miri? She better qualify.

Matilda opens Ms. Barnes's desk drawer and rummages through it.

"What are you doing?" I blurt out. "You can't go through her drawer!" Uh-oh. I'm for sure getting witch detention for insubordination. I wonder what witch detention is. There are so many options! They could lock you in a dungeon, or zap you over to Kenya. They could trap you in the Civil War if they wanted to.

Would I get a hoop dress?

Matilda chuckles. "A witch with a conscience," she says. "Impressive. How about this, then?" She snaps her fingers, and the entire contents of Ms. Barnes's private drawer are now on display on top of her desk. "Now we're not going through her drawer."

Creative way of solving the problem. I think I'll shut up now.

"Let's see . . . we have a packet of crackers, a Twix bar. . . . We can work with this. Rachel, please turn to page seven hundred and fifty-three in your copy of your spell book."

I stall. "You mean *The Authorized and Absolute Reference Handbook to Astonishing Spells, Astounding Potions, and History of Witchcraft Since the Beginning of Time?*"

Matilda raises an eyebrow. "That would be the one."

"Here?"

"Of course here."

Oopsies. "I didn't bring it to school."

She clucks her tongue. "Even on test day?"

"I didn't know it was test day." I've been waiting all week for test day! "Should I zap it here?"

"No, I shall write out the spell." She zaps the board, and the equation I was in the middle of copying disappears. She lifts her finger and magically inscribes on the board (in what I hope is chalk and not permanent white marker):

½ piece of colored chalk

1 piece of chocolate

1 cup

Place chocolate in cup. Crush chalk and sprinkle on top of chocolate while chanting:

You shall bake
A chocolate cake.
Make it hasty,
Colorful, and tasty.

I reread the spell and peek at the clock. The period is going to end in about two minutes. What if I don't finish in time? What if the kids in next period rush in and see Pause-apalooza?

"Take your time," Matilda says.

Not!

I hurry to the desk and pick up a piece of green chalk, Ms. Barnes's chocolate bar (sorry, Ms. B! I'll get you a new one—promise!), and her coffee mug. I dump her coffee into the garbage can and carry all three elements back to my desk. I unwrap the chocolate, drop it into the mug. Time to crush the chalk. Need something hard. Calculator? I pick up my calculator, stand the chalk up, and attempt to grind it into my desk. Not bad. Once done, I slide the chalk into my palm and then recite the spell while sprinkling the chalk into the cup.

The room gets cold and the ingredients contract, swirl, and begin to expand. Kabam! A small chocolate cupcake materializes on my desk. On it, in tiny green frosting, is written *See you on Saturday!*

Wahoo!

Matilda claps. "Congratulations, Rachel. I'm looking forward to teaching you this fall." With that, she steps back into the recycling bin, tosses the pink powder into the air, and immediately disappears.

I guess that's it. Well done, me!

Everyone in the room un-pauses. Including Ms. Barnes, who now looks thoroughly perplexed. Because instead of a math equation on the board, there is a baking spell. Not to mention that the contents of her drawer are on top of her desk, on display. Minus one chocolate bar.

"What . . . ," she begins.

I focus on the board and think:

The spell looks obscene.
Let the board be wiped clean!

As if people aren't confused enough, a gush of cold air storms through the room and the spell disappears from the board.

Tammy points to my desk. No, to the cupcake on my desk. Whoops. "Want some?" I offer. She shakes her head, clearly confused. I shrug and then I gobble it up. Yum. What can I say? Must get rid of the evidence.

"So," I say, dropping my knapsack on the kitchen floor after school. "Did you pass? Did she show up during social studies? Did she use the pink pausing dust?"

Miri is slumped in a chair, her socked feet up on the table. "She showed up during lunch! She froze the entire cafeteria for fifteen minutes!"

"No way!"

"Way. When she unfroze them, the bell rang and no one understood what happened to their lunch period." She giggles. "It was super-awesome!"

"Super-awesome?" I repeat with a laugh.

"Yes! Admit it: you're excited."

"I'm not admitting anything," I say, sitting down beside her. "I'm reserving judgment till tomorrow."

She rolls her eyes. "Speaking of tomorrow, I don't want to be late. Class starts at one, so let's plan on being there for twelve-thirty. We'll transport, of course, since it's in Arizona. I'd like to leave at twelve, 'kay?"

" 'Kay," I say, bopping in my chair. Okay, fine, I'm a little excited. Maybe class will be fun. It might even be awesome. Or super-awesome.

"I hope we can take notes!" Miri says, eyes dreamy.

Or super-geeky.

10 Welcome to the Witch World

Miri cracks open the bathroom door. "I told you I wanted to leave at noon! If you wanted to straighten your hair, you shouldn't have slept in!"

"I'm ready, I'm ready," I say, unplugging my Chi, aka the world's best hair straightener. "What are you wearing to this thing?" I open the door wide. Miri is in jeans and a T-shirt. "Isn't Arizona hot?" I ask. "Should we wear shorts?"

"I get cold when I travel," she says. "Do you want to go together or separately?"

"Together," I say. "My batteries are dead."

"Your batteries are *always* dead. What is so hard about getting new ones? They sell them everywhere. They have them at the pharmacy down the block."

"I know, I know. I've been meaning to go."

"You just went yesterday. You bought gum."

"Right. I can never remember to get all the things I need when I'm there."

"Why don't you keep a list like a normal person?"

"Why are you so obsessed with lists?" My sister types them up and pins them to the bulletin board above her bedroom desk. *Homework Assignments for the Month! Things I Need at the Drugstore! Reasons I'm a Geek!*

Anyway, except for the acquiring of the batteries, the transport spell is easy. You think of the place you're heading to; hold two lithium batteries together, positive and negative charges facing each other; say the spell; and go.

After I finish getting dressed (jeans, my back-to-school top, and my summer sandals that I haven't seen in at least two weeks—hello, sandals!), we say good-bye to Mom and grab our copies of A^2. Miri scoops up her batteries, I take the address, and we're ready!

Almost ready.

"What are you doing?" Miri asks me, annoyed.

"Just texting Raf."

"Hurry!" She crouches to the carpet.

`See you at 7:30! Rachel.` He finally showed me how to punctuate and I am now a texting machine. The queen of texting. The master of my technology. The—

"Rachel! Get on! This position isn't comfy!"

I hit Send. "Done. Hey, do you want to give me the batteries? I don't mind playing pony."

She springs up, I crouch, and she hops on. I pick up the batteries, one in each hand; make two fists; twine my thumbs together; and say:

"Transport me to the place inside my mind.
The power of my fists shall ye bind."

I picture the address, 122 East Granger, and a jolt of electricity runs through my body, like I just stuck my finger in a socket. My body begins to feel weightless, like I'm an astronaut in a spaceship, and my skin feels hot and dry, like it's being blow-dried by a thousand hair dryers all set on high. Instead of our beige living room couch and wood floor, there're a kaleidoscope of dots and swirls of blue, red, and yellow. Eventually, the wind stops, the colors settle into a flat desert yard and a wide blue sky, and my feet touch—

Ouch!

—the tip of a baby prickly pear cactus. About a hundred pins insert themselves into my right heel. Ow! Ow! Ow! Ow! Why am I stepping on cactus needles? I look down to see one sandaled foot and one bare foot standing on a row of cactuses. Cacti? Either way, it hurts!

"Get off, get off, get off!" I shout at Miri. "You're making it worse!"

She hops off my back and steps away.

I peel my foot from the cactus. I am a human porcupine. Ow. I begin picking out the offending needles. Ow, ow, ow. This had better be the last one. . . . Ow!

Now. Where's my shoe? "I lost a sandal!"

"Where?"

"If I knew where it was, it wouldn't be lost, would it?" I hop away from the attack plant and look around. We're about ten yards away from a small white stucco cottage.

"I mean, is it in Arizona?"

"It could have fallen off on the way." It could be anywhere from Chicago to Topeka.

"So what do you want to do?"

"Find it," I whine.

"We can zap up a multiplying spell for the one you still have. Hold on. Let me find it. I think it's on page seven hundred and two."

Ow. Ow. Ow. I hop over to her. "My foot hurts too much. I can't think!" I pluck out one of the needles. And another. And another.

"Weird," she says. "I could have sworn it was here. But there's a heat spell on page seven hundred and two instead! Where is that multiplying spell? I'm so confused!"

"Miri, can't you just make something up?" Ow. Ow, ow, ow.

"You know I prefer to use the spells in the book," she says haughtily. "They're far sturdier."

Gimme a break. "You know what would make me sturdier? A second shoe. Just do it, please!"

"All right, hold on. I'll try."

She takes a deep breath, bends on one knee, touches my sandal, and says:

"Missing shoe,
Give me two!"

Poof! A second sandal blossoms on the ground.

"Yay, Miri! Way to go! I'm so proud of you."

She preens. "Thank you. I thought it was pretty clever."

I slip my foot inside, but something feels wrong. My toes are sticking out the other side. What's up with that? Oh. She copied the original sandal. Both shoes are made for my left foot.

"Does it fit?" she asks.

"Yup! All good," I say quickly. No reason to undermine her confidence. There must be a spell to right the right. Right? I'll fix it later in the bathroom. I hook her arm through mine. "Shall we?"

We start toward the cottage. "It looks so plain," she says as we approach the one-story nondescript white building.

"What did you expect? Sparkles?"

She giggles. "Something like that."

When we reach the door, I say, "There's no doorbell. I guess I'll knock."

No answer.

"Miri, we're not going to be the only ones at these lessons, are we?"

"I hope not," she says. "The whole point is to meet new people. Maybe this just isn't the right place. Look." Miri points to a window on the left. The shades are drawn, but it looks dark inside. "I bet you took us to the wrong address."

"Oh, sure, assume I'm the one who screwed up. Maybe you wrote down the wrong address."

She cocks her head. "It's a little more likely that you messed up, isn't it? Don't deny that I'm the superior witch."

Puh-lease! I kick up my second left shoe. "Oh yeah, Ms. Superior? Do I look like I have two left feet?"

She flushes. "Well, I have seen you dance."

"Hello there," says a low voice behind us. A male voice.

We spin around to see a boy. He's on the small side—maybe five foot five—is thin, and has light brown messed-up hair. He's wearing faded jeans and a green untucked shirt.

And he's cute.

"Do you live here?" Miri asks. "Because if you do, we're in the wrong place. 'Cause you shouldn't be here. I mean—"

What is she saying? That girl has got to learn how to talk with boys! "Not that there's anything wrong with you," I say. "Or with where you live. . . ." I look at Miri. I'm not doing much better.

He breaks into a smile. "Judging from the lithium batteries you're holding, I'm thinking you're in the right place." He opens his hands and reveals two batteries. "Transportation spell, right?"

Omigod! He's a *boy* witch. A *cute* boy witch. I'm *talking* to a cute boy witch.

"You're a warlock?" Miri asks him. "That is so cool! We've never met any warlocks our own age before."

"How old are you guys?" he asks, stepping closer.

Oh, look at his blue eyes. Big blue eyes that crinkle when he smiles!

"I'm twelve and Rachel's fourteen," Miri says. "I mean thirteen. I mean, I'm thirteen, and Rachel's—"

"Fifteen," I interject. "I just turned fifteen on Thursday."

He gives me a crinkle-eyed smile. "Happy birthday, Rachel."

He knows my name! How does he know my name? He is an all-knowing warlock! Oh, wait, Miri just said it. "Thank you." Now we're just smiling at each other. This is weird. Must stop!

"I'm Adam." He puts out his hand.

Adorable! We're going to shake hands. I stick out my hand and we shake. I don't expect his hand to be so . . . warm. "This is my sister, Miri."

Now they shake. There's a whole lot of shaking going

on. Is he still smiling at me? He is! I look down at my identical shoes.

"Nice to meet you," he says. "You've never been here before, have you?"

"We're newbies," I say.

"Where are you from?"

"New York," Miri says.

"New York City," I clarify. He should know that we are city girls, and therefore super-cool. "You?"

"Salt Lake City." Oh! He's a city boy too! He's also super-cool!

Do cool people know they're cool? Or does wanting to be cool automatically make you uncool?

"So, Adam, what are you doing here?" Miri asks. "Isn't this the place for Samsorta lessons?"

"I'm studying for my Simsorta," he says.

"Your what?" I ask.

"Studying for my Simsorta," he repeats.

"No, I heard. I'm just wondering what a—"

"Can we continue this conversation inside?" Miri interrupts, fidgeting. "I don't want to be late."

"Miri," I say, "we're not late. We're here."

"Isn't Samsorta class at one?" Adam asks.

"Yeah," Miri says. "And it's already a quarter to."

Adam taps his watch. "It's only a quarter to ten. There's a three-hour time difference."

Miri's eyes widen. "I forgot that part."

I laugh. "Good work, Mir."

"I'll show you guys around, then," he says. "Should we go in?"

"I tried knocking," I say. "But no one answered."

"Did you try *umrello*?" Adam asks.

I don't know what to do with that sentence. "Is it raining?"

He laughs. "Not umbrella. *Umrello*. It means 'open' in Brixta. It's the secret code."

Guess Matilda was too busy pausing to give us the password.

"Watch." He approaches the door, knocks three times, and says, "*Umrello!*" The door creaks ajar. He opens it the rest of the way.

Miri and I gasp. What looks like a small cottage from the outside is gigantic inside. It's the size of my school. We follow Adam through the doorway, down two steps, and into the atrium. Even though we couldn't see in from outside, from inside we can see out. The walls and ceiling are all windows. Blue is everywhere. It feels like we're suspended in the desert. Wow. I take a deep breath. It smells like cinnamon incense. Around me, I hear sounds of wind chimes. Wind chimes and . . .

Teens. Teen witches and warlocks. Boys laughing! Girls gossiping!

"Are you sure we're in the right place?" Miri whispers.

Boys and girls flirting on window ledges!

Adam laughs. "Welcome to the LWCC. The Lozacea Witch Community Center."

Boys and girls floating above window ledges!

Miri squeezes my hand. "Who are all these . . . these . . . people?"

"Witches and warlocks."

"But why are you all here?" she asks. "For lessons?"

"The guys are studying for their Simsortas. And there's a game room downstairs. And advanced Brixta starts at eleven, so people came for that."

"Oh, we should take that!" Miri says. "We need to learn some Brixta for the Samsorta."

"Beginner's Brixta isn't till next semester," Adam says. "I took it last year."

"But what's a Simsorta?" I ask.

"You really are newbies," he says. "A Simsorta is a Samsorta. For boys."

"Aha."

"Except since we're not allowed to participate in the group celebration on October thirty-first—"

"Wait," I say. "Why not?"

He shrugs. "Girls only. Tradition."

"That sounds kind of sexist," I say.

"Tell me about it. So since boys can't be in the main one, it's become a tradition to do our own stand-alone events on Friday nights throughout the year. Mine is next month, so I'm here to practice." He smiles. "And to meet cute witch girls."

My cheeks burn. Am I a cute witch? I think I am!

"Let me show you the caf," he says, and we follow him through the atrium and into a hallway. "Here it is," he says, opening another door.

A cluster of small round bar tables is in the center of the room, and four white-and-black-checkered stools surround each one. There are girls and boys at about half the tables, and everyone is eating. But I don't see where they bought their food. Not a lunch lady in sight.

"Is there a kitchen?" I ask, looking around. "I don't see any place to get food."

"Watch," he says. He sits down on one of the stools, places both hands facedown on the table, and calls out, "Fresh OJ! Cheese and mushroom omelet! French fries! A side of crispy bacon! Ketchup!"

The table rumbles and—*poof!*—his breakfast, as well as a set of cutlery, appears in front of him.

Cool!

"Can I order you guys some breakfast?" he asks us. "It's all free."

Miri's eyes are wide. "I'm good. We ate three hours ago. In New York. When it was really ten o'clock."

Who cares? I can't wait to test this baby out. I splay my hands on the smooth surface. "Tall white chocolate mocha decaf latte! With whipped cream! And brown sugar!"

Poof!

"Yay!" I squeal, dipping my finger in puffy cream. "It worked! What else can I do?" I place my hands back in their positions. Something fun! Something crazy! "Cotton candy!" *Poof!* Omigod, it's on a cone! How did it know I like it that way? "This is the coolest trick ever! How does it work?"

"Who knows?" Adam says, eating a forkful of egg. "The founders of this place thought of everything."

"No kidding. So tell me more about these Simsortas. Are they also in Transylvania?"

"Romania," Miri says.

"Whatever." I take a big sip of my drink. Ouch! Hot! Need something cold! Water! No—frozen yogurt. I place both hands on the table. "Pinkberry!" *Poof!* Abracazam. My favorite frozen yogurt appears right in front of me. I ingest a spoonful. Yum.

Adam is watching me, clearly amused. "You're a riot," he says.

I take another spoonful of yogurt. "I aim to entertain. But back to the Simsortas. Where are they held?"

"They're everywhere. Mine is going to be at the Golden Gate Bridge."

I drop my spoon. "Seriously?" I've always wanted to go to San Francisco! Maybe now that I've amused him, he'll invite me.

"Yup. Erik Bruney had his at Disney World last night. We could go on any ride we wanted to. I went on Space Mountain like ten times in a row."

"Wow," I say.

"They rented out the whole place?" Miri asks. "That must have cost a fortune."

His eyes crinkle. "They *enchanted* the whole place. I doubt any money changed hands."

Miri makes a face. "Doesn't sound very gray."

"It wasn't," Adam admits. "Hey, do you guys know Amanda Hanes? She's from Manhattan. She was there."

Hello, do you know how many people live in New York? Like . . . well, I don't know exactly, but it's a lot. We shake our heads.

"She's my age," he says. "Sixteen."

"Oh! I didn't realize you were older," I say. "You're a junior?"

He nods.

"How come you're just having your Simsorta now?"

"Boys usually get their powers later than girls do. Do you know Michael Summers?"

"We don't know anyone," I say, and get annoyed with my mom. Why did she have to keep us so secluded? We're never going to win at witch genealogy. We're, like, the worst players ever.

"We know Wendaline Peaner," Miri pipes up. "Do you know her?"

"Of course! She was on my summer teen tour last year."

"Oh! She mentioned going on a teen tour," I say. "But I thought she was kidding!"

"No, it was real."

"Where did you guys go?"

"We visited all the Wonders of the World."

"How long did that take?" Miri asks. "All summer?"

"No, only a few days. We skipped the airplane part, obviously."

Obviously.

"Wendaline's going to Charm School, though, right?" Adam asks.

"Yeah," Miri says sadly. "Our mom studied there too."

"You're lucky you were able to convince her to let you come here, then," he says. "This place is a million times more fun than Charm School."

"Why's that?" Miri asks.

"We have Ping-Pong," he says, "and the coolest caf in the history of the world. And unlike Charm School, we're coed."

Yes, that's certainly an advantage.

"Do you know Praw?" he asks next.

"No," I say, focusing again on my yogurt. "Is he from New York too?"

"No," says a new voice. "But I just sat down at the table. Hey, y'all."

"Hey, Praw," Adam says. "What up?"

I look away from my snack and at the new boy at our table. He's younger than Adam, younger than me, maybe thirteen or fourteen. He has sandy red hair and pale white skin and is covered with freckles. He looks just like Archie! No—he looks just like Ron from *Harry Potter*!

"Hi," I say. "I'm Rachel. Nice to meet you. This is my sister, Miri."

"Hey, Rachel," he says to me, then turns to Miri. "Is it Marie?"

Instead of responding, my sister squeaks.

Praw leans in closer. "Pardon?"

"Eeek," she squeaks again.

"It's Miri," I say for her, and give her my what-is-wrong-with-you look.

"Pretty name," he says.

A flush of red creeps up Miri's neck. She looks like she's having an allergic reaction. Or maybe she's choking on something? I need to get her a drink. I place my hands back on the table. "Water!" *Poof!* A stream of water begins sprouting from the center of the table. Uh-oh.

"Stop water!" Adam says. The water stops. "You have to be more specific. I've done that a few times too."

I try again. "Bottle of water!" *Poof!* It works. I hand my still-flushed sister the bottle of Evian. Fancy! I wonder if I can order extra and take some home.

Miri takes a long sip and gives us a forced grin. She then turns even redder. Redder than Praw's hair. No, redder than the bottle of ketchup.

"Are you talking Samsorta lessons?" Praw asks her.

She nods very slowly. What is up with her? I know she gets weird around boys, but she doesn't usually go mute.

"I'm here for Advanced Brixta," he says.

"Are you having a Simsorta too?" I ask, trying to alleviate some of the awkwardness.

"Not till next year. I just got my powers over the summer."

"When did you get them?" I ask Adam.

"Last September."

"You're practically a veteran," I tease.

"How do y'all know each other?" Praw asks. He looks at me, but his eyes keep darting back to Miri. He smiles at her. He has a nice smile. Dimples too. She takes another sip of water.

"We go way back," Adam says.

"Waaaay back," I say. "Years."

"Decades," he counters.

"Lifetimes." Tee hee. Adam might be my new best friend. My new *cute* boy best friend. I've never had a boy best friend before. Fun! Someone to talk to, someone besides my possibly male unborn half sibling to help me understand the inner workings of the boy brain. Adam will be just like a brother! But not related. And cute. A BBF (best boy friend) of my very own. That's *boy friend*. Two words. Not *boyfriend*. One word. See the difference? Good thing I learned how to make spaces on my cell phone, or things could get really confusing.

A girl sashays into the cafeteria.

"Adam," she calls, "where have you been? I've been looking for you."

"Hey, Karin," he says. "Did you stay late last night?"

"Yeah. I'm wiped." She flicks her long blond hair behind her right shoulder. How about that? She's the first blond witch I've encountered so far. She's also like six feet tall, and super-curvy. She's Barbie Witch. People shouldn't get to look like Barbies and be witches. You should get one or the other. Fair's fair.

What does Barbie Witch want with my new BBF? Are they a couple? I bet they're a couple. Not that I care. I have a boyfriend, you know. A boyfriend I'm meeting tonight at seven-thirty.

"Hey, Praw," Barbie Witch says, and pinches his cheeks. "What's up, cutie? And who are you guys?" she asks us, wedging between us at the table.

I look at Miri to see if she's going to answer, but apparently she's still comatose. "I'm Rachel. And this is Miri, my sister."

"Nice to meet you. How come we've never met you before? Did you just move to the U.S.?"

"No," I say with a sigh.

"I thought we knew every teen witch in the country," Adam says with a laugh.

I'm seriously going to kill my mother. "We were kind of kept in the dark until the last year," I admit.

"Well, welcome!" Karin says. "I love meeting new witches."

Praw hops off his stool. "I gotta get to Brixta class. See y'all later. Karin, you can have my seat."

"Thanks!"

"I have to go too," Adam says. "One month until my Sim and I still have no idea what I'm doing. We'll see you guys later?"

"Definitely," I say. "Have fun!"

Miri squeaks good-bye.

The three of us watch the boys go. Karin squeezes our hands. "So, are you guys doing the Samsorta class too?"

"Yeah," Miri says, finally regaining her voice.

"Fun!" she chirps. "I want the full scoop. Who are your parents? Do they both have powers? When did yours kick in?"

The Q and A session goes on for the next two hours. Karin takes a brief lunch break to devour her Caesar salad, but quickly resumes after the last bite.

I worry she'll go on indefinitely, but the lights begin to flicker.

And when I say flicker, I don't mean on and off. A rainbow of green, gold, red, and yellow washes over our faces, like there's a disco ball overhead. Maybe this place turns into a dance club at night? A witch-rave? A wave?

A voice from the sky screams, "Ladies, please enter the auditorium! Samsorta class is about to start!"

"Let's go!" Karin says, pulling us by the hands. "I want to get a seat up front! I have a lot of questions!"

No kidding.

We let Karin lead us out of the cafeteria, back into the atrium and then, along with a herd of other girls—no, a herd of other witches—through the double auditorium doors.

11 The Girls of Sam

"What you experienced this year was the most amazing transformation of your life. You went from notch to witch. Less than a hundredth of one percent of the world's population has the capabilities you do."

"I wish I'd brought a sweater," I whisper to Miri. "It's freezing in here. What's with the insane air-conditioning?"

"Shush!" she says. "I'm trying to take notes."

Of course she is. Student Miri is adorable. She doesn't doodle. She highlights. She listens intently. She nods along with our turtle-shaped (round body, tiny arms and legs) teacher, Kesselin Fizguin. No, Kesselin is not her first name. Apparently, it means *teacher* in Brixta.

Fizguin hasn't said much worth noting so far. First she took attendance; then she welcomed us to the center. Only a few of us had never been here before. She told us that we were expected to come to every class and that there would be a fifteen-minute break halfway through every lecture. Boo on the first part, but yay on the second. Maybe I can use my break to order another hot drink to warm me up.

"The Samsorta is how we witches honor this extraordinary moment. It's our way—a way that has endured for centuries—of introducing you to the rest of the magical world."

"You're really not cold?" I whisper. How is that possible? It's like minus twenty degrees in here. My arms are covered in goose bumps. Other than that, the classroom is pretty comfortable. It's all white. Every seat is covered with a fluffy white cushion. The floor is a lush white carpet. I feel like I'm at an Apple store. Or inside a marshmallow.

"Over the next seven weeks, I will be talking about the history of witches, the ethics of magic, a witch's responsibilities, magic and family life, and magic in the modern world. And of course, we'll practice the spells you're required to perform during the Samsorta ceremony."

Unfortunately, Fizguin occasionally spits when she makes the S sound, and Karin led us to the front row. There are fifteen girls in class, all between the ages of about ten and fifteen.

I'm pretty sure I'm one of the oldest girls here—if not the oldest.

Miri is sitting to my right. On my left is Karin. Next to Karin is Viviane. Karin introduced us. Viviane lives in Sunset Park in Brooklyn. She has cool bangs, has hipster square glasses, and is wearing a funky vintage maroon tunic and gray leggings. When Miri heard she's in the eighth grade too, her eyes lit up.

I squeeze my sister's arm. "You guys can be BFFs!" I whisper, like a real matchmaker.

She shushes me.

But seriously, they can be! And then we can call her Viv, which is the best name ever. Plus she can teach us how to shop at vintage stores! I've always wanted to but I'm nervous I'll accidentally bring home outfits infested with moths.

"There are three parts to the ceremony," Fizguin is saying. "The first is the opening march, when all Samsorta witches walk in by school affiliation."

I lean over to Miri and whisper, "But how many witches could there be at each school? JFK only has two, and I thought that was a lot." One too many, if you want my opinion.

"She means by *witch* school," Miri whispers back. "Here. Lozacea."

Right.

"Once the opening march is complete," the teacher continues, "your alimity will stand before you in the circle. Your alimity is a female relative, usually your mother, who has already been Samsorted. One at a time, each alimity asks each Samsorta if she is willing to join the circle of magic. Once you—the Samsorta—agree, the alimity will use the golden knife to remove a lock of your hair."

Seriously? How third grade.

"Once that part of the ritual is complete, your alimity will approach the central cauldron and make her offering. We shall go clockwise around the circle, beginning with the oldest Samsorta."

Oh God. Is that going to be me? I bet it is. So embarrassing.

The teacher points in my direction. "Ms. Weinstein?"

Whoa. Why is she calling on me? Is she trying to tell me I *am* the oldest? She'd better not want a piece of my hair right now. I can't give it! I need to strategize with Este! What if she accidentally lops off an important piece? "Yes?" I ask.

"Not you, Rachel," Fizguin says. "Your sister has her hand raised."

Oh! I forgot that Miri is a Ms. Weinstein too.

"What," begins Miri, "if two girls share the same alimity? Is that an issue?"

"If the alimity is shepherding more than one of you," Fizguin says, "she will collect all the locks before approaching the cauldron. After all the alimities have completed their offerings, they will be returned to their seats."

I wonder where they're sitting. Isn't it supposed to be at a cemetery? Are they going to make themselves comfy on burial plots? Kick their heels up on a gravestone? Creepapalooza.

Fizguin paces the front of the auditorium and continues. "The third part of the ceremony is the Chain of Lights service. Each of you will recite the light spell, in Brixta, and set your candle aflame."

In Brixta? Uh-oh. Hopefully we can get it written out phonetically.

"This time we will go counterclockwise. The final girl will bring her candle to the central cauldron and set it aflame."

Karin raises her hand. "Is it going to be a Charm School girl again this year?"

"Yes, it is customary for a Charmori student to cast the wonderment spell. Their school is the oldest and most traditional."

Everyone grumbles.

"But you're all chanting the wonderment incantation together, since the gift the spell creates, the *giftoro,* must come from all of you. Can someone list some of these gifts for those of us who are not familiar? Don't be afraid to go back a few years."

Karin raises her hand. "The Panama Canal, Niagara Falls, the Empire State Building, playing cards, the Pyramids, the Great Barrier Reef, iPods, the Leaning Tower of Pisa, the polio vaccine, Mount Everest—"

"Well done," Fizguin says, cutting her off.

Was that for real? I glance at the other girls. No one is laughing, so apparently it is. No way! My witchcraft sisters created the Pyramids! And iPods! I bet we also did the Chi. We must have. It's too brilliant to have been concocted by mere mortal minds. Maybe TiVo?

Perhaps this year we can work on some sort of boob enlarger?

"Those are some of the more successful gifts," Fizguin continues. "Of course there have been others that have been less successful, or at least less attractive. Like those"—she wrinkles her nose with disdain—"Croc shoes."

I guess witches don't always have good taste.

"Unfortunately, as Samsortas, you can't control what you give. Your *giftoro* is created from deep within your collective unconscious." She taps her temples for emphasis. "And often it takes a few weeks, if not months, for your legacy to become clear. And that's the end of the ceremony. Afterwards there is the dinner and dance. Your table can be any size you'd like from two to three hundred seats, but we do need to know final numbers at least twenty-four hours before the Samsorta. Oh, and of course you're each responsible for your own invitations. Any questions?"

Karin raises her hand. "Can we bring dates?"

"Of course. The first dance after the ceremony is for the Samsortas and their dates. But remember to count them as part of your table. Any other questions?"

No date for me. Sorry, but I cannot bring Raf to this freak show. No way. Not happening. Whatever. It's not like Miri's going to bring a date. I'll just have to sit that first dance out.

Karin raises her hand again. "Who's the band?"

"That's a surprise. Anything else?"

Karin raises her hand again.

"Anyone else?"

Karin raises it higher.

"Yes, Ms. Hennedy?"

"How many girls will be doing their Samsorta this year? From all the schools, I mean."

"Eighty-four. Next?"

I'd better not be the oldest of eighty-four girls! Beyond humiliating. I'd be like a parent at a pop concert.

"That's it? Let me ask a question, then. How many of you haven't taken Brixta 101 or its equivalent?"

Miri and I are the only students who raise our hands. Thanks again, Mom.

"Well, girls, you're in for a real treat. Brixta is one of the most beautiful languages ever spoken. It's very melodious. Like music to the ears."

What I'm not looking forward to is having to study this so-called music. All this Samsorta stuff is going to seriously cut into my TV schedule.

Miri raises her hand again. "How would you suggest studying Brixta at this point?"

"It's too late to study it now," Fizguin says. "We'll get you a language potion."

Now, *that's* music to my ears. Television-theme-song music.

"Do you know that at Charm School they make you study Brixta for two years before you take Samsorta lessons?" whispers Heather, from the row behind us.

Heather is sitting between Shari and Michy. And they are—wait for it—triplets. Imagine! Witch triplets!

If you're witch triplets, you definitely get a TV show.

According to Karin, they're identical triplets. They all have stick-straight light brown hair, pale skin, and tiny bird-like features. They are dressed differently, though. Heather is the earthy triplet; she's wearing faded jeans and a loose-fitting hemp shirt. Shari is the preppy triplet—beige cords, a striped sweater, barrettes. And Michy is the glamour triplet; she's in designer jeans, a fitted shirt, and patent leather flats.

I wish I were a triplet. Or a twin at the very least. Then I could ask my twin to try on outfits and go outside to see if they looked good. Much more effective than a mirror, since it's always the outdoor light that gets you.

Although I'm thinking it would be even more fun to dress up in identical outfits. To play pranks on people. How hilarious would that be? We could pretend to be each other and go to the other's classes, go shopping with each other's friends, hang out with each other's boyfriends. . . .

Omigod. What if Other Rachel tries to kiss Raf? He would have no idea it wasn't me. She could totally go Sweet Valley on me and try to steal him away!

Forget about Other Rachel. She's obviously up to no good. I'll stick with Miri. "Do you think we should dress alike?"

She shushes me. Again.

After zapping up a plate of nachos during my break, I fix my sandal and then sneak into a deserted corner to call Raf.

"Hey!" I say. "Happy Saturday."

"A happy Saturday to you too. What's up?"

"The roof?"

"Ha. Where are you, Grand Central? Sounds busy."

"Me? Oh. Um . . ." Where *am* I? "I'm shopping. Yeah! I'm shopping!"

"Where?"

"At H&M." Hexes & Magic, that is. "On Eighteenth?"

"No way! I'm at Union Square! Want me to come say hello?"

"Oh! No. Don't. We're on the move. And we're in a rush. A big rush. Huge."

"I don't mind. I'll come by for a second. I'm only a block away."

Yikes. "No, we're really already gone. We're getting into a cab. Next time! But I'll see you tonight at seven-thirty?"

"Oh. Okay," he says, sounding deflated.

We make plans to go to T's Pies for pizza (I might seriously turn into a pie) and then pick up a movie at Blockbuster. Dinner out, then cuddling with Raf!

Perfect. As long as he doesn't pepper with me with more questions about my shopping experience.

When class ends, Miri and I follow the other girls back into the atrium. I glance at the clock on my cell, which has conveniently adjusted to Arizona time. So smart, my little guy! I bet the cell phone was a collective unconscious Samsorta gift. I bet the regular phone was one too. Maybe Alexander Bell was a warlock. I should have paid more attention to the history of witchcraft part of the lecture. Anyway, it's 4:01 here, which means it's 7:01 New York time. Time to get home to get ready for my date with Raf. The seven of us congregate in the atrium to say good-bye. Apparently, I have a witch group. A witch clique. A *wique*?

I spot Adam across the atrium. I wave.

He hurries over and gives us a lopsided grin. "Do you guys want to come surfing with us?"

Surfing? Hello? We're in Arizona.

"Who's going?" Karin asks.

"Me, Praw, Michael, Fitch, and Rodge." As he lists them, four other boys join our group. "We're celebrating

Fitch's last study day, since his Sim is on Friday." He points to me and Miri and says, "Rachel and Miri, meet Michael, Fitch, and Rodge. And you already know Praw."

"Hey," they say. Michael is dark-skinned, tall, and lanky. Fitch is short and pasty, and wearing thick glasses. Rodge is super-muscular and has gelled-back black hair. I'm guessing they're all sophomores or juniors. At least I'm not the oldest person in the building—just the oldest one who doesn't shave. My face, I mean. Of course I shave my legs. My mom tells me I shouldn't, because she claims it'll grow back twice as thick, but that makes no sense, because if it did, then wouldn't bald men shave their whole heads? Although if they're bald, they have nothing to shave. What was the point of all this? I forget.

"Hey," I say.

Miri just squeaks. What is up with her and the squeaking?

Omigod. I know! She likes Praw. Miri likes a boy! Yay!

"So are you in?" Adam asks. "Surf's up."

"I'm in," Karin says.

"I'm kind of tired," Glamour Triplet says, putting on her oversized sunglasses. "But I'm happy to rest on the beach and soak up some rays."

"What beach?" Karin asks. "South Beach?"

"No," Michael says. "It's already seven-fifteen on the East Coast. We need to go west. How about Hawaii?"

Are they seriously going to pop over to Hawaii for sun and surf?

"Yo, let's go to Hanauma Beach," Viv says. "It has a great vibe."

"I'm in if y'all are," says Praw.

"I'm in," says Michael.

"We're there," says Preppy Triplet.

"Cool," says Rodge.

"Me too," says Karin.

"*On y va!*" says Fitch. Huh? Is he French?

Sand, surf, sun . . . fun. Plus Miri can talk to her crush! "Us too!" I exclaim.

Adam breaks into a huge grin. "Excellent. Let's go."

Wait a sec. What am I thinking? I look at my watch. I have to get home! Raf is going to be at my apartment in fifteen minutes. I can't go to the beach. "Sorry, sorry," I say. "I can't go. I forgot. I have to get home."

To see my boyfriend. But I don't say the last part aloud.

Why don't I say the last part aloud?

Because no one cares that I have a boyfriend. Did anyone ask if I have a boyfriend? No, they did not.

Sucks that I can't go surfing, though. I mean, I love hanging out with Raf, but I've never been to Hawaii! I even know all the lingo from when Dad and Jennifer went there on their honeymoon! And, well, if I went to Hawaii with my wique, we could talk about Sam class and the big party and all the stuff I can't mention to Raf.

"Rough," says Glamour Triplet.

"Next time, man," says Earthy Triplet.

Karin fluffs her long blond hair. "Miri, you're coming, right?"

Such pretty blond hair. I wonder if she's nervous about the lock-chopping too?

Miri glances at Praw, turns bright red, and shakes her head.

"Miri, you should go," I tell her quietly. She totally

should. First of all, the very reason we signed up for this Samsorta was so that Miri could meet people like her and not be stuck at home. And now people are asking her for plans. Plus the guy she obviously likes is going. She can flirt while working on her tan! Best setup ever!

She shakes her head again, looking at the floor.

I am going to kill her. "Miri. Go."

She gives me a pleading look. A look I take to mean "Make me an excuse, because for some reason my tongue is superglued to the top of my mouth."

"Neither of us can," I say begrudgingly, narrowing my eyes at my wimparoo of a sister. Liar, liar, pants on fire. "We have a . . . family thing."

Viv motions for the crew to follow her outside. "Yo, whoever is coming, let's move! Have you suckers used the new go spell? It rocks."

"I've been meaning to try it," Michael says.

"Bye!" the triplets say to us. Most of the group moves toward the door.

Adam trails behind. "Too bad you can't come," he says to us. To me.

I nod. "Next time."

He looks like he wants to say something else, but instead he follows them, and we follow him, out the door.

Viv pulls a bag out of her purse, scoops out a handful of an oatmealy concoction, tosses it up into the air, and chants:

"Through space we flow.
To Hanauma Beach in Hawaii
We shall go!"

The group begins to disappear in pieces. First a leg, then an eye, some hair. Cool.

Eventually, the only human body parts left outside belong to me and Miri.

"No batteries required," Miri says. "And it worked on a whole group. We need to whip some of that up."

"Oh, look who found her voice!"

She blushes.

I take the batteries out of my purse. "Miri and Praw, sitting in a tree. K-I-S-S-I-N-G. First comes love, then comes marriage—"

"Stop!"

"Why didn't you go? You could have flirted with him!"

"I couldn't talk to him, how was I supposed to flirt with him? Can we just go home?" she begs. "Please?"

"All right, let's go," I say. "As punishment for wimping out, you have to be the pony."

She pouts but gets into the crouched position.

I hop on.

She turns back to me. "But isn't he cute?" She giggles and off we go.

12 Sweet Dreams

The second our feet touch my bedroom carpet, I storm the bathroom. I have to brush my teeth before Raf gets here! Why did I have to zap up a plate of nachos, why oh why?

"Rachel? Miri? You're home?" I hear my mom say.

Can't talk! Brushing teeth!

"How was it?" I hear. "Tell us everything."

How cute. She's calling herself and Lex *us*.

"It was fascinating," I hear Miri say. "During the first half of the class, we learned all about the ceremony, and during the second, we learned about the history of witchcraft."

I spit toothpaste into the sink. "Miri fell in love," I call out.

"Rachel!" Miri screams.

I laugh and gargle simultaneously.

"Will you come for Thai food with us?" Mom asks. There's the *us* again. Twice.

"I guess," Miri says.

Dinner with Mom and Lex . . . surfing in Hawaii . . . dinner with Mom and Lex . . . surfing in Hawaii . . . What's wrong with that girl?

Raf and I pick up a new James Bond movie, then get a table at T's Pies in a booth in the back. We hold hands most of the time. Not when we're eating, obviously. That would be weird. But we smile at each other a lot.

Until I suspect that I have a piece of pepperoni stuck between my teeth and I sneak into the (cramped) single-stall bathroom to remove it.

The second snag is when Raf asks me what I got.

"Got where?" I ask, carefully chewing my delicious pie.
This pizza *is* good.

He takes a long sip of his Diet Coke. "Didn't you go shopping?"

"Oh! Right. I got . . . nothing." Wow, I'm the worst liar ever. I can barely remember the stories I made up less than two hours ago.

"How come?"

I squeeze his hand across the table. "I'm a very picky girl."

Back at my apartment, we make ourselves comfy on the couch and pop in the movie.

About five minutes in, I discover something hilarious about Raf.

He talks to the TV.

"What are you doing?" he asks Jack, a bit player in the movie who is about to get whacked by the bad guys. "Don't be a moron! Don't you know you're going to get killed if you go in there?"

Adorable, right?

"No, no, no! Turn around! Oh, man." Raf covers his face when Jack gets shot in the chest.

I kiss his cheek. "He's not a real person," I assure him. "It's just a role."

Raf laughs and snuggles me closer.

As the movie continues, Raf keeps talking to the characters—the ones who are still alive, that is. I, on the other hand, find myself yawning. And yawning again. Eyes. Getting. Heavy. Too much excitement for one day. Must stay awake! Why didn't I wish myself up a caffeinated beverage when I had the chance?

Eyes. Very. Heavy. Maybe if I close them for a second, I'll feel refreshed.

Yes. Close them. For a sec . . .

The next thing I hear is Miri saying, "She's out?"

"Like the macarena," Raf says, and then laughs self-consciously. "Apparently I'm very boring."

I spring up. "No! You're not boring! I'm just tired! From my day of shopping."

"Right," Miri says, plopping down beside me on the couch. "We did lots of shopping."

"Where's Mom?" I ask, stifling a yawn. I don't want Raf to think he bored me to sleep!

"She and Lex just went for a walk. They'll be back in ten. Where'd you guys eat?"

"T's," Raf says. "It's the best. The delivery sucks, though. You have to eat there." He stretches. "I should get going. It's getting late." He stands up first, then peels me off the couch. "See you Monday?"

"Okay." I'm waiting for Miri to go to her room so I can have a moment alone with Raf for some good-night kissing, but she doesn't get off the couch. "I'll walk you out," I say with exaggeration, but instead of getting the hint, Miri follows me like a shadow.

"Good night, Raf," I say.

"Good night, Raf!" Miri chirps.

"Good night, ladies." He plants a soft kiss on my lips.

I close the door behind him. Then I throw my hands into the air. "Miri! Couldn't you have left us alone for two seconds?"

She looks confused. "But you were alone all night."

"I wanted to give him a proper good-bye kiss," I grumble, and then return to the living room. I gave up surfing in Hawaii, and I don't even feel we had much of a date. My fault for falling asleep, but still. I guess I just wish I could have told him a little bit about what was on my mind. You know, about magical cottages in Arizona and witch ceremonies and stuff.

"See!" she calls after me. "This is my problem!"

"What?"

She sinks into the couch and hugs her knees to her chest. "I don't know how to act around boys!"

"Is this about Praw?"

She nods. "I think he's really cute."

"Aw, you do like him. That's great!"

"It's not great if I can't speak around him! My mind goes all hazy, like the phone when you're using the microwave."

"Huh?"

"Haven't you noticed that you can't speak on the phone and use the microwave at the same time?"

"Um. No. But back to the boy."

"Right. Praw. I don't know what's wrong with me! What do I do?"

"Flirt with him!"

"But how?" she asks. "I don't know how to flirt. Teach me."

"I don't know if it's something I can teach. It's something I just do. Like walking or breathing."

She snorts. "Tell me this: how did you get Raf to like you? Naturally, I mean. I want him to like me for me."

"Are you implying that I'm not likeable?"

"Stop being annoying and just tell me how you did it!"

Hmm. "Let's see. I joined the fashion show. Since Raf was doing it too, I not only got to spend time with him, but I showed him we shared similar interests."

"Modeling overpriced clothes?"

"Noooo." Sheesh. "Well, maybe. That and dancing. So those are my two recommendations. Be around and share his interests."

"How do I do that?"

"For one thing, when his friends invite you to surf in Hawaii, you go."

She nods. "I see your point. I don't want to be fake, though."

"A little fake won't hurt, I think. What do we know about him?"

"He's a redhead."

"Cute, but not helpful."

She leaps off the couch. "I know! I'll check out his profile on Mywitchbook!"

"Perfect!"

We hurry into her room and turn on her computer. Miri signs in to the site, and I check out her page.

Miri Weinstein's Mywitchbook.com
Profile
Hometown: New York, New York
Magicality: Gray
Favorite Activities: Tae Kwon Do
Hero: Mother Teresa; Princess Diana;
my sister, Rachel
Relationship Status: Single

"You're so cute," I tell her. "You picked me!"

She blushes and clicks over to Praw's. Luckily, his profile isn't set to private.

Corey Praw's Mywitchbook.com
Profile
Hometown: Atlanta, Georgia
Magicality: Gray
Favorite Activities: Karate,
saving the world
Hero: Bono
Relationship Status: Single

He sounds like he's running for Miss America.

"He likes martial arts!" she shrieks.

"I know."

"And he's single!"

"I know," I say, laughing. "What is magicality?"

"His views about how to use magic. And he's gray too! We're interested in all the same things! I won't have to fake anything!"

"Clearly, you two are a match made in witch heaven."

Miri nods excitedly.

"Why don't you friend request him?" I ask.

She stares at me, horror-stricken. "What? No!"

"Why not?"

"Because then he'll know I like him!"

"So don't request *just* him," I say. "Request all the people we met at Lozacea."

She considers the idea. "Okay. But should I start or end with him?"

"I don't think it matters."

She clicks on the Add Him as a Friend button. And then clicks on the button that shows his friends—all fifty-two of them. We scroll through them, searching for familiar faces.

I point. "There are the triplets! Friend them!"

She does. "And here's Karin." She friends her, too. "And Adam."

"Let me see his profile," I say. When we click on his name, a photo of him with a big smile appears.

Yup. Still cute. "Omigod. He has three hundred and seventy-five friends!"

"That's a lot of friends," Miri says.

"How does he know so many witches? I barely know that many people." I read the rest of his information.

Adam Morren's Mywitchbook.com
Profile

Hometown: Salt Lake City
Magicality: Pink
Favorite Activities: Surfing, watching football, hanging out, traveling, spells
Hero: My dad
Relationship Status: Single

Interesting. Very interesting. "What's pink?" I ask. "Sounds kind of feminine."

"It means he uses magic for fun."

Good to know. I am *so* pink. I am shiny pink. Sparkly pink. "He's kind of cute too, huh?"

"I think he might like you," she says, and I feel her watching me.

I don't meet her eyes. "As a friend, maybe."

"I don't know," she says. "He kept smiling at you."

I point to his picture. "He's a smiley type of guy."

"Still."

Did he like me? I'm not sure. Do I like him? He is cute. Not that it matters. I finger the tiny heart Raf gave me for my birthday.

My heart belongs to Raf.

"He accepted!" Miri sings, bouncing on my bed.

"I'm trying to sleep!" I say, pulling up my covers. "What time is it?"

"Only a little after twelve."

"It's practically one in the morning and you woke me up because—"

"Because Praw accepted my friend request! And he wrote me a note! He asked me about my Tae Kwon Do! Isn't that awesome? So I wrote him back telling him all about my Tae Kwon Do! And guess what! Now I have fifty more friends!"

I don't say anything. Because I'm sleeping. Or trying to. Is she still here?

"Should I not have written him back so fast?" she continues. "Will he think I'm desperate?"

"Probably."

"Oh, no!" she cries. "Seriously?"

I open my eyes and see that her forehead is all creased with worry. "I'm kidding! Relax. I'm sure he'll fall madly in love with your adorableness and nondesperateness. In fact, I'm sure right now he's saying to his big sister, 'Wow, that Miri Weinstein is not desperate at all.' "

"How do you know he has a big sister?" she asks.

"I don't. I was being funny." Ha-ha?

"But he does have a big sister. She's sixteen and her name is Madison. I saw it on Mywitchbook."

I close my eyes. "Great. Now can we go back to sleep?"

"No! He's still online. I need to strategize with you."

"Go bug Mom."

"She's sleeping."

"See? Normal people are asleep," I say woozily. "And I want to be normal."

"Too late. You're a witch. By definition, you're the very opposite of normal."

I flip my pillow. "Speaking of the opposite of normal, are you coming makeunder shopping with me and Wendaline tomorrow?"

"Of course! Not that I think she needs a makeunder. But I want to hang out with her."

"Good. Now go to sleep!" I pull the covers over my head and drift off.

Until Miri crawls into my bed. "Fitch invited us to his Sim this Friday," she whispers.

I open one eye. My room is pitch-black. "What time is it? And what exactly is a Fitch?"

"It's two, and you remember Fitch! He's the short French one. Do we want to go?"

"I want to go to sleep."

"Focus, Rachel, focus. He's having a party. This Friday night. He invited us to come."

"Where is it?"

"The Eiffel Tower!"

"Huh? In Paris?" Now both eyes are open. I can kind of make out her outline in the dark.

"No, in Oklahoma. Yes, in Paris," she says in a low voice. "His family is originally from France."

"But still. The Eiffel Tower?"

"Boys have them in crazy places."

Like a cemetery isn't crazy.

"So do you want to go?"

"If you want to." I like France. I like French fries. French manicures. French kissing.

"Do you think there's dancing? Will we have to dress up? What if Praw is there?"

"Then you'll dance with him," I say.

"How am I going to dance with him when I can barely talk to him?"

Silly Miri. "You don't need to talk if you're dancing."

"But we're going to go? I want to RSVP."

"You have to ask Mom first." I close my eyes. "Wait! What about Dad? Next weekend is his. What are we going to tell him? We already have to come up with a way to disappear for three hours on Saturday for our Sam class. Do you think we could just pretend we're napping?" We could put pillows under our covers in case Dad comes in. Although

Prissy would probably rip the covers off. Maybe we can give her a napping spell. We can give the whole house a napping spell! It will be just like *Sleeping Beauty* except for three hours instead of a hundred years. Of course, we could always pause them, but then they would be weirded out over having lost three hours. Hmm . . .

"I think we should tell him the truth," Miri says.

"About the Simsorta? Yeah, that would confuse him just a little. *Excuse us, Dad. We're hopping over to Paris for a few hours for a party.*"

"No. You don't understand. I want to tell him the truth. About us."

I spring into a sitting position, my heart racing. "What?"

"I want to tell Dad the truth."

"Yes, I heard, thank you. I just can't believe what I

heard. Why would you want to do that?" We can't tell him. We just can't.

"Why not?"

"Mom never told him the truth. If she didn't want him to know, we can't go behind her back." The words tumble out of my mouth until I'm out of breath.

"Times have changed. Witchcraft doesn't have the same stigma it used to." She talks about witchcraft as though it's as American as pie baking. "Anyway, Mom always said we could tell Dad if we wanted to. I wanted to wait until I finished my training, and I'm pretty much done. And now I feel like he should know. I mean, we got mad at Mom for not telling us important things, right? Don't you think Dad has a right to know? I hate lying to him."

"You've been lying to him for half a year!"

"I know, and it makes me feel bad. I don't want to lie anymore. And I want him to come to our Samsorta. Don't you? We can't have a huge coming-out party and not invite our father! It's just not right."

"He's going to tell Jennifer. You want her to know too?"

She frowns. "He doesn't *have* to tell her."

"Yes, he does," I say. "They're married. Married people tell each other things. It's the rule."

She wrinkles her nose. "We'll ask him not to. He's our father. He loves us."

"Then he's lying to *her*." Ha! I got her there.

She hesitates, then says, "Let me think about it. Maybe we should talk about this during daylight hours."

I nod. Then. Or never.

"But what about Fitch's Sim?"

"If you want to go, we'll go," I say. "But you have to figure out what to tell Dad."

Her eyes brighten. "Technically, we don't have to tell him anything. Paris is six hours ahead of New York, so the party should be done at six p.m."

"Oh, sure, *now* you remember time zones."

She ignores my dig. "We can be at Dad's at our regular time. We can skip the train and transport ourselves right from the Eiffel Tower to the Long Island train station. Smart, huh?"

For someone who's so insistent on not lying, my sister can sure make up stories.

Miri hops out of my bed and sneaks back into her room. I close my eyes, but unfortunately, I can hear Miri's typing through the walls.

Click, click, clack, click.

I open my eyes and stare at the ceiling. Miri might be the loudest typist in the history of the world.

I can't believe she wants to tell Dad. We can't tell him. I flip onto my stomach. But don't I want to share something this important with him? Don't I want him to know who I really am? Won't he love me anyway? He has to, right? He's my dad. If you truly love someone, don't you love them no matter what? And when you really love someone, don't you love them not despite their quirks, but because of them? I need to think this through. I need sleep.

Clack, clack, click, clack.

What I really need are earplugs. I focus and chant:

> "*It's really late.*
> *I need to hit the sack.*

Please give me plugs
So I don't hear her click-clack."

Not the world's best rhyme, I know, but give me a break. It's the middle of the night.

Anyway, it works. Sort of. Two identical bathtub plugs materialize on my night table.

Too tired to cast another spell, I bury my head under my pillow and finally, *finally* fall asleep.

13 Makeunder Madness

When I open my eyes the next morning, I discover I've slept right through the pillaging of my closet. Half my outfits are splayed on the pink carpet, no longer in their original forms. Meaning my first-day-of-school shirt is now a minidress; my last year's green prom dress is now blue; my sandals are now strappy stilettos; and my running shoes are now heels. My sister sits in the eye of the tornado, in just her underwear and a sequined top. I believe the top was once a necklace.

"Um, Miri? What are ya doing?"

"I have nothing to wear," she wails.

I stretch my arms above my head and yawn. "To what?"

"What do you mean, 'to what'? To the Simsorta! To see Praw! I need to look pretty! And I have nothing pretty! Nothing!"

"Mom said we could go?" I ask.

"Kind of," she says. "She said we weren't allowed to miss school for someone we barely know, but that we could go for the dancing. So we'll come home right after school, get ready, then go to Paris. But only if I have something to wear!"

"Calm down. We'll find you something nice. You'll come shopping with me and Wendaline today. We'll make you beau-ti-ful."

"You scare me when you speak in syllables."

I cackle for effect.

That afternoon, while we're waiting for Wendaline at Bloomie's, a woman in a black smock asks us if we'd like her to do our makeup.

"Yes! Start with her," I say, pushing Miri forward. "She really needs it."

Miri shakes her head. "I don't wear makeup."

"Do you want to look pretty or not?" I ask, arms crossed.

"Have a seat," Smock Lady says. "I promise not to bite."

Miri hesitates. "Can you make it look really natural?"

"Absolutely."

Miri reluctantly climbs onto the stool.

"I'll start with your eyes. You know, really make them pop. Bring out the green." She peers at my sister's face.

"She has brown eyes," I say quickly. "Like I do. I haven't agreed to have a color-blind makeup artist paint my sister, have I?"

"You haven't," Smock Lady says, picking out a thin

brush. "Your sister's eyes are definitely brown. But she has some gorgeous flecks of emerald I'm going to bring out."

Who knew? I step toward one of the seven hundred mirrors and examine myself. Do I have flecks of emerald in my eyes too?

Is that one? No.

There? Also no.

It seems my eyes are fleckless.

Smock Lady pulls out a palette, studies Miri, looks back at the colors, studies Miri again. "I'm going to try a new shade called Perfectly Pretty on you."

I love how all the shades have fun names. I flip over the containers to see what the other colors are called. Lady in the Water, Lucidity, A Dozen Roses—who comes up with these names, anyway? I bet I could do it. That would be a fun job. When I grow up, I want to be an eye shadow namer. Fun!

I turn back to Miri.

Smock Lady applies eyeliner and mascara and then swings Miri's stool around to face one of the seven hundred mirrors. "What do you think?"

"I don't know," she says, looking at herself. "It's so makeup-y."

"She'll take them!" I exclaim. She looks amazing. Her eyes are popping all over town. "What do you have in a lip gloss for her?"

"I don't need lip gloss," she says.

"You do too," I say. "Don't you want to look kissable?"

She turns bright red.

"I don't think she needs a blush," I say.

After Miri's done, I climb onto the stool and let Smock Lady do her magic. "Use everything," I say. "Mascara, shadow, blush, lip liner . . . the works!" I've always wanted to see how to apply my makeup without getting that punched-in-the-eye look.

When she's done, I admire my many reflections. Yes! She dusted my eyes in mauve and lined them in gray and now they are popping! And I thought I had cheekbones before? Hah! *Now* I have cheekbones. Rusty pink ones. And my lips! Beautiful, glossy, kissable lips. "Fantastic!" I exclaim. "I'll take them!"

Miri shakes her head. "Didn't Mom say we could only spend two hundred dollars?"

Mom was nice enough to hand me her credit card, with the instruction that I could spend two hundred dollars on a new dress for Miri. But I'm sure that didn't include accessories, so I dismiss her with a wave of my hand. "Don't worry. It'll be fine. I don't need a dress, since I have the one I wore for prom."

Miri raises an eyebrow.

"What?" I say, defensive. "I'm not a celebrity, you know. I do wear things more than once."

While I'm charging the purchases, Wendaline arrives. She's wearing another ridiculous outfit—red lace skirt, draping black velvet top—but at least she arrived by foot.

"Don't you two look pretty!" she says.

I curtsey, charge the makeup, and then lead the way up the escalator.

"Okay, ladies, here's what we need!" I rub my hands together. I feel like a football coach. "We are looking for a new dress for Miri. Something that shows off how cute she is. Something fun. Something flirty. Something—"

"To bring out my green eyes?" She bats her mascara'd lashes.

"Not green, Miri, *fleckled* with green. Supposedly."

"You mean flecked," she says, rolling her eyes.

"Anyway. For Wendaline we're looking for jeans," I say. "Not too tight, not too flared. The perfect boot cut. She also needs some tops."

"Can't I wear the shirt I have on with jeans?" she asks, gesturing to the black velvet number that is draped over her upper body.

"No," I say simply. "You cannot. And for me—"

"I thought you weren't getting anything," Miri interrupts.

"I'm keeping an open mind."

"What do you need a dress for?" Wendaline asks.

"A guy named Fitch invited us to his Sim."

"No way! This Friday? On the Eiffel Tower? I'm invited too!"

"Yay!" Miri cheers. "We can all go together."

"My whole family is invited," she says. "My mom went to Charm School with his mom."

"No time for chatting," I say. "Let's move. We'll meet back at the changing room in fifteen. Go, team!"

The troops disperse.

Fifteen minutes later, Wendaline returns with three pairs of jeans that are clearly wrong. (Too big! Too low! Did I say bell-bottoms? No, I did not.) Miri also gets it wrong.

The dresses she picked are the most awful pieces of clothing I have ever seen. Seriously. They're hideous. One has hot pink embroidered tulips and one has fluorescent orange crinoline. Luckily, I have good taste and have made more appropriate selections. Unfortunately, I spent so much time finding clothes for them, I had time to pick out only three shirts and a pair of black jeans for myself. The black jeans are too advanced for Wendaline, but I've been noticing them on a bunch of the A-listers.

For some reason, we all crowd into one dressing room.

The jeans I picked out for Wendaline are *perfect*. They elongate her legs and make her butt look small.

"They're so tight," she says. "Are you sure this is the right size?"

"Yes," I say adamantly. "They stretch."

"I hope so. They're not that comfortable. There's a button pushing into my stomach."

"You have to get used to them. Now try on this top." I pass her two T-shirts, one long-sleeved and one short-sleeved. "Layer them," I instruct.

Miri slips on a red dress. "What are we supposed to wear for *our* Samsorta? Is Kesselin Fizguin going to talk about that?"

"We all have to wear heliotrope dresses," Wendaline says.

I zip Miri up. "A what?" Sounds like a circus act.

"Purple," Wendaline says. "Purple-pink. Like the flower. The color has magical properties—it supposedly enhances beauty."

If only I had known that last month. It would have been the perfect color for my back-to-school shirt.

"Where do we get these dresses?" Miri asks. "Anywhere?"

"I'm not sure," Wendaline says. "I have to wear my

mom's. She's kept it preserved for thirty years especially for my Sam."

"Do you think Mom still has her dress?" Miri asks me.

"I doubt it," I say. "Although it could be in the cleaning closet. Anyway, we'd still need one new one. It's not like we could both wear it."

"Dibs!" Miri calls.

She's more than welcome to wear Mom's Windex-scented number while I get myself something brand-spanking-new. "Fine with me," I say, and then admire her reflection. "That looks sexy."

Miri pushes in front of the mirror and turns sideways. "It's too red. Makes me look like I'm trying too hard."

I roll my eyes. "If you don't want it, let me try it on." I can always zap it bigger if it's too small. Or ask for a larger size. Whichev. I turn to Wendaline, to see how she's doing. "No, no, no. You have it on wrong," I bark. "The short-sleeved shirt goes over the long-sleeved one."

"Then you can see the sleeves!" she says. "Why would I do that?"

I roll my eyes. "You're supposed to see the sleeves. That's the style. Switch it up."

She shrugs and pulls them both off.

Omigod! "Wendaline, you have huge boobs! I had no idea. What cup size are you?"

She models her bra in the mirror. "I'm a C."

"You need to wear tighter shirts," I tell her as I shimmy into the red dress. Nice! Yes! I love it! Why should I wear my old prom dress to the Sim when I could be wearing this?

And what if Miri's magical tantrum with my wardrobe this morning did any lasting damage? I need something new so I can look hot. Red hot.

Do I want to look red hot? Why do I want to look red hot?

Miri pulls her tulip number off the hanger.

"That one looks like fun," Wendaline tells her.

"Are you guys blind?" I ask. "Honestly, you are not even allowed to try that on." I pull it out of her hand and throw it over the dressing room door. "That does not say 'pretty.' That says 'fiasco.' If it were an eye shadow, that's what it would be called. Fiasco. Try this on instead." I hand her a simple green silk dress. "It's stunning and simple."

She slips into it, I zip it up, and we both look in the mirror.

Miri smiles at her own reflection. "Not bad," she says.

"Not bad?" I say dismissively. "Please. It's gorgeous. If *it* were an eye shadow, it would be called—"

Wendaline winks. "Simply Stunning."

Exactly.

My game plan is destroyed on Sunday night. Mom freaks at the Bloomie's receipts and makes me promise to return my new dress and the black jeans. "I said two hundred dollars total!" she says.

"Why does Miri get to keep all her stuff and I have to return everything?"

"Because you already have a dress you can wear. And you spent a hundred dollars on back-to-school clothes two weeks ago!"

Oh. Right. Prom dress it is, then. Perhaps with some magical modifications.

On Monday, Wendaline wears her new jeans and T-shirt to school . . . and Cassandra ignores her. Yay! I'm not sure if it's because Cassandra doesn't recognize her, or if she just discovered a new person to be rude and obnoxious to, but I don't care. I'm glad to have avoided another sticky situation.

Tammy seems a bit distracted.

"How was your weekend?" I ask during French. "Wasn't Bosh in town?"

"Yeah," she says. "It was good." She sighs.

"What's wrong?"

"Can we have lunch today, just us? It was a bit of a weird weekend, and I so need to talk about it."

"Sure," I say. "Wanna go down the street to Cosi's?"

She nods, relieved.

At lunch, she dives right into it. "I really care about him. And I know he really cares about me. But he's only been gone for a few weeks, and it's already so tough."

"Like how?" I ask.

"Well, my moms won't let me go visit him, for one thing. They say I'm too young to stay overnight, which I understand."

I nod.

"So I only get to see him when he comes into town. And how often can he come in? He doesn't want to miss out on all the college activities, and I don't want him to either! I just don't know what to do. Long-distance is so hard. And we're in such different places right now. He has all these college friends, and college jokes, and college stuff . . . and I'm still here. And there's such a big age difference . . . I just wonder if we should break up."

I gasp. "You can't break up! You guys are, like, the world's best couple."

She takes a small bite of her turkey sandwich. "But we have nothing in common anymore. Nothing at all. We live in different worlds." She sighs again. "I don't know what to do."

"Can't you give it more time?" I ask. "Like till Thanksgiving or something?"

She laughs. "They call that Black Monday, you know. When all the college freshmen go back to school after breaking up with their high school sweethearts on Thanksgiving."

"Yikes," I say.

"I know."

"But I bet some of them work out. Not everyone breaks up with their high school boyfriends. Some people must get married." Like Raf and I. We're totally going to get married. Maybe. What's a little distance in a relationship? Raf and I don't share every detail of our lives. And we're fine. We're great.

"Like one in a million couples," Tammy says. "But maybe you're right. I can give it a few more weeks. At least a month."

"A month sounds reasonable."

"Thanks, Rachel," she says. "You rock."

"Yes I do," I say, smiling. I'm a good friend, school is going well, I'm going to Paris . . . life is good.

On Wednesday, Wendaline screws everything up.

Tammy and I are walking to chemistry, which happens to be by the seniors' lockers. Wendaline is on her way to bio. She waves to us. We wave to her. The three of us spot Cassandra in her all-in-black outfit (trendy new black jeans like the ones I was forced to return, black running shoes, black sweater, black headband) simultaneously. Flanked by her posse, she closes her locker and then inserts a stick of bubble gum into her mouth. She tosses the wrapper on the floor.

That's when Wendaline does it. When she passes Cassandra's locker, she picks up the discarded wrapper, offers it to her, and says, "You dropped this."

Noooooooooooooooooooo!

Clearly, Wendaline is a masochist.

Cassandra stares at Wendaline as if she has three heads, four eyes, and a tail. Or as if she's wearing her cloak and sitting on a broomstick.

I'm afraid to move. It's like I'm paused.

"Why, thank you, *Wendaline*," Cassandra says snidely, drawing out her name so that it sounds ridiculous. She rips the wrapper out of Wendaline's hand.

"You're welcome," she says, smiling self-consciously, and continues walking.

Cassandra smoothly stops Wendaline after a step. "Your hair is so long," she says, patting Wendaline's as if

Wendaline were a child, "It's like it's never been cut. How very unusual."

Her friends snicker, and the entire posse travels down the hall like a school of sharks.

Wendaline crosses the hall toward us. "See? She's not so bad."

That's when I see it—a wad of chewed gum lodged in her hair.

Tammy and I gasp.

Wendaline asks, "What now?"

Another sticky situation, courtesy of Wendaline.

14 How Do You Say **Party** in French?

Bonjour! Vive la France! “We’re here! We’re here!”

Paris. The land of romance. Of fashion. Of cheese.

It’s ten o’clock in Paris, six hours later and much darker than it is at home. It also smells different. Better. Perfume-y. New York smells like egg rolls and dryer sheets.

Imagine if instead of lavender or garden spring, you could buy scents like Paris and New York. Maybe I should become a professional perfumer.

“Look how big it is!” Miri exclaims, gazing up at the Eiffel Tower. She slides off my back. “Both your shoes still on this time?”

I drop the batteries into my silver clutch (aka my magically altered schoolbag). “Yup! You?”

“Yup. Let’s go!” She teeters ahead in my mom’s shoes, not used to walking in heels.

"I think that's a bouncer," I whisper, motioning to a woman in a black cloak in front of the door. "We're on the guest list, right?"

Miri nods. "I hope. I heard that they enchant the whole place so notches and norlocks can't even see the party. How cool is that?"

"But what if some tourist tries to crash?"

"The bouncer tells him it's closed for a private party."

"But what about the person who runs the Eiffel Tower? Someone has to know what's going on!"

Miri shrugs. "Maybe they just pause him or something."

"*Votre nom?*" the bouncer asks.

"I'm Miri Weinstein," my sister says.

The bouncer studies her list. "I 'ave you." She turns to me. "And you are Rachel?"

"Uh, *oui*." Magic bouncers are the best bouncers ever. Not that I've ever been to anything that's required a non-magical bouncer before. But still, she seems very effective.

"Give me your 'ands," she barks.

Huh? "You need a hand? Do you need us to help you with something?" Maybe she's not as good as I thought.

"Your 'ands." She takes my hand and stamps the back of it with a hologram of the Eiffel Tower. She stamps Miri's next.

"Touch!" she instructs.

Miri and I look at each other, shrug, and then simultaneously touch our stamps. *Vroom!* We're vaulted to a restaurant at the top of the tower. After landing, I reach out for something to steady my trembling body, and accidentally yank the edge of a black tablecloth. Uh-oh. I watch the glasses on top of said tablecloth all tip over in slow motion. I slam my eyes shut and wait for the sound of breaking glass.

Instead, I hear "You sure know how to make an entrance."

I open my eyes to see Wendaline wiggling her fingers. Glasses magically upright themselves.

"Thanks," I say gratefully.

She smiles. "It's all good."

At least we didn't disrupt anyone's dinner. No one is sitting at the table. All the guests (I'm guessing about a hundred) are dancing to a live band.

"You look great!" I tell her. And she does. She's in a dark black gown beaded with shimmering black pearls. "Your hair is perfect!" Her hair has been styled into a short bob. After the gum trauma, we called Este's salon and begged them to squeeze Wendaline in that afternoon. She definitely doesn't look like Rapunzel anymore, that's for sure. More like Snow White. Plus, I convinced her to get rid of the black nail polish and paint her nails baby pink.

We're standing right beside the crowded dance floor. Everyone is in formal wear. The adults are in dark suits and long dresses. The teens are also all dressed up. The girls are wearing tea-length dresses, and the boys are wearing suits.

"Where do we put our gift?" Miri asks her.

Wendaline walks us to a pile of presents near the bar. We wondered what to get. What do you buy for a guy who can zap up anything? Wendaline told us it's traditional to bring jars of rare spices to a Sim. So the guy can make up new spells maybe? We weren't sure what to spend, so we went to a fancy rare-spice store called Penzeys and bought him an eight-jar bakers' assortment gift box. We attached a card thanking him for having us. I hope he doesn't stare at the "from Rachel & Miri Weinstein," then turn to his family and say . . . "Who?" Or "*Qui?*"

"My mom is motioning to me," Wendaline says with a sigh. "She wants to introduce me to all her Charmori friends. I'll be back soon. . . ."

"Do I look okay?" Miri asks self-consciously when it's just the two of us.

"Still amazing," I say for the fifth time. Her green dress looks gorgeous. And she did a great job with the eye shadow. We only went through a half bottle of makeup remover.

I look pretty good too, if I must say so myself. Miri insisted I change the color of my prom dress from green to silver, because her dress is green and she didn't want us to look like twins. Of course, I wanted to look like twins (fun!), but she was strongly against it. I tried to turn my dress heliotrope, but the shade I came up with made me look like a grape. I hope the Samsorta cosmetologists know what they're doing.

I straightened my hair too, and it's extra-glam.

"I hope Praw's coming," Miri says.

After all this effort, he'd better be. "Didn't he tell you he was?"

"Yeah, but what if he doesn't? And I got all dressed up and he's not even here!" She turns white. "I see him! He's here! He's dancing! Don't look!"

I look.

Praw is indeed on the dance floor, boogying it up and looking extra-adorable and freckly in a dark gray suit.

"I told you not to look!" Miri cries. She nibbles at her fingers. "What if I freeze up again?"

"Calm down," I say in my most soothing voice. I pull her fingers away from her mouth. I should have gotten her a manicure after the makeup lesson. "What are you so nervous about? You've been Mywitchbooking with him all week. You'll have plenty to talk about."

"Mywitchbooking isn't the same as talking in person. Help! What do I do?"

"Eye contact. Smile. And relax," I instruct.

Just then, Praw spots us, smiles, and comes over. "You're here!"

"Yup," Miri says, looking at the ground. "Hey."

"Hi, Praw," I say. I poke Miri in the side. "Eye contact," I whisper.

She looks up.

"Y'all look nice," he says, but keeps his eyes on Miri.

Aw.

"You look very nice too," I say.

He blushes. "How was your French quiz?" he asks Miri.

"Not bad," she says. "How was your Spanish one?"

"Not awful."

Silence.

More silence. Uh-oh. Miri gives me a desperate look, so I jump in. "Have you ever been to Paris before?" I ask him.

"Yeah," he says. "I was here last Sunday for brunch with my parents. I mean, my mom and stepdad. My parents are divorced. Did I tell you that already?" He turns red.

He's babbling! Talking to Miri is making him nervous! How cute! I squeeze Miri's arm.

"Oh," Miri says, picking at her fingers. "Cool. Not cool 'cause your parents are divorced. Cool because . . ." She drifts off and looks helplessly back to the floor.

Because mine are too? She is really struggling here. Should I cause a distraction? Pull on another tablecloth?

"Praw," Miri says decisively, "let's dance."

Omigod! Miri! I did not see that coming! But . . . way to go! Now she doesn't have to talk at all. But she does have to make it to the dance floor. She teeters in her heels, and I worry she is going to do a face dive, but Praw takes her hand and steadies her. Aw.

I look around the room for someone to talk to. Adam, where are you? The dance floor is too crowded to make people out. Hmm. I could stand here alone like a wallflower or . . . I head outside to see the view. Pretty! The lights of the city shimmer.

"Don't you want to dance?" I hear a voice behind me.

I smile when I see Adam. He looks very handsome in his suit. "There you are."

"Looking for me, huh?"

I flush. I don't want him getting the wrong idea! "I . . . well . . ."

"I'm teasing you," he says. "You clean up nice."

"Why, thank you. So do you."

He motions inside. "Wanna dance?"

Would Raf care if I danced with Adam? As a friend, of course. "I would," I say, "but I'm the world's worst dancer."

"I'm not exactly *Dancing with the Stars* material either," he says.

"There's a dancing spell, you know."

"I haven't tried it. You?"

"Oh, yeah," I say. "You do not want to hear that story."

"I think I do," he says, his eyes crinkling.

"Okay, you asked for it." I put my hands on my hips. "My school had a fashion show and I really, really wanted to be in it." Then I giggle. "I can't believe I'm telling this ridiculous story." I've never had anyone to tell it to. Or really I've never had anyone I *could* tell it to.

"Let me guess," he says. "You were the star."

"Not quite," I say, giggling again. "See, my mom reversed the spell one minute before the show."

"No!"

"Yes. I was a disaster. Actually, I beheaded the faux Eiffel Tower."

He presses his index finger against my lips. "Shhh, don't say that too loud here. It might get you tossed off."

A boy is touching me. Touching my lips. A boy who is not Raf is touching my lips.

I take a step back, away, and grip the railing behind me. I don't think Raf would want another boy touching my lips. I don't think I want another boy touching my lips. "I better hold on tight, then." I giggle again, this time out of uneasiness. "Um, what about you?" I ask, anxious to keep this light. "Ever done any crazy spells?"

He holds on to the railing beside me. "When I first got my powers, I wanted to be on the football team."

"Who doesn't?"

"Exactly! So I found a strong-arm spell and then tried out for quarterback."

"Did it work?"

"I shot the ball about a thousand yards." He does a slow-motion impression of himself throwing the ball, which includes funny facial expressions. "They thought I was bionic."

"So you made the team," I say, laughing.

"Yup. Starting quarterback."

"Congrats!"

"Not so much. I had strength, but no aim. My first throw, I accidentally hit the coach. Broke his nose." He does a slow-motion impression of the coach grabbing his face.

I wince and then laugh. Adam *gets* what I'm going through. He gets my pain. He gets *me*.

The band finishes its song and a crowd of people come out for air.

Karin, Viv, Michael, and the triplets join us, and then Wendaline and her friends from Charm School, Imogen (who's English) and Ann (who's Scottish), come out and once again we're a group.

"Hey, have you tried the go spell?" Karin asks me.

"No," I say. "Should I?"

"It's the best," Glamour Triplet says.

The rest of the group murmurs their agreement.

"That's the spell you used to go to Hawaii, right?" I ask.

"Yeah," Michael says. "It's made from brown sugar and baby powder and some other stuff, too."

"Do you want me to write it out for you?" Karin asks.

"Sure," I say. "Thanks."

She zaps up paper and a pen and magically maneuvers the latter to write out a spell.

"We have extra mix," Preppy Triplet says. "I can give you some if you want to try it home tonight."

"Thanks!" How awesome are my new witch friends? So awesome! "Did one of you make it up? Do you share spells?" Do they all get together and trade them like recipes?

"It appeared in the spell book last week," Adam says.

"Spells appear in the book?"

"Every so often," Viv says.

"Haven't you noticed?" Karin asks.

"Oh, yeah, for sure," I say, biting my lip. Not.

"You so never noticed," Adam says, teasing. "That's why the page numbers get messed up. People add content. That's how they stay current."

"It's like Wikipedia," Michael explains.

"I've added a few," Viv says. She's wearing a very cool black flapper dress. "I made up the clear skin spell last year."

"No way! I used that spell!" I give her a high five. "How do you add spells? I didn't know you could."

"Yo, you know the blank page at the end? Just write it in there. If it works, the book absorbs it."

"Cool!" I wonder if it would like my bathtub plug spell. Nah, probably not my best one. But my outfit color-changer definitely deserves its place in the canon.

When it's time for dessert, I pile my plate high with freshly baked cookies, fancy French pastries, and fruit. Yum. Now, where to sit? Where's Miri? I spot her on the dance floor still boogying it up with Praw. Those two have not taken a break all night. How are her feet not killing her? Mine are all blistered and I haven't even danced. I look down at her feet and realize that she's shoeless. Aha. Smart girl.

"Rachel, come sit." Adam pulls out the chair beside him.

Isn't he sweet? I sit down and kick off *my* heels. I put my plate between us. "Dig in."

"Having fun?" he asks, helping himself to a cookie.

"Yeah," I say. "Sims are wild and crazy."

He leans back in his chair. "You're gonna have to come to mine, you know."

Yes! An invite! "I'd be happy to. How long have you had your powers, again?"

"Since last September," he says, reaching for another cookie. "You got them over the summer, yeah?"

"Yeah. But get this." I motion him closer and he leans in. "My lucky-duck sister got them four months before I did."

"Ouch," he says. His breath smells like chocolate.

"Do you have any siblings?"

"Two younger brothers. I was the first to get powers, though. But both my parents are witches, so I've pretty much spent my whole life waiting for them."

"At least you knew what to expect. My mom didn't tell us that we were witches. She was a nonpracticing witch! I knew nothing about"—I wave my arms around the room—"any of this!"

"Seriously?"

"Seriously," I say.

He moves his chair closer to mine. "So you grew up like a notch?"

"Yeah." We're only a few inches apart, and his knee is grazing mine under the table. Is he doing that on purpose? No. I'm sure he isn't. I pull away anyway. "Hey. They don't know you're a warlock at school, do they?"

"No way," he says. "I keep my lives separate. Magic life, regular life. Witch friends, school friends."

"Does everyone do that? Because if it were up to Wendaline, she would have told the entire school about us."

He laughs. "I think it depends on the family. And on where you live. New York City is pretty liberal."

"I'd rather keep my witchiness a secret. Any tips? I'm a newbie."

"It helps to tell your school friends that you have a country house. So they understand why you're never around on the weekends."

"Clever," I say. "But I'm not sure that my dad would believe that I bought myself a country house."

"Your dad doesn't know? That's rough." Our eyes lock. He touches my shoulder.

I freeze.

Call it witch's intuition, but I think now would be the right time to tell him that I have a boyfriend. It doesn't have to be a big deal. I can just casually introduce it into the conversation.

Such as "My dad doesn't know. And neither does my boyfriend."

Or "Will you excuse me for a second? I have to call my boyfriend."

Or maybe "Did I mention I have a boyfriend?"

Now.

Okay, now.

Now.

His hand is still on my shoulder. I have to get it off.

How am I supposed to do that without mentioning I have a boyfriend?

I glance at my watch. It's almost six in New York. "Gosh, it's late!" I blurt out. "I have to go!"

His hand drops to his lap.

I push my chair back, slip my shoes back on (ouch), stand up, and pick up my clutch from the table. "I gotta get back to my dad. Have you seen Miri?"

The band starts playing a slow song.

He puts his hand back on my shoulder. "One dance before you go."

"But—" I have a boyfriend! I should leave. This second.

But if I leave now, Miri won't get to have her slow dance with Praw.

Before I realize what's happening, my right hand is in his, my arm is around his neck, and we're dancing. I am dancing with someone who's not Raf. I'm *slow* dancing with someone who's not Raf.

It feels nice. Easy. Safe.

It's just a dance.

His hand is warm. He pulls me in a little closer. He smells good. Musky and outdoorsy. And the muscles in his arm feel . . .

Ack! Don't care! What's wrong with me? I close my eyes and picture Raf.

My boyfriend Raf. He might not be a warlock, but he's sweet and smart and creative and he makes my heart swoon. When the song ends, I step back immediately.

Another slow song begins and he murmurs, "One more?"

"I can't," I mumble. "I really have to go. Good night!" Giggle, giggle. "Thanks for the dance!" I head straight for Miri and Praw. "Excuse me! Sorry to interrupt. We have to go!"

Miri and Praw are startled out of their embrace. They both have dopey looks on their faces. "Already?" She glances at her watch. "It's late!"

Praw reluctantly lets her go. "You'll be at Lozacea tomorrow though, right?"

"Yeah." They're looking at each other like they've just turned on the TV and discovered a new favorite show.

"Bye," she murmurs.

"Bye, Miri," he says softly.

"We should transport from the terrace," I say. "No reason to go all the way downstairs."

We push through the dancing crowd. How lucky all these people are not to have to go home! Not to have anyone to lie to.

Miri's lips are set in a long straight line.

"What?"

"You got mad at me for hanging around when you were saying good night to Raf! I'd think you'd know better when I was trying to say good-bye to Corey."

"Who's Corey?"

"Praw! He has a first name, you know!"

"Oh!" Omigod! She wanted to kiss him. "I'm so, so sorry, Mir." I smile.

She gets a worried look on her face. "You think he likes me, right?"

"Miri! You danced the entire night. He did not talk to

anyone but you. He likes you. Can we talk about this later? We have a train to pretend to be on. Dad is expecting to pick us up at six-twenty."

I pull the traveling concoction and Karin's note out of my clutch. "Look what I got. It's called the go spell."

"Is that what we saw them using last week?"

"Yup. Ready?"

"Good-bye, Paris! Good-bye, city of love!" Who is this lovesick tourist and what has she done with my grumpy sister?

I toss the mixture into the air above us and chant:

"Through space we flow.
To the Port Washington Long Island Rail Road station
We shall go!"

I feel the familiar rush of cold and then *whoosh!* We are sucked into the air, and the next thing I know, we are standing in a bathroom stall in the train station.

"Ew," I say. A piece of toilet paper is stuck to my heel.

"Could have been worse," Miri says. "Could have been the men's."

"Mir, you have some of the spell still in your hair." I pluck at the dandruff-like flecks. Note to self: don't use this spell when wearing black. "Is it on me?"

After she picks it off, we check ourselves out in the bathroom mirror, and we're ready.

Her eyes go wide. "Rachel!"

"Miri!"

"Why are we in these dresses?"

Did the go spell wipe out her memories? "Because we were at the Sim?"

She flicks my arm. "I mean what's our reason for Dad? Unless you want to tell him the truth."

My heart speeds up. "Now? No! Definitely not. Let me think."

"We should just tell him! He'll be excited! Trust me, I know he will." Her eyes are lit up with so much hope and love that it makes me nervous. Miri has always kept my dad on a bit of a pedestal. Nothing is ever his fault; it's always Jennifer's. But what if we do tell him, and what if he doesn't react the way Miri thinks he will? What will happen to Miri?

"Miri," I say carefully, "we can't just tell him now. That's insane. It's too spur-of-the-moment. We need to think it through."

She sighs. "We'll just tell him we went to a party."

"Why are we at a dress-up party that ends at six? That makes no sense. Let's use the transformation spell to change into something more casual."

She hugs her new outfit with her arms. "No way! I'm not zapping this dress!"

Oh, sure, my wardrobe was fine to play magical chairs with, but her dress is too precious. "Then let's just go home and change."

"By magic?"

"No, by train. Of course by magic! And then we'll come right back." I check the time on my phone. "We have seven minutes. We'd better be fast."

I toss the concoction into the air and chant:

"Through space we flow.
To our apartment in New York
We shall go!"

Vroom! I feel like I'm in a race car with this spell.

"This stuff makes me dizzy," Miri says as our feet land on our bathroom floor.

"It helps to close your eyes," I say, opening mine. "But why do you think we keep ending up in bathrooms?"

"Maybe 'cause it's private? So no one will see us? Like Superman's phone booths?"

"Ha. But what if someone is using the bathroom? Like Lex?" Gross.

"Hey, it's Friday night. What if he's here right now? What if they're—" She wiggles her eyebrows.

Gross to the power of two. "No time to throw up; we gotta move. Mom!" I scream. "Are you home? We're here!"

No answer. That had better mean they're out and not otherwise engaged.

I throw open the door. The lights are all off, and my mom's door is open. "All clear."

Miri motions to her back. "Unzip me!"

I undo her dress, she undoes mine, and then we both run to our respective rooms, throw on jeans and tops, and meet back in the hallway.

"Ready?" I ask, gasping for breath.

"Ready."

I toss the concoction again.

> *"Through space we flow.*
> *To the Port Washington Long Island Rail Road*
> *Station*
> *We—"*

"Wait!" Miri yells.

"What?"

"Try specifying a place not in the bathroom!"

"But I don't mind the bathroom. We don't want to pop up in a public place, or on the train tracks and get run over."

"Squashed like grape," she says, and then laughs.

"Like what?" I ask.

"It's a *Karate Kid* reference. Corey would get it."

Begin rolling of eyes. I try again.

"Through space we flow.
To the Port Washington Long Island Rail Road Station
We shall go!"

With a jolt we return to a bathroom stall in the railway station. I creak open the door and spot a woman applying lipstick in front of the mirror.

"Hello," I say nonchalantly.

She ignores us.

I hurry out, push open the bathroom door, rush to the aboveground platform, and hide behind a pillar while we wait for the train to arrive. I check my phone. "With a minute to go! Way to go, us. We are the masters!"

"We are pretty good," she agrees. "So," she says, "what's the story with you and Adam?"

My heart speeds up, but I try to ignore it. "No story. Why would you ask that?"

"I saw you dancing with him. *Slow* dancing."

"It was just a dance," I say, paying way too much attention to the tracks.

"Does he know you have a boyfriend?" she asks.

I shrug. "It hasn't come up."

I feel her eyes on me. "It hasn't come up, or you haven't told him?"

The train pulls in, so I don't have to answer.

The passengers file out and we join their march down the stairs to the parking lot. We spot Dad, Jennifer, and Prissy waiting by the car. Could we have planned this any better? We might never take the train again. Why should we? We'll just pretend to be on it.

We wave and hurry over.

"Hi, girls," he says.

"Hi, Dad!" we chirp.

Jennifer looks at us and then around us. "Where are your bags?"

Miri and I look down at our empty hands and then at each other. Whoopsies.

We were so busy getting ready for the party that we forgot to pack. Sure, we leave toothbrushes and pajamas at Dad's, but never *good* clothes. ('Cause why would we need good clothes in Long Island? If we liked them, we'd want to wear them to school.)

"Did you forget your bag on the train?" Dad asks, getting ready to sprint for it.

"No," I say. "We forgot them at home."

Both Jennifer and my dad look at us as though we are total morons.

"Your homework too?" Dad asks.

"Yup," I say.

Dad shakes his head. "That was dumb."

"Yup," we admit.

"You can borrow whatever you want of mine," Jennifer offers.

"Me too!" Prissy chirps. "Borrow mine! Mine! I have a princess dress and it's pink and it would look pretty on both of you."

Excellent. Miri and I will be sharing a princess dress to Samsorta lessons. We'll look really hot.

Not that I care about looking hot.

Because I don't.

My dad unlocks the doors with a click. "I'm getting you guys some new vitamins. B12 is good for forgetfulness."

"Maybe we'll get you some new clothes, too," Jennifer says. "Clothes you can leave here."

Yay! Jennifer is so thoughtful. And we should forget our stuff more often. "You know," I say, climbing into the backseat, "I could really use a pair of black jeans."

15 Kiss, Kiss

After dinner, Jennifer puts Prissy to bed, and we all sit down in the den.

"So, what's new with you two?" Jennifer asks. "Tell us everything!"

Miri gives me a hopeful smile.

Is she kidding me? Now? I shake my head. We can't just tell them our secret on a whim. We need to think it through. Have a plan. Warn Mom.

"Not much," I say in a rush. "Nothing important. We're really busy at school."

Jennifer raises a perfectly arched brow. "So busy that you didn't bring your homework?"

"We *forgot* our homework," I say. Which is a bit of a problem. I'm supposed to study the difference between *imparfait* and *passé composé* for a French test on Monday morning, plus finish *Animal Farm*. How exactly am I going to do that? Maybe I should zap myself over to the library, or back to Paris for a tutor. And I still haven't figured out how Miri and I are sneaking out for three hours tomorrow. . . . Wait a sec. Problem solved! I am a genius. "Dad, could you drop us off at the library tomorrow for a few hours? I bet they'd have some of our books."

"Sure," my dad says. "Good idea. In the afternoon?"

"Say from four to seven? After shopping, of course," I add.

Miri smiles.

Dad nods. "The library is right near the restaurant we're going to for dinner. We'll pick you up when you're ready and go straight over."

"Great!" I say. No napping spell necessary. Although *pretending* to be at the library won't exactly help me with my French conjugation or reading *Animal Farm*. One problem at a time, I suppose.

After lots of chitchatting about homework, the weather, and morning sickness (fun times), we're off to bed. My ears are still ringing from the music, but I close my eyes, ready for sleep.

"I have a question for you," Miri says.

"Am I tired? Why, yes, I am."

She giggles. "Not the question. Will you tell me how to kiss?"

I sit up. Adorableness!

Her face flushes. "To be honest, even though I was mad you didn't leave us alone tonight during the good-byes, I was also relieved. I don't know what to do if he kisses me. How do I know what to do with my tongue?"

"Miri, Miri, Miri." Adorable, adorable, adorable. "You'll just know."

"Do you open your mouth right away? Or wait?"

"Don't open your mouth right away. If you attack him, you're definitely going to lose kissing points."

"What points? There are points?"

"I'm kidding. Don't worry. It'll come naturally."

"But what if I naturally want to open my mouth right away?"

"Keep your mouth closed. But parted a little." I separate my fingers a half inch. "That much."

She nods, looking very serious. "What about the tongues? Do they really touch?"

"They really touch."

"I think I'd be less nervous if I could practice."

"Practice on your pillow." I pick mine up. "Oh, Corey," I say fake lustfully, then smother my face in it.

"Don't kiss my boyfriend!" she says. "You already have two of your own!"

I pick up my pillow/fake boyfriend and (gently) hit her with it.

Of course, after our little discussion, Miri falls right asleep. She's smiling, too, and making kissy noises, so it's not hard to imagine what she's dreaming about.

But me? I'm back to staring at the ceiling. The room is too hot. My bed is too hard. My pillow is too fluffy.

And I'm wondering if kissing a regular guy and kissing a warlock feel any different.

After breakfast the next morning, we get dressed in yesterday's clothes, then head to the mall. My dad agrees that it's ridiculous for us not to have clothes at his place.

"Buy whatever you need for the winter," he says. "Within reason, of course."

My dad loves saying "within reason." Not sure what he thinks Miri and I would do otherwise. Are we that unreasonable?

Don't answer that.

Jennifer takes us to pick out extra undies and socks, and then we all meet up to get the black jeans and a few tops. The only problem is that both the tops I get are sweaters, which is perfect for the upcoming winter, but not ideal for Samsorta class in Arizona.

Actually, it was pretty cold in the classroom. Never mind. Maybe I'll double up.

"Miri!" I scream up the stairs. "Let's go! We're going to be late!"

"You're going to be late for the library?" my dad asks, grabbing his keys from the vestibule.

Whoops. "Late for *studying*. We have lots to cover."

A few minutes later she bounds down the stairs. Her eyelids are all sparkly. I see she's dug into Jennifer's makeup case.

"Got all pretty for your boyfriend?" I tease.

She blows me a kiss. "Got all pretty for yours?"

Not funny! Fine, I might have explored Jennifer's

makeup case too. But it's not because I care how I look. I just wanted to test out her colors. Note for next time: brown eye shadow is not a good idea. Prissy said I looked like a raccoon.

"I'll pick you up at seven-fifteen," Dad says, pulling up in front of the library. "We have a seven-thirty dinner reservation at Al Dente."

"Thanks!" we say. Once he drives off, we head inside, find a deserted corner, and use some of the remaining go spell to zap ourselves into the girls' bathroom at Lozacea.

In front of the mirror, we pick the concoction out of our hair.

"I think I prefer the battery spell," I tell her. "At least it doesn't leak on me."

"Ready?" she asks. "Let's go find the boys."

I pinch her side. "Not boys, plural. Let's go find Corey."

"Sure, whatever you say."

But as soon as we exit the bathroom, the lights begin to flicker, so we go straight to class.

Kesselin Fizguin is drawing a pentacle on the board. And when I say drawing, I mean using chalk. And not pointing her finger at the board and wiggling it, which is what I would always do if I were a witch teacher.

"Who can tell me what this stands for?" she asks.

About half of the thirty or so girls in the room raise their hands, including my sister.

She points to Miri.

"Teacher's pet," I murmur.

"The five pillars of witchcraft," my sister says, giving me a dirty look.

Fizguin nods. "Very good. Can you tell me what the five pillars of witchcraft are?"

"Truth, trust, courage, love, karma," Miri sings.

How does she know everything?

"In Brixta, please," the teacher says.

Miri blushes. "I don't . . . I don't know."

Guess she doesn't know *everything*.

The teacher frowns. "You haven't taken the Babel potion yet?"

Miri shakes her head. "No. Was I supposed to?"

"Go get some from the Potionary at the break," Fizguin says. She points to Preppy Triplet. "Shari. Tell me what the five pillars of witchcraft are."

"*Mouli, misui, mustrom, mantis, macaney.*" Preppy Triplet's teeth are very white. I glance at the other triplets' mouths to see if their teeth are as pearly. Yup. Do they all go to the dentist at the same time? Can one get a cavity on her own, or is it across the board?

"Let's start with the first one," Fizguin is saying. "*Mouli*. Truth. Tell me. Who does a witch have to be true to?"

"Her mom and dad?" someone says, and everyone laughs. Everyone except me and Miri.

"Yes, a witch should be truthful to her parents. But who's even more important than her parents?"

Her boyfriend?

Viv raises her hand. "Herself."

"Exactly. You should never lie to yourself. Pay close

attention now as I tell you the story of Briana, one of our most important foremothers. . . ."

It's Saturday! I don't want to pay attention! I want to watch TV and zone out.

"And what about *misui*?" Fizguin is asking.

Hmm? No idea what she's talking about. Good thing Miri is still scribbling away.

Earthy Triplet raises her hand. "It means *trust*," she says.

"Excellent." Fizguin turns to write something on the board but keeps talking.

Ring! Ring!

Someone's phone! How embarrassing.

Ring! Ring!

Oh, crapola. It's mine. It's not loud enough for Fizguin to hear, but it might be if she shuts up for a sec. I reach into my purse and fumble to turn it off. How do I make it stop ringing? There's a Mute button somewhere. Where is it? I really should have read the instruction manual. . . . I look at the caller ID. Raf. *Raf!* I know I shouldn't, but what else can I do?

"Hello?" I whisper, sinking into my seat.

"Hey!" he says, his voice sexy as always. "What's up?"

"Um . . . nothing. You?"

"Why are you whispering?"

Because I shouldn't be on the phone! "Because I'm . . ." Where could I be? Ack! "At the dentist."

Miri snorts. I elbow her in the side.

"On a Saturday?"

"He's a weekend dentist. It's, um . . . his hobby."

"You're not allowed to talk when you're at the dentist?" he teases.

"My mouth hurts. I have a cavity." Just brilliant. "Can I call you later?" Fizguin is going to turn around any second!

"Sure. I'm going to the park, but I have my cell. Good luck."

"Thanks," I whisper, and close the phone.

Why didn't I just tell him I was at the library? That would have made a lot more sense. I'm at the library studying *Animal Farm*, verb conjugation, trust, and truth.

And to be honest, I'm having some issues with that last one.

At the break, we all spill into the atrium.

Corey is sitting on a window ledge, obviously waiting for Miri.

"There he is!" my sister squeals. "What should I do?"

"Laugh!"

"Why?"

"It'll look like you're having fun!" I explain. "Guys like girls who have fun!"

"But I have nothing to laugh at."

"Pretend I said something funny! Ha, ha, ha!"

"You're so weird," she says, and laughs.

"You're doing it! Well done!"

"I'm not faking," she says. "I'm laughing at you."

Meanwhile, Corey is smiling at her. So cute! He is

pulling a thread off his shirt, trying not to look overeager. He likes her! He really likes her!

We smile back and join him by the ledge.

"Did you guys get home okay?" he asks.

"Yup. No problems." I scan the room and spot Adam on the other side. Should I wave? I don't want him to think I like him. I don't want him to think I don't. Why am I so confused? I give him a half wave to cover all bases.

Adam sees us and hops over. "What's up?"

"Hey," I say, flushing. "Will you show us where the Potionary is? We need to get the Babel potion."

"Sure," Adam says, and we follow the two boys down a long yellow hallway. At a purple wall, he knocks four times in a row and says, "*Gazolio!*" The wall morphs into a counter.

A ponytailed man in a lab coat pops up behind it. "What can I get for you?"

Adam motions for me to approach.

"Kesselin Fizguin sent my sister and me to get the Babel potion?" The counter smells like a mix of a grocery store and my chem class. The wall behind him has built-in shelves lined with glass vials filled with multicolored liquids.

"No problem," he says, handing us a pen. "I just need you both to sign in."

When I don't see a book to write in, I ask, "Where should we sign?"

"Oh, in the air is fine."

Miri and I give each other a look but do as we're told.

"Babel, right?"

"Yes," Miri says. "So we can speak Brixta."

"Got it," he says. "*B*, where's *B*?"

"After A and before C," Corey says.

Hey, Miri's boyfriend is a wannabe comedian.

The man—potionist?—pulls a vial off the shelf, and a second one immediately appears in its place. He pulls that off too. "Here we go. One for each of you. It lasts about three months."

I hold my vial up to the light. It's yellowish green. I remove the stopper and lift my vial to Miri's. "Cheers."

"Cheers," she says.

We clink and then chug it down. Not bad. It's sweet and tangy, like honey, lime, and green apple. My tongue begins to tingle.

I wait.

"It takes about ten minutes to kick in," the potionist says.

"Have either of you ever taken it?" I ask the boys.

They shake their heads.

"I learned the boring, traditional way," Adam says.

"It's not going to stain my teeth, is it?" I ask the potionist.

"It shouldn't," he tells me.

"Thanks for your help," I say, and then lead the group back to the atrium. "Have you noticed how the go spell leaves a residue in your hair?" I ask them.

"I have," Adam says. "But the running spell? That's the worst. Your toes are webbed together for a week."

I laugh. "You tried out for the track team, huh?"

He winks.

"What about the singing spell?" Corey says. "It makes your teeth itch."

"How come you tried a singing spell?" Miri asks.

He turns red. "I'm in my school chorus."

Wow, he's just as geeky as she is. "I should try the singing spell," I say. "I've always wanted a good voice. How good of a voice do you get? Like rock-star good?"

"Yup," he says.

"Ooh! You know what we should do?" I say. "Ask the potionist for the singing spell and then try out for *American Idol!*"

The three of them groan. "I don't think they're having tryouts right now," Adam says. "But we can practice with karaoke tonight."

"Yeah," Corey says. "I know the best place to go in Tokyo. All the songs are in English."

Japan. Why not?

"Can you guys come?" Corey asks eagerly.

Tell me, who goes to Tokyo for karaoke? Besides Japanese teenagers, of course. "We can't," I say slowly. "We have to have dinner with our dad."

Miri looks crestfallen. On one hand, I'm disappointed—Tokyo! Cool! Sushi with witch friends! On the other hand, I'm relieved. If we don't hang out, then I don't have to tell Adam about Raf. If we don't hang out, I'm not doing anything wrong.

Corey looks crestfallen too. "Too bad. Another time."

"Maybe we could all do something later this week," I add. Why did I say that? I shouldn't have said that.

The lights begin to flicker.

"Mywitchbook me!" Miri calls out to Corey as we head back to class.

Maybe I should join Mywitchbook. Maybe I shouldn't make plans to hang out with boys who are not my boyfriend.

"Now," Fizguin says when we're all reassembled, "let's talk about *mustrom*. Who can tell me what that is?"

Wait a sec! I know what she just said! I understand! "Courage!" I blurt out. Whoops. Indoor voice, Rachel.

"Very good!" Fizguin says. "I see you took Babel. Can someone tell me what we witches should have the courage to do?"

"Embrace our magic?" says a girl in the back.

"Yes!"

"Follow our convictions?"

"Yes!"

Miri scribbles in her book and then passes it to me to read. *Tell your father you're a witch?*

I pick up my pen and write back: *Gut giken vy!* Which translates to *Stop annoying me*.

But it sounds more musical in Brixta.

16 Urla (Brixta for You've Got to Be Kidding Me)

We're about to order at Al Dente when Jennifer asks my dad if he knows what *polpetti* is.

"Meatballs," I say, studying my menu.

"And *pesci*?"

Miri takes a sip of water. "Fish."

"Are you guys taking Italian this year?" my dad asks.

"No," we say.

Miri kicks me under the table. "How did we know that?" she whispers.

"I have no idea." But how cool? I speak Italian!

"I'm so impressed!" Jennifer says. "What does this mean?" She points to an item in the menu.

Miri pushes back my chair. "Rachel, come with me to the bathroom for a sec?"

"*Certamente*," I reply.

Prissy thumps her tiny hands against the table. "Me too! Pony ride to the bathroom!"

"No ponies at the restaurant," Jennifer barks. "Would you girls mind taking her?"

"Whatever," Miri says, rolling her eyes.

Jennifer bites into a bread stick. "How do you say *thank you*?"

"*Grazie*," we respond, then look at each other. I'm thinking maybe we should stop answering translation questions before Jennifer starts giving us weird looks.

Prissy grabs hold of our hands and drags us toward the bathroom. "How do you say *pretty*?"

"*Carina*," Miri says.

"Miri," I warn.

"Tell me I'm pretty!" Prissy says. "Tell me I'm pretty!"

I open the door. "You're pretty."

"Noooooo, tell me I'm pretty in Italian."

"How crazy was that?" I say to Miri. "I guess the spell works for more than just Brixta."

"I wonder if it works for every language." Miri pushes Prissy into an empty stall. "Pee. Now."

I hope it works for French, too. That would certainly make studying for my upcoming test easier.

"You have to put paper down on the seat for me," Prissy orders. "Mommy says so."

Miri lines the seat while muttering, "*Rompicoglioni*."

I could translate that, but I won't.

It's not very nice.

Back at my dad's, we decide to call Wendaline to see what she can tell us about the Babel potion. I try to encourage Miri to call Corey, but she's too embarrassed. Obviously, I'm not calling Adam.

Wendaline's voice mail clicks on. "No answer. Should we text her? Or get in touch on Mywitchbook.com?"

"Just leave a message," Miri says. "It's already ten. She's probably out doing fun magic stuff."

"Hi, Wendaline, it's Rachel Weinstein. If you could call me back when you have a chance—"

Boom!

There's a blast of cold, and Wendaline Appears in the center of our room. "Hi, guys!"

Miri and I both shriek.

"You called?" Wendaline asks.

"You scared me!" Miri says.

"Wendaline," I say, "what did I tell you about Appearing?"

She smiles sheepishly. "I thought that since we weren't at school, it was okay?"

"It isn't! Normal teenagers do not Appear in other teenagers' bedrooms. Here's how it works: I call you. You call me back. We make plans. You do not just Appear!"

She digs her heel into the carpet. "Sorry."

"Keep your voice down," I order. "My dad is right on the other side of the wall."

Wendaline sits on the edge of Miri's bed. "I'd love to meet him."

"Not gonna happen," I snap. "Anyway, we have a question. Have you ever used the Babel potion?"

"Oh, I love the language potion!"

"You've used it before?" I ask.

"Mm-hmm. I spent a weekend in Rio during sixth grade. I would have preferred to learn Portuguese more organically, but—"

"When you used it, could you understand every language or just Portuguese?" I ask, cutting her off.

"Just Portuguese, but I've heard that the spell has evolved. Let me ask my friend Imogen. She might know."

Wendaline snaps her fingers. "Imogen?"

The lanky girl Appears beside Wendaline. "Hello," she says with a thick British accent.

What, now we're having a party? Have these people never heard of the phone?

"You're up!" Wendaline says. "Isn't it like three in the morning in London?"

"It absolutely is. I was playing on that dreadful Mywitchbook. Have you tried the iSpell application? I'm obsessed! Hello again," Imogen says to me, then turns to Miri. "Lovely to meet you. What can I do for you?" she asks Wendaline.

"Do you know if the Babel potion works for multiple languages?"

She sits down beside Wendaline. "Hmm. Have you checked the book?" She snaps her fingers, and her copy of the spell book materializes in the center of the room. The cover is decorated with pink and silver glitter. I'm so jealous! I want mine to be all sparkly!

"Miri? Rachel?" we hear from outside. My dad knocks on the door. "Can I come in?"

"Disappear!" I tell Wendaline and Imogen.

They look at me in confusion. Without thinking, I open the closet door and motion for them to hurry inside.

They follow, intrigued. "Is there a secret passageway back here?" Wendaline asks.

"Yup, see if you can find Narnia," I say before firmly closing the closet behind them.

"Come in!" I say, trying to keep my voice even.

My dad opens the door. "Everything okay in here? It sounded like you were screaming."

"I was just showing Rachel a new Tae Kwon Do move," Miri says.

Quick thinking, Miri! Or 잘 했어요! That means *good job* in Korean.

"Are you guys going to sleep soon?" He looks from me to Miri, then down at Imogen's pimped-out copy of A^2.

Uh-oh.

His forehead wrinkles. "What's that?"

"Huh?" I say, stalling.

"That book," he says, transfixed by it.

Miri gives me a meaningful look.

She wants to tell him. Right here. With Wendaline and Imogen in the closet.

I shake my head. No, no, no!

"Dad, there's something we've been wanting to tell you," she begins.

She's going to tell him! What if he freaks out? What if he's scared of us? What if he looks at us differently?

What if he doesn't love us anymore?

He fell out of love with Mom, a little voice inside me says. *What's stopping him from doing the same with us?*

Miri clears her throat. "Last February, Mom told us that—"

No! I can't let her! "We needed to keep a scrapbook."

Dad's eyes dart between me and Miri.

"Yes," I continue, "Mom said that we need to better catalog our lives. So we're creating memories—photos, poems, drawings—and taping them into that book."

"That sounds like a fun project," Dad says.

"It is," I say. "It's great fun. Lots of bonding. I'm wondering if you . . . um . . . if you kept the bill from tonight's dinner? I thought I could put it in."

He scratches his head. "Sure, I'll save it for you."

"Thanks, Dad. You're the best." I force a smile.

"Good night, girls. Love you." He closes the door.

"Love you," Miri calls.

"Love you," I say, then whisper fiercely at my sister, "I'm so mad at you."

"*You're* mad at *me*?" She throws up her arms. "I'm mad at you! That was the perfect opening to tell him!"

"It's not just up to you," I say, and storm out of the room. I'm done talking about this. I'm getting washed and going to sleep. Miri follows me into the bathroom, where we brush our teeth, floss, and scrub our faces. We can't tell him. We don't know how he'd react. I mean, I know he wouldn't really stop loving us the way he stopped loving Mom. He's our dad. And it's not like he stopped loving Mom because he found out about the witch stuff. He never even knew.

Wait a sec. Is it possible that he stopped loving her . . . because he never knew? Because she was keeping such a big secret from him? I think this over as I make my way back to my room, drop my clothes in a pile on the floor, and pull a new pair of pajamas out of a drawer. I'm about to get into bed when I remember Wendaline and Imogen. They probably zapped themselves home by now. They can't still be in our closet.

"Wendaline?" I whisper. "Imogen? You're not here, are you?"

No answer.

Miri slides open the closet door and gasps.

Our closet is now huge. They've turned it into a den. They're lounging on a long L-shaped couch.

"What did you do?" I squeal, leaping off my bed.

"It was a bit cramped in here," Imogen says.

"We'll change it back," Wendaline says.

I step inside. They zapped up a flat screen! Excellent.

"It's not Narnia," I say, spreading out beside them. "But it's not bad."

On Sunday night, I stay up way too late talking to Tammy.

She tells me that things were even weirder with her and Bosh. They were quickly running out of things to talk about.

I tell her that no matter what happens, she'll be okay. "And who knows?" I say. "Even if you guys break up now, you could still get back together one day. Maybe when you're in college."

"Maybe. I don't know. If you want to know the truth, I think we're going to break up for good."

"That's so sad."

"I know, huh?" She sighs. "Let's talk about something else. Tell me about your weekend."

I wish I could tell her about the Eiffel Tower, or about class in Arizona, or about my fake den, or about becoming multilingual. I wish I could tell her about everything. My heart skips a beat. Could I? She loves magic stuff! She wouldn't think I was a freak. She plays with sharks! She won't be afriad of me!

Maybe I *could* tell her. Maybe I should. She's my BFF. Isn't that what a BFF is for? To be your friend no matter what?

Although . . . well, Jewel was my BFF too, wasn't she? And look how well that turned out.

What if Tammy went the way of Jewel? What if she too is more of a BFFN—Best Friend For Now?

I could always tell her and then give her a forgetting spell if we stopped being friends. No, that won't work. Spells on people only last a few months. If I gave her something to forget the truth, it would rub off. I would have to keep giving it to her again and again and again. . . .

"Rachel? You still there?"

"Yeah! Sorry! What was I saying? I forget."

I ace my French test on Monday morning. *Quelle surprise*. I checked the spell book, and apparently I can speak every language in the world for the next few months! I'm for sure going to get an A in French this semester. Wahoo! I wonder if I can speak computer languages too. I bet if I took C++, I could get an A++.

At lunch, Raf and I sit together eating burnt mac and cheese.

"How's your mouth feeling?" he asks.

"You mean because of the mac and cheese?"

"No." He laughs. "Because of your trip to the dentist. You were there on Saturday?"

Riiiiight. The dentist really wasn't my best lie. Do I want him thinking about my bacteria-riddled mouth when he's kissing me? No, I do not. But what else am I supposed to tell him?

The truth?

Right.

He'd either think I was crazy, or he would run screaming. Most people would. Look at how everyone reacted to Wendaline—and they all thought she was kidding!

No one wants to date a freak.

"So, are we hanging out after school?" I ask.

He looks at me strangely. "You just totally zoned out and didn't answer my question. The dentist?"

"Oh! All good." I wave my hand to change the subject. "Back to plans. What do you wanna do?"

He rips open a packet of mustard and squeezes it onto his food. "A bunch of people are heading to Washington Square Park. We could go."

"What are you doing?" I ask, gesturing to his food.

"Adding mustard."

"To mac and cheese?"

He grins.

"That is so disgusting! Condiments do not go on mac and cheese. Ketchup, maybe, but even that is kind of gross."

I'm teasing him, but for some reason, seeing him eat this, this weird mustard and mac and cheese concoction fills me with hope. Why? Because it's weird. Raf does weird things too! Just like me! He talks to the TV, doesn't he? I don't like him any less because he has quirks, do I? Definitely not! I like him even more!

Maybe he would like me more if he found out my one little quirk?

"Wanna try?" he asks. "You know you want a taste." He spears a noodle with his fork and waves it at me. "Pretend it's an airplane."

I open up and he scoops it inside. See, Raf? I am open to new things. The "new thing" almost makes me gag.

"Not bad," I lie, washing it down with a gulp of juice.

"I'm happy to share the rest of my mustard," he says, waving his leftover packet.

"Give it to me, baby," I say with a wink.

Wendaline approaches our table. "Hi, Rachel. Hi, Raf."

"Hi," I say. Didn't I rule against her sitting with me? At least she looks almost normal now in her new jeans.

I too am sporting a new outfit today—my new black jeans and sweater. Yeah, I know I was supposed to leave them at my dad's, but come on! That would have been a huge fashion waste.

"I have a question," she says, sitting down.

"Shoot," Raf says.

"Why is Cassandra popular if no one likes her?"

Raf laughs.

"No, I'm serious," she says. "Doesn't *popular* mean *well-liked?*"

"No," I say. "It means people want to hang out with you. It means you get invited to lots of parties."

"But why would anyone want her at a party if she's mean?"

She's got me. I look at Raf and shrug. "I don't know. But they do."

"She's popular right now because she has power," Raf says. "Fashion show tryouts are after school on Thursday, and she decides who makes it."

My heart sinks at the mention of the fashion show. I've seen the posters around school, but I've been pretending I haven't. Because if Raf tries out for the show, he's going to make it. Not only was he in it last year, he was amazing. He is a great dancer, he's super-cute, and everyone loves being around him. He's definitely getting in. Of course, I'd rather he not get in, since fashion show rehearsals take up a ton of time—time he'll be spending with Melissa, who I'm sure will also make the show.

Perhaps I should give him an antidancing spell? Maybe I could make him hear one song when another is playing so his rhythm is off?

No! What a terrible thing to think! I love him and want him to be happy! Of course, I could always test it out on Melissa. . . .

"So once that's over, she'll stop being popular?" Wendaline asks.

"Probably not," he admits.

"But she's such a bully!" Wendaline says.

I tense. "What did she do to you today?"

She crosses her arms. "It's the way she says my name. It drives me nuts. She draws it out like it's an insult."

"Tell her to back off," Raf says.

"No!" I say, giving Raf a warning look. "Just ignore her."

"I don't get these people," she mutters. "I'll see you later." She wanders off.

"So," I say to Raf, playing with my food. "Are you going to try out for the fashion show this year?"

"Not exactly," he says.

"Oh, good," I say, relieved.

"No, I'm not trying out because I don't have to. Cassandra said I don't need to try out. I'm automatically in."

"Oh. So you *want* to be in the show."

"Well . . . I'm not sure. I'm not dying to do it again, especially if you won't be in it. But see, here's where it gets complicated. For some reason she really wants me to be in it—"

"Because you're an amazing dancer," I say.

He blushes. "I don't know about that. But she said that I was good last year and that she wants experienced sophomores in the show. And she said that if I did it, Kosa Coats could outfit the all-guys number."

Last year, half the guys in school showed up in the Hugo Boss bomber jacket one of the A-list guys had worn in the show. "Great way to get your stuff noticed. Could you use one of your own designs?"

"If I wanted to, I guess. If they were good enough. What do you think? Should I do it?"

No! "Yes."

He nods. "You could do it too."

"No way," I say quickly.

He takes another bite of his concoction. "Why not? We had fun last year."

"We had a great time practicing. The show was a disaster."

"So this time the show will be great."

"No thanks," I say. "I'm over it." Even if I wanted to be in the show, it's not like I have the time. I mash up my mustard mac and cheese.

I have too much on my plate.

That afternoon, on the way from English class, Tammy is talking about *The Crucible*, our next reading assignment, and I'm trying to change the subject. I haven't read it yet, but Mr. Johnson said it was about the Salem witch trials.

I can't think of anything I want to do less than discuss the Salem witch trials in English class. Seriously. I'd rather have my eye poked out with a broomstick bristle. So I try to bring the conversation back to *Animal Farm*. Good old *Animal Farm*.

"I forgot *Animal Farm* at my mom's," I tell Tammy. "*Ib dul brink io mysine!*"

She looks at me strangely. "What did you just say?"

"*Ib dul brink io mysine*." Wait. That didn't sound right. I was trying to say "I had to stay up all night finishing it."

"What is *ib dul brink io mysine*?" she asks.

"*Intis ghero tu jiggernaur?*" That was supposed to be "Why can't you understand me?"

"Rachel, are you speaking pig Latin or something?"

"*Dortyu!*" Ah! That was supposed to be "Sorry." I can't speak English! What just happened? I think I'm speaking . . . Brixta? How did that happen? What do I do now?

She peers into my face. "You're not choking on something, are you?"

I shake my head.

"Are you sure? Say something."

"*Guity oj.*" I'm fine. This is not good. I point to my throat and lift a finger, trying to motion that I'll be right back, and then I hurry to the bathroom. Inside, I thump my chest and try to cough up the Brixta.

I turn to a random girl washing her hands beside me.

Maybe I should see if it worked, and try to say hello. I take a deep breath and then say, "*Ho!*"

Her eyes slit, and she mutters a not-so-nice word under her breath. (Clue: it rhymes with witch.)

Ho? Ho is how you say *hi* in Brixta? I can't go around school telling random people *ho*! Argh! What is wrong with me? I need Wendaline. I hurry through the hall, near the freshman row of lockers, hoping to spot her. Why is it that the one time I'm looking for her is the one time I can't find her? I try her cell, but no answer. Last time she Appeared when I called her. Appear, Wendaline. Appear!

I see Tammy across the hall, her forehead creased with worry. I wave. What do I do? I can't go to class like this, can I?

I turn to escape down the stairs, but I spot Raf on his way up. I definitely can't talk to him like this!

Hi ho, hi ho, it's off to math I go.

I avoid speaking for the rest of the afternoon by claiming laryngitis. Not claiming, exactly, since I can't speak, but by pointing to my throat and nodding emphatically when Tammy asks, "Is it laryngitis?"

Unfortunately, my writing skills have also been compromised, so every time Tammy passes me a note, I have to respond with a doodle.

I zap myself home between classes to look at A^2 but I can't figure it out. I need help! I finally find Wendaline by stalking her locker after the final bell. She shows up with her two new friends. I look up at her sheepishly. "*Jeffle.*"

"What's wrong?"

"*To froma,*" I say, taking her arm and leading her back to the bathroom. In private.

I spend way too much time in bathrooms. Perhaps Wendaline can whip up a Narnia for us at school so we can have a more comfortable place to chat?

The stalls look empty, so I say, "*Hot jeou sofy, ki frot kirt doozy,*" which means "For some reason, I can't speak English."

She looks into my eyes. "Since when?"

"*Umpa ooble.*" After lunch.

"Did you eat anything funky? Besides the mac and

cheese, I mean. That stuff is gross. This is why it's better to learn languages the old-fashioned way. Fewer complications."

"Ki biz com hindo ut ficci. Diut! Raf fir bitard bi ry. Dout sak vu tre ry?" The mustard! Raf's mustard!

"I don't see why any of those would affect the Babel potion." She plays with the tip of her short hair. "I'm wondering if it's something else. A witch is supposed to speak from the heart, you know? And language is a tool to speak from the heart, to communicate what's inside. If you hide what's inside, the language gets tangled up, and if you're tangled, your words are tangled, especially if it has something to do with your magic. Following?"

I shake my head.

"You need to be honest and true!"

I slap my palm against my forehead. *"Ahhh!"* Apparently, *"ahhh"* is the same in Brixta as in English. *"Ig bin Ig dkhy nor!"* I'm as honest as I can be!

She looks at me dubiously. "Are you?"

"Yes! I'm not telling anyone anything," I huff in Brixta. "Do you know how to fix me?"

"I may be able to whip something up if you come by after school. I'm hoping to be a potionist one day, you know."

Why am I not surprised? *"Bur that yitten Raf."* But I have plans with Raf. *"Isht ik faten igo?"* What am I supposed to tell him?

"The truth?"

Not! I'll take the non-potentially-life-altering fix, thanks. *"Kip kifel, fo tribe,"* I tell her, miming the act of writing for her. I'll speak, you write.

She zaps up a pen and paper. Normally, I would chastise her for using magic in school, but I think we're beyond that at this point. She translates my Brixta as follows:

> *Dear Raf, Emergency tooth issue! Have to go back to the dentist. So sorry! I'll call you later! Let's hang out tomorrow after school instead!!!*

I instruct her to use lots of exclamation points.

"How should I sign it?" she asks.

Argh! There is no time to make such a potentially relationship-altering decision right now. XO? Hugs & wishes? Not. Love? He wrote *love;* I can write *love*, right?

But that was on a birthday card and this is at school! A school note should not show as much affection as a birthday card. A school note gets tossed; a birthday card gets saved. Luv, maybe?

Yes. Luv.

I somehow manage to find the Brixta words to explain to Wendaline the difference between *love* and *luv*.

"Are you going to give it to him?" she asks.

"*Ooga!*" I say, which means *no*. Which makes me laugh. Ooga? That's supposed to be musical? Maybe for a band of gorillas.

I tell Wendaline—in Brixta—to slip it into Raf's locker, and off we go.

17 Rocks Ahead

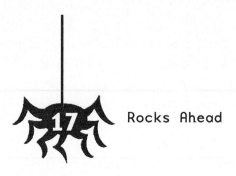

"Oh, good, Rachel, you're finally home," Mom says later that afternoon. She and Miri are sitting at the kitchen table, a stack of papers in front of them. "Where were you?"

"Communication difficulties," I say.

Miri raises an eyebrow. "You okay?"

"Nothing that olive oil and a chopped onion couldn't cure," I say with a sigh. Wendaline reversed the effect, and now I'm back to being multilingual. "But I wouldn't get too close to me if I were you. I'm kind of smelly. What are you doing?"

"Our Samsorta invitation list!" Miri squeals.

Huh? "But we have no one to invite!"

Miri points to a list of about thirty names. "Not true! Mom has a ton of family who would all be insulted if they didn't get invitations."

I glance at the names. Regina and Stephen Kelp. Moira

Dalven. Jan and Josh Morgenstein. Who are these people?

"Mom, this is crazy. You excommunicated yourself from the witchcraft community. You haven't spoken to any of these people in at least twenty years. I've never even heard of them."

Mom shrugs. "They're extended family. If we're going to do this, we have to do this properly."

"Why? I thought you didn't even want to do this!"

"Rachel," Miri says, "it's a great opportunity for us to be more in touch with our roots."

"I guess." I spot Liana and Sasha Graff on the list and my fists clench. "Why are you inviting them?"

"I have to. Sasha's my sister," Mom says.

"Your *evil* sister! And anyway, Liana didn't invite us to hers."

"Maybe, but two wrongs don't make a right. Besides, we weren't speaking then."

"But you're barely speaking now!"

"Rachel, please don't be difficult."

"Why not? My life is difficult! I have to go to school for six days a week instead of five and I smell like onion!"

She looks me in the eye. "Don't act like I didn't warn you that having a Samsorta was a major undertaking."

Humph. I hate I-told-you-so's. I mean, if she had something important to say, then she should have told me how important it was before! Er. Anyway. "I'm going to do my homework."

"Okay, but sit here for a second," Mom says. "Miri was right: the Samsorta is a great opportunity for the three of us to spend some quality family time together."

I knew that this Samsorta was going to be trouble. I begrudgingly pull up a chair.

"Oh, and don't make any plans for tomorrow after school," Mom adds.

"Too late," I say. "I have plans with Raf." Kind of. Proposed plans, at least.

"Cancel them!" Miri exclaims. "We're going to Georgina's Paperie!"

"What's that?"

"You mean 'who,' " Mom says. "She's the stationer. I've heard she's all the rage. And the best part is that she's here in New York. We were lucky to get an appointment. This is her busiest time, you know."

"You heard? Who did you *hear* from?" The only person she talks to is Lex. "You didn't join Mywitchbook too, did you?" She has a profile before I do? Hello, that's so embarrassing.

"No, dear, I finally started reading the newsletter." She shuffles the papers in front of her. "We need you, Rachel. You have a good eye."

Flattery will get you everywhere. "Fine, I'll be there." Not sure why we can't just zap up invites, but maybe it's like a haircut. Sometimes you gotta trust a professional.

"Also, don't make plans for Sunday morning," she says. "I have a special surprise for you two."

I perk up. "What is it?"

"If I told you, it wouldn't be a surprise."

After fifteen minutes of bonding time, I'm allowed to go to my room to start my homework and call Raf. Big surprise—I decide to call Raf first.

"How's your tooth?" he asks. "Is your mouth still frozen?"

"Yes," I say, then realize I should make my mouth sound frozen. "Ya." How do I make it sound frozen? I stick my finger between my lips so it doesn't close all the way.

"So, are we on for tomorrow?"

"Oh, uh . . . umorrow's no 'ood—" Ouch! I just bit my finger. Forget it. I am not going to make it through this whole conversation with a fake speech impediment. I'm just going to speak normally and hope he doesn't notice. It's not like he'd think I'd *make up* a cavity. Who does that? "I forgot I promised Miri I'd help her with something." Not a terrible excuse. Vague and less gross than getting cavities filled. No frozen mouth necessary. I jiggle my bitten finger till it stops stinging.

"I can help too, if you want," he says. "I don't mind."

"Oh! Thanks! That's so sweet of you . . . but it's a girl thing."

"Oh, okay." Pause.

"So what else is up?" I ask.

"Um, on Saturday, my parents wanted to invite you for dinner. It's my dad's birthday, and he wants to take all of us out."

Awkward. The last time I had dinner with the Kosravis, I went as Will's date. And Raf brought Melissa.

It was pretty miserable.

"Great," I say. It has to be better this time if I'm going as Raf's date. And I really like Will's girlfriend, Kat. I've barely seen her since school started. She must be super-busy with student council. She is the president, after all. Maybe I should run for student council president when I'm a senior.

Or maybe I should run for president of the United States! The first witch president!

Unless there already have been magical presidents.

"What time is dinner?" I ask.

"Seven-thirty at Kim Shing in Midtown. I'll come get you and we can go together."

"I have a busy weekend," I say, taking a deep breath. "I better just meet you there."

The next day, after school, we're in Georgina's Upper East Side apartment, looking at sample invitations.

Georgina is stunning. She has long glossy black hair and could easily be a model if she ever wanted to give up stationery. She does more than just Samsortas, too. She has Simsorta invites, wedding invites, and Wishing invites.

"What's a Wishing?" Miri asks.

"Oh, you know," Georgina says with a wave of her hand. "When you have a baby, you invite all the witches in your family over so they can bestow her with a wish. Brains, beauty, compassion, a beautiful singing voice, painting skills, dancing skills . . . I'm sure you girls had one." She smiles knowingly.

Wow. Just like *Sleeping Beauty*. I wonder what I got. Um . . . not dancing skills . . . not beauty . . .

My mother giggles nervously. "That was so long ago, who remembers?"

"I think that means we didn't have one," Miri says.

"Thanks, Mom. It's not like brains and beauty are things we could use."

"You guys are perfect just the way you are," Mom says. "And you both have fantastic skills all on your own! Like your math skills, and your Tae Kwon Do skills . . . Let's try to focus on the present."

Grumble.

Georgina's invitations are not in sample books. They wouldn't fit, because Georgina's invites are not your typical invitations. Some examples:

A sunflower, with the date, time, and place inscribed on the petals.

Candles that, when lit, write the information in smoke.

Fridge magnets that magically spell out the info.

"Anything you like?" she asks us.

"I like all of them!" Who needs boring paper invites? These are in 3-D.

"Do you have a theme in mind?" she asks.

A witch ball isn't enough of a theme?

"Since we're doing it together," Miri says, "maybe it can have a sisters theme?"

"Sisters. I like it. Let me think." Georgina rubs her fingers against her temples. "I'm seeing paper dolls. Two of them!"

I love paper dolls! "The linked kind?"

"Yes! Fabulous!" says Georgina, hands flailing. "When you open the envelope, they'll burst into song with the pertinent information! I'll make the girls look just like the two of you! They'll even sing like you! And dance like you!"

My mom picks at her thumbnail. "Hmm, maybe not. They're not exactly the best dancers. Or singers."

"Whose fault is that?" I snap. "You deprived of us of our Wishing!"

"I thought we were perfect just the way we are," Miri says.

She ignores us both. "Georgina, can we see the sunflower invitations again?"

An hour later, we've settled on a New York theme—a snow-globe-sized Times Square replica. The news ticker will list all the party info. Very cool, no?

When I get home, I head to my room to do some homework, and Miri heads to the computer to check—wait for it—Mywitchbook. I think she might be addicted.

A few minutes later she stomps through the apartment. "Mom?" I hear her yell through the walls. "Corey and his friends all went skiing! Can I meet them?"

"It's already seven o'clock! It's getting dark!"

"Not here. In the Canadian Rockies! In Whistler! It's only four there. Can I go? Please? Only for a bit!"

"It's still September in Vancouver! There can't be snow!"

"They make snow!" Miri says. "And it's really high up. Please?"

"Is Rachel going?" Mom asks.

"No!" I scream back through the wall.

"Yes," Miri says.

Mom laughs. "You're too young to go out with boys on your own. You can only go if Rachel goes."

Gee, thanks, Mom. No pressure.

"And since it's a school night, you have to be back by

nine—New York time. And you both have to wear your helmets. And one of you has to call me as soon as you get there."

Miri bursts into my room. "Get dressed!"

I look down at my jeans and T-shirt. "Am I naked?"

"For skiing."

"Miri, I don't want to go skiing. I need to do my homework."

"But everyone is skiing! It's not just Corey! It's everyone! Adam's there." She gives me a mischievous grin.

My heart skips a beat. I have no time for Raf, but I have time for Adam? "I don't know, Mir—"

"Mom won't let me go without you. Please? How perfect would it be if my first kiss was on a chairlift? That is so romantic! Please!"

I do like to ski . . . and I haven't been since the trips to Stowe. . . .

The view from the mountain is like a postcard. Blues, greens, and whites swirl around me like I'm doing some sort of motion spell. I take a deep breath. Ah. As soon as we zapped ourselves over to the ski hill (we Appeared in a bathroom in the chalet at the very top), I transformed my regular shoes into ski boots, a lip gloss into poles, and pieces of spearmint Trident gum into skis. My poles are pink and my skis are mint green. They definitely clash, but I had to work with what was in my purse.

Miri and Corey are snowboarding, but I prefer old-school skis. I call my mom to tell her we made it in one piece.

"Be careful," she warns. "Stay on the bunny hills. You haven't skied in a while."

"Yes, Mom."

"Where's Miri?"

"Talking to Corey." I wave to my sister, and she waves back. I make a kissy face. She turns beet red. Tee hee.

"I can't wait to meet the infamous Corey," Mom says. "Have fun. Don't be home too late. No night skiing."

"Yes, Mom."

"Love you," she says.

"Love you too."

I'm about to stuff the phone into my jacket pocket when it rings again. It's Raf.

"Hi!" I say.

"What's up?"

I glance around at the mountainous view. If only I could tell him! "Not much. You?"

"Finishing homework. Are you almost done with your sister? Want me to come over for an hour?"

"Oh! I can't. We're not done yet."

"What? Sorry, I can't hear you. There's lots of static."

Ya think? It's not like I'm in another country and on top of a mountain or anything. I lurch to the right, in case it helps, and then yell, "I said, we're not done yet!"

"With math?"

Sure, why not? "Yes, with math."

"It's still . . . 'aticky. Let me call you . . . on your landline?"

No! "I can't talk now! I'll call you later!"

"What?"

"I'll call you back when I'm home! I mean, when I'm done. Yeah, done."

"Okay. Have fun."

"You too! Love you!" I say.

And then I realize.

Did I just say that? I did not just say that. I did not just tell Raf Kosravi that I love him. I didn't mean to say that. Now what?

I press the End button.

Omigod. I just hung up on my boyfriend. Right after I accidentally told him I loved him.

Crapola.

Aaaah!

What do I do now?

Maybe he didn't hear. Reception is terrible; he said so himself. But what if he did hear? Did I mean it? Do I *love* him? I know I always joke that I *love* him, but do I really?

Sure, he's sweet and funny and adorable. And he makes my heart go all fluttery.

Why did my mom have to tell me she loved me on the phone? I had love on the brain.

Maybe I should call him back. And do what? Tell him that it was a mistake? Is it a mistake? It's all his fault, anyway. He started it with the whole love-in-the-card thing.

Aaaah!

"Rachel!"

I stumble at the sound of my name and drop my phone in the snow. Great.

I look up to see Adam approaching me. "Ready to hit the slopes?"

I pick up my phone and jam it into my pocket. I'll have to deal with this later. "Hi! Ready!" I pull down my goggles (aka transformed sunglasses).

"Then let's go!" He pushes off toward the top of the mountain. "I'll race you."

I turn back to see Miri deep in conversation with Corey. I guess she can take care of herself. I spot the triplets and the others already flying down the hill. Not flying, obviously. Skiing really fast. Okay, fine, Glamour Triplet might be flying.

I hang back on top of the run.

"What's wrong?" he asks.

It looks kind of steep. "I haven't been skiing in a long time."

He laughs. "It'll all come back to you. It's just like riding a broomstick."

"Ha-ha. All right. I'm ready." I push off, and while I'm a bit shaky, I'm actually quite good. I can slalom! I can turn! I can—

Smack!

—fall on my butt.

I push myself back up. Ouch. That is gonna sting in the morning.

"You okay?" Adam asks, swishing up beside me.

"Just rusty. Ready to race? On your mark, get set, go!" I take off. I'm a bird! I'm a plane! I'm Rachel the skiing witch! He's right behind me, and then he's next to me, and then I pull ahead again. We pull up together at the bottom.

"What a rush," I say. "Again! Should we use the go spell to get back on top?"

"Nah, I'm tired of Appearing in bathrooms," he says.

I giggle. "You've noticed that too?"

"Yeah. Let's take the chairlift like normal people. It'll be fun."

We hold our poles in our hands and look behind us to catch the incoming chair. "I haven't done this in a while," I say.

"You'll be fine. Here it comes," he says, and then, swoop, we're sitting!

As we rise up the hill, I spot the triplets skiing down below. I wave but they don't see us. Beyond the run, our chair glides over a patch of forest that separates two trails.

I soak up the view. The sky is blue, the air is crisp . . . it's all so pretty.

Creak. The chairlift grinds to a stop.

We sway back and forth, back and forth. "I hope this thing is sturdy!"

"I'll protect you," he says, casually putting his arm around my shoulder.

Uh-oh.

He leans in to kiss me.

18 It's a Small World

Should I? Do I? No!

I pull away about a half second before his lips touch mine.

"Adam," I say. "I have a boyfriend."

Did I just almost kiss one boy less than ten minutes after telling another boy I loved him? What is wrong with me?

"I'm sorry," Adam says. "I thought . . . I thought you felt the same way. I didn't know you had a boyfriend. I—I think you're really cool, Rachel." He covers his face with his gloves. "I'm sorry."

"I . . ." I'm not sure what to say. "It's my fault. I should have told you." I don't know why I didn't. Okay, I do. 'Cause I didn't want him to know. 'Cause I might like him.

"Who's your boyfriend?" he asks. "Do I know him?"

"No. He's not a warlock. He doesn't even know about"—I motion around me—"any of this."

"So it isn't serious?"

"No—it is."

"Doesn't sound serious," he mutters.

Hey! "I heard that."

"Well, he doesn't know anything about you!"

"Yes, he does."

"Not the most important part. Don't you want to date someone you have more in common with? Someone who gets what you're going through?"

"I . . ." My voice trails off.

As if this moment can't get any more awkward, my cell phone starts to ring.

I know it's Raf without even having to look. Stupid intuition. I let it ring. And ring.

Adam doesn't comment. And neither do I.

I have got to get out of here. Why won't this stupid chairlift start working?

"Chairlift, start to run,
'Cause this awkwardness is no fun!"

The chairlift jerks to a start.

I arrive home feeling lousy. Partly because of the Adam incident, partly because Raf has called three times and I haven't picked up, and partly because my butt hurts from my tumble down the mountain. Also, I'm almost out of go spell. I need to make more of that stuff pronto.

Miri, on the other hand, is on cloud eleven.

"We took the chairlift up together!" she tells me while we get ready for bed. "He put his arm around me! Did you see him board? He was even worse than I was! Tee hee! I had to show him how to turn. It was so cute! He's so cute! And then he—"

I zone her out, a pit growing in my stomach. Adam didn't say one word to me after the chairlift debacle. We quickly joined up with the rest of the group and then froze each other out.

I wait until I'm in bed before calling Raf back. I hope he didn't hear what I said before. You know, the L word? I really, really hope he didn't hear. There was static! Lots of static. I'm sure he didn't hear.

"Hi," I say, my heart pounding.

"Hi," he says.

He did not hear. I'm sure he didn't. "Sorry it took so long to call you back."

Silence.

He heard and he doesn't feel the same and now he's going to break up with me. He heard and he somehow knows that I almost let another guy kiss me and now he hates me.

"About what you said before . . . ," he begins.

I hold my breath.

"I love you, too," he says.

I drop the phone but then quickly pick it back up. "Really?"

"Yeah."

Another silence.

He said he loves me. The boy I've been crazy about since the first day of freshman year just told me he loves me.

Raf Kosravi loves me. Officially.

I should be thrilled. I should be dancing up and down. Fine, maybe not dancing. I don't want to scare the neighbors. But I should at least be shaking my arms with joy or cartwheeling.

But instead, my eyes prickle with tears.

"Cool" is all I can choke out.

"And I'm so happy you said it. You've been acting kind of weird lately and I was worried that . . . I don't know. That you didn't, you know, like me anymore."

"That's crazy!" I say. "How could you even think that?"

"Well, you didn't want to meet up with me when you were shopping and then you fell asleep when I was over and you kind of blew me off today. . . ."

My heart sinks. "I'm so sorry. Honestly. I've just had a lot going on. You know. With family and stuff. None of my weirdness had anything to do with you. At all. Really. Nothing makes me happier than having you as my boyfriend."

"Good," he says.

"Good."

We talk about classes and school and his jackets, and when we finally get off the phone, I hug my pillow to my chest, tears in my eyes.

'Cause I love Raf. I really do. And yeah, he said "I love you," and he might even believe it, but it doesn't mean much if he doesn't love the *real* me. It's no better, no more *real* than him being enchanted with me because of a love spell.

I sigh. And the next time he feels like I'm distracted . . . what happens then?

"So," I say when I sit down in homeroom, "how was your weekend?"

Tammy turns to me, her lips quivering.

And I know. "Omigod, you broke up!"

She nods.

I leap up and hug her.

"It was tough, but I think it's the right thing to do," she tells me.

"You broke up with him?"

"Kind of. I think it was mutual. I know people always say that, but this time it really was. We care about each other, but we're just in different places. We're still going to stay friends, though."

"When did it happen?" I ask.

"Last night."

"You should have called me!"

"I would have, but we got off the phone at like three in the morning and I figured it was too late."

"It's never too late when it's that important!"

"I was going to text you but I was too drained." Her eyes tear up. "But thanks, Rachel. I know you're here for me." Then Tammy says she's sick of talking about her and Bosh. "Your turn to tell me what's been bugging you lately."

"What? Me? Nothing's bugging me; why would you say that?"

She shrugs. "I can tell when something's bothering you."

I swallow. Now she's going to be mad at me too? "I just have a lot going on right now."

She studies me. "Anything bad?"

"No," I say quickly.

"If you need someone to talk to, you know I'm always here to listen."

"Thanks," I say, and my head pounds.

Why does everything have to be so complicated?

Reading *The Crucible* doesn't put me in a better mood.

Do you know what happens in *The Crucible*? Do you know what they do to alleged witches in that book—no, that horror novel? They take them to the gallows—i.e., they hang them.

I rub my neck as I read.

This is exactly why I can't tell anyone my secret. What if they tell someone who tells someone who tells someone and then people try to kill me?

Fine, they probably wouldn't send me to the gallows per se, since New York doesn't have the death penalty.

But they could still do bad stuff! I've seen high school mobs and they're usually evil.

Case in point:

The next day, Tammy and I are on our way to chemistry when we spot Wendaline.

"Hey, Wendaline," we both say.

Unfortunately, our greeting is followed by "Weeeeenda-liiiine. Weeeeeennnnndaliiiine. Weeeeeennnnndaliiiine."

It sounds like the wailing of a ghost, but as far as I know, JFK is not haunted. Instead, it's Cassandra and her posse chanting my friend's name.

Her cheeks bright red, Wendaline is staring at

Cassandra. She tugs a lock of her short hair behind her ear and then fidgets with the shirt I bought with her.

"Weeeeeennnnndaliiiine. . . . Weeeeeennnnndaliiiine. . . . Weeeeeennnnndaliiiine."

"Why are they doing this to her?" Tammy asks, fists clenched around her notebook. "I'm going to tell them to stop."

I grab hold of her arm. "Don't." I don't want Cassandra going after Tammy, too! I've been the target of the A-list, and it's no fun. "She can handle it."

"What kind of a name is Wendaline, anyway?" Cassandra says. "Sounds made up to me. Just like your story about being a witch, *Weeeendaliiiine*."

"This is ridiculous," Tammy mutters.

I keep shaking my head. I want to tell Cassandra off too, but I can't. I just can't. I can't be too obvious! I can't have everyone staring at me.

"Do you know what they used to do to witches?" Cassandra continues. "They used to throw them in the ocean to see if they would use magic to float. Maybe we should take you for a swim in the Hudson?"

I think I'm going to be sick. It's *The Crucible* come to life!

"That's it." Tammy slips out of my grasp and storms across the hall to Cassandra. "You better shut up," she orders.

Cassandra laughs. "Or what?"

"Or I'll report you to Mrs. Konch for threatening the life of a student."

"Oh, really?" Cassandra says, crossing her arms. Her

curls stick out at jagged angles like weapons. She's like Medusa.

Now Tammy crosses her arms. "Really. Then you'll get expelled."

What is Tammy doing? She's going to get *herself* thrown into the Hudson. And that's a polluted pool of water that even she wouldn't want to explore. I press my back against a locker and try to be invisible. Not really invisible, obviously, 'cause that would really be giving myself away. Or not. I'm confusing myself.

"And why would anyone believe you?" Cassandra snaps.

Tammy juts out her chin. "Who do you think they're going to believe? A sophomore with a 4.0 GPA or an obnoxious fashion show poseur?"

Ouch.

Cassandra narrows her eyes. "You better watch yourself."

"You don't scare me," Tammy says, grabbing Wendaline's arm and leading my flabbergasted friend into the bathroom.

The chant begins again immediately: "Weeeeeennnnndaliiiine. Weeeeeennnnndaliiiine. Weeeeeennnnndaliiiine."

I keep my head down and hurry into the bathroom behind them. I had no idea Tammy was so strong. Wow. I'm both incredibly impressed and incredibly terrified. Tammy and Wendaline are both holding on to the sinks.

"Are you crazy?" I ask Tammy. "Now you're on her hit list too!"

"I'm not afraid of her," Tammy says, but the trembling of her legs gives her away. She turns to Wendaline. "You okay?"

A wide-eyed Wendaline nods.

"I need to sit down," Tammy says breathlessly. "Coming, Rachel?"

"You go ahead," I say. "I'll be two secs."

Wendaline moves to follow her out the door but I hold her back.

"You have to stay out of Cassandra's way," I tell her. "Or we're all going to find frogs in our lockers. Is that what you want?"

"Of course not!" Wendaline cries. "I'm trying. What else can I do?"

"From now on, we stay away from her locker," I order. "Got it?"

Wendaline throws up her hands. "But how am I supposed to do that without Appearing—or disappearing—in school? You told me not to do that!"

"No magic! Just take the back stairs up to bio and away from her evil lair. Can you do that?"

She nods.

"And there's one more thing."

"What?"

"Your name is too witchy-sounding. Cassandra is right. From now on, tell everyone"—I take a deep breath—"to call you Wendy."

Her shoulders hunch, deflated. "Wendy," she echoes.

I nod. Maybe that will help. They can't make fun of a nice, normal name like Wendy, can they?

Adam was right. You have to keep your witch world and your school world separate. It's too dangerous otherwise.

Although he also said I should be dating a warlock. Was he right about that, too?

No. He can't be! How can I date a warlock when there's a norlock I'm crazy about?

I open the bathroom door and peer out to make sure the coast is clear.

Wendaline—I mean, *Wendy*—follows me down the hall. I swallow the lump in my throat and hope I'm leading her in the right direction. Symbolically, I mean. (I do know my way around school, you know. I've only gotten lost that one time.)

Receiving my first Sim invitation that night cheers me up.

The package arrives right before bed. It Appears smack in the center of our living room. It's a big red box wrapped in a black bow. In silver glitter it says *For Rachel and Miri Weinstein*.

"Mom, is that from you?" I yell.

"Is what from me?" she calls out from her bedroom.

Guess not. I tap it twice to see if it explodes. Nope. Probably not a bomb, then. "Miri, come look. We got something."

Inside the box stands a shining two-foot-tall gold Oscar statue.

"Um . . . did you secretly try out for the school play or something?" I ask.

Zap! Suddenly, the box disappears and out rolls a red carpet. Except instead of rolling straight, it spells out cursive letters on our living room floor.

Please join me
When I become Simsorta
Friday, the thirteenth of October
At seven-thirty in the evening
In the Kodak Theatre
6801 Hollywood Boulevard
Los Angeles, California

Michael Davis

"That's where they hold the Academy Awards!" I say.

"Cool," Miri says. "I can't wait. Who are we with that weekend?"

"Dad," I say.

She plays with her fingers. "Maybe it's a good opportunity to tell him."

"*No*," I say forcefully. "Why are you so obsessed with telling Dad? Mom never told him."

"But she told Lex," Miri says. "And anyway, not telling Dad was different. She didn't want to be a witch then. We're making witchcraft part of our lives. Why should we hide who we are?"

"We can't go around telling everyone what we are! Not everyone is going to think it's hunky-dory that we're witches, okay? Some people are going to find it weird. Some people are going to find it scary. Some people might even try to send us to the gallows!"

Miri rolls her eyes. "You're being insanely paranoid."

I jab my finger into her chest. "You read *The Crucible*, then talk to me about being paranoid."

"We don't live in 1692," she says, waving her hand in the air. "It's the twenty-first century! Anyway, our father is not going to send us off to be hanged."

"Obviously not, but I still don't think it's a good idea. He'll have to tell Jennifer and they could get freaked out, or be afraid of us."

"Well, we have to tell him *something*," she insists.

"No, we don't," I say. "It's called for seven-thirty, which is ten-thirty our time. We'll just tell him we're going to bed early and sneak out."

She sighs. "I would rather just tell him the truth."

"Well, I wouldn't," I snap. I have enough on my mind without having to worry about telling Dad—Adam and Raf and almost being exposed at school. I shake my head and then try to change the subject. "So, where are all your witch friends tonight?"

She frowns. "Everyone was invited to some guy's Simsorta at the Bellagio in Vegas."

"Someone from Lozacea?"

"Yeah. But no one we're friends with. I mean, I'm Mywitchbook friends with him, but that's it."

"Wanna crash it?" I ask.

"No, I want to be invited." She sighs and sits down in the middle of the red writing. "Do you think we'll still be invited to Adam's, or are we both on the outs?"

"You noticed that, huh?" I sit down beside her and rest my head on her stomach. "He tried to kiss me on the chairlift."

She groans. "How come your non-boyfriend knows to try to kiss you on the chairlift, and my maybe-boyfriend doesn't?"

"Because Adam is sixteen, and Corey is only fourteen. Guys get more suave with age."

She giggles. "So what did you do?"

"I pulled away! What else could I do?" I pause. "I told him I have a boyfriend."

"Do you like him, though? Adam, I mean."

I try to unravel the way I feel before answering. "I do. He *gets* me. But Raf makes my heart beat a little faster. You know?"

"Oh, I know," she says. "Corey does both of those."

Show-off.

19 Dateless in Lozacea

The next morning in Samsorta class, safely in the back row and away from Fizguin's spraying-and-saying, the girls are all buzzing about Samsorta dates.

"Are you bringing Praw?" Karin whispers to my sister.

Miri turns bright red but continues taking notes. "Maybe. I haven't asked him yet. Who are you going with?"

"My boyfriend, Harvey. He already had his Sim last year."

Great. Everyone has a date but me.

"Are you going with someone too?" I ask Viv.

She nods. "Zach. My boyfriend."

"Has he already had his Sim?" I ask.

"No. He's a norlock."

My jaw just about hits the desk. "He is? Seriously?"

She stares me down. "Yo, you have a problem with that?"

"What? No! I just didn't know you could bring a norlock to the Sam!" My heart races.

"Of course. You can bring whoever you want."

I poke Miri. "Did you hear that? Viv is taking her boyfriend! Her norlock boyfriend!"

"Yeah, I heard."

"Do you think I could take Raf?"

"You could. But you'd probably have to brief him on the whole witch thing first. Otherwise a couple hundred people in cloaks casting spells in a Romanian cemetery might confuse him."

I turn back to Viv. "Does Zach know that you're a witch?" I whisper.

"Obviously," she says, combing her fingers through her bangs.

"Do a lot of people know? I mean, the people at your school?"

"*Yes*. I'm not ashamed of who I am."

"I'm not either! I thought . . . well, I thought people kept their worlds separate, you know?"

She adjusts her glasses. "I don't. I'm me. Take me or leave me."

"And no one thinks you're weird?"

She shrugs. "I don't really care what other people think."

Right. There's the problem.

I do.

"Through space I flow.
To Kim Shing in New York
I shall go!"

Zap!

Class is done, and it's time for me to join Raf and his family for his father's birthday dinner.

I appear in the bathroom.

I try to pick the go spell from my hair to save it. I wonder if I can reuse the spell. Probably not. I am really low on it. I probably have enough for only one more trip.

Miri was not happy when I told her I would not be accompanying her and the gang to Epcot to watch the fireworks. "You know I can't," I said. "I have that dinner with Raf's family." It wasn't like I wanted to go, although I am excited about the Chinese food. Yum. My favorite is General Tso. Since it's family style, can I suggest what I want, or should I just be polite and eat whatever they order? Please, please, please let them order General Tso.

At least Miri convinced Mom to let her go to Epcot without me. She used the "it's not a date, it's just a bunch of friends hanging out" line.

Adam didn't seem to care that I wasn't going. In fact, he didn't even say hello. He's obviously avoiding me.

I push open the door.

The scents of friend onion and spices waft through the main dining room. I peer at various tables but don't see the Kosravi crew anywhere. Maybe I'm early?

I approach the maître d'. "I'm here with the Kosravi party," I say in my most grown-up voice. "Am I the first to arrive?"

He peers into his book. "I'm sorry, but we don't have a Kosravi reservation. Might it be listed under another name?"

"Um . . ." Maybe Raf's dad's first name? It's . . . I know his name! I do! When you're crazy about a boy, you remember every minute detail about him, including the color of his favorite pair of socks: soft brown. To match his gorgeous eyes. Now, why can't I remember his dad's name? I'm just nervous. It's something with a *D*. Doug . . . David . . . Dorian . . . "It's a party of eight. At seven-thirty?"

"No, we don't have a party of that size at this time," he says. "Are you sure you're at the right location?"

Oh, no! "Is there more than one?" Raf didn't tell me there was more than one. He said it was in Midtown!

"Yes, there are a few. There's one on South Beverly, and

one on Ventura Boulevard."

I've never heard of those streets. "Where are we now?"

"On Sunset Boulevard."

I've heard of Sunset Boulevard. In *California*. "Uh, isn't that street, um, in L.A.?"

He turns up his nose. "West Hollywood, actually."

I swallow. Hard. That doesn't sound good. "I'm in Hollywood?"

"*West* Hollywood. West."

Did I not specify the city I wanted to go to? I must not have! And the spell took me from Arizona to the nearest Kim Shing restaurant . . . which is in California. Ah! "I have to go!"

I hurry back to the bathroom and slam myself in a stall.

I reach into my Ziploc and sprinkle the last few bits of go spell crumbs into my palm. This better work, 'cause after this I'm out of go spell.

"Through space I flow.
To Kim Shing in New York City
I shall go!"

Zap!

I definitely said "New York City." One hundred percent. When I open my eyes, I'm in another bathroom stall. A single stall. At least, I think it's a bathroom stall. There's a sink, but instead of a toilet, there's a small porcelain hole in the ground. Maybe the toilet broke and they took it to be fixed? Or . . . I think I'm in the men's room!

Yes, that must be it.

I open the stall door and peer outside. Maybe I'm in the right place? Please, please, please? The overhead lights are off. The only light in the room is faintly shining through the two windows. But yes, I'm in a restaurant. Except I'm the only person in the restaurant. No staff, no cooks, no anyone. The writing on the wall is in Chinese, which makes sense. It's supposed to be a Chinese restaurant. But where is everyone?

Maybe it had to close down for some reason? Mouse problem?

The clock overhead says eight-twenty-five. Hmm. Either I lost an hour, or I'm really not in the right place. Where could I be that's an hour ahead?

Bermuda? Canada? Maybe I'm in a Chinese restaurant there? But how did that happen? I definitely said New York this time. What could have gone wrong? Something obviously did, 'cause this is not the right time.

I pull open the blinds. The early-morning sun spears my eyes. I watch people pass by the window. Chinese people.

The signs are all in Chinese.

The flag of China is flapping in the wind.

Am I in a Chinatown? Or . . .

Maybe it's eight a.m., not eight p.m. Maybe that missing toilet was a Chinese squat toilet.

I reach for my now empty Ziploc. I'm stuck. And not stuck in Chinatown—I'm stuck in China.

Great. Just great. I drop the blinds and pace the length of the restaurant.

Think, Rachel, think. Yes, you're stuck in a Chinese restaurant without go powder, batteries, or your copy of A^2.

And yes, you're going to be late for dinner with Raf and his family, which will send a terrific impression.

But don't panic. You're a witch! You can find a way out of this mess!

Maybe I should make up a go home spell. Yes! People are always needing a go home spell. Even Dorothy needed one. Hey, maybe *The Wizard of Oz* chant would work.

I close my eyes and click my heels together three times, repeating, "There's no place like home, there's no place like home, there's no place like home. . . ."

I open my eyes. I'm still in the Chinese restaurant. The *Chinese* Chinese restaurant.

Maybe now's not the time for new spells.

I should just make another batch of the go spell. Yes! There's a full kitchen here at my disposal. All I have to do is remember the ingredients. Now, what were they? There was brown sugar. There was . . . What else was there? I run my fingers close to my scalp. Yes! It's still there, just like dandruff. Or lice. Yuck. I sniff it and run the texture between my fingers.

Baby powder. And what are those hard pebbly bits? Oh, right—pepper!

Hi ho, hi ho, it's off to the kitchen I go. I sneak through the dining room and push open a set of swinging doors. This time I block my nose. Fish! There are fish everywhere! Eels! Salmon. It smells like the seafood section of a grocery store on a hot July day.

Tammy would feel right at home, but I think I'll keep my nose blocked.

I frantically look for pepper, which I find, and then brown sugar, which I find too. It helps that I can currently read Chinese. But my luck runs out at baby powder. There is no baby powder in this kitchen. And why would there be? Who has baby powder in their kitchen?

Now what?

Argh! I need to call Miri.

I flip open my phone and pray that it works. It does. I do not even want to think about how much this call is going to cost. I dial my sister's phone, complete with country code. She answers on the fifth ring. "Hi, Rachel! You would not believe how cool this is. . . . What? Yeah, I know! Rachel, hold on a sec!"

"No, Miri!" I yell, but instead of listening to me and my problems, she's saying to Corey or whomever, "Funnel cake? I'd love one, thanks so much!"

"Miri, there is no time for funnel cake at a time like this!"

"I had to send him off so I could tell you the news! Guess what!" she chirps. "I asked Corey to be my date for the Samsorta! And he said yes!"

Oh, excellent. Now not only am I about to miss my boyfriend's father's party, but my sister has a date and I don't.

Absolutely perfect.

"Great, Miri, I'm happy for you, but—"

"He's so excited. He's going to zap up a tux! He asked me what kind of corsage I want but I'm not really sure. He still hasn't kissed me, though. Do you think I should kiss him? Or should I—"

"Miri! Stop talking! I need help!"

She pauses. "What's wrong?"

"I'm stuck in China!"

"Huh?"

"I'm in China!"

"Why?"

"I wanted to see the Great Wall. Why do you think? The go spell messed up!"

"Really? That's strange. It works perfectly for me."

"Terrific. I'm so happy for you. Can we get back to me now, since I'm the one stranded on the other side of the world?"

"Maybe it's not the go spell that's the problem. Maybe it's your *mouli*."

"I don't even know what you just said."

"Don't you pay attention in class? *Mouli?* Hello? It means your truthfulness."

"Yeah, thanks, I speak Brixta too. But what does that have to do with me?"

"You're insisting on disguising your true self from Dad and Raf, so your magic is getting funky."

Why is everyone so obsessed with my truthfulness? Honestly, it's getting annoying. "But I'm always disguising my true self! And my magic usually works!"

"Well, your magic has always been funky. But maybe magic can sense that you're feeling guilty. . . . I don't know. I think it depends how many of your *m*'s are blocked and how hard the spells are."

Terrific. "So what do I do?"

"See if you can find a broom?"

"Not funny," I say, close to tears. "It would take me a month to get home."

"Don't cry, Rachel."

"I'm going to if I don't figure out how to get out of here!"

"Where are you, again?"

Is she purposely being annoying? "I told you! Stuck! At a restaurant in China!"

"Which one?"

"What's the difference?" I yell. "Just help me!"

"I'm trying to, but I need to know where you are!"

"Why?" I scream.

"So I can come get you!" she screams back.

Oh. "The Kim Shing. In China."

She hangs up. A few seconds later she Appears beside me, tight-lipped.

"Thanks," I squeak.

"Whatever," she grumbles, tossing the go spell into the air.

"Through space we flow.
To our apartment in New York City—"

"Actually, Mir, I'm kind of in a hurry. Would you mind dropping me off at the Kim Shing in Midtown?"

"Fine," she says, giving me a dirty look. "But you're so taking a cab home."

20 That's the Way the Fortune Cookie Crumbles

I hurry into the restaurant and find the Kosravis' table.

"I am so, so sorry." I am forty-five minutes late. I am the worst girlfriend ever. "I had transportation issues."

Raf leaps up to greet me. "Don't worry about it. Have a seat."

Embarrassed but grateful to get off my feet (my legs are a bit wobbly from all the transporting), I sit between Raf and Kat at the circular table. Next to Kat is Will; next to him is Mitch (the oldest Kosravi brother); next to him is Janice (his new girlfriend); next to her is Mrs. Kosravi (or Isabel, but she has never told me to call her that); and next to her is Mr. Kosravi. (It's Don! Sure, *now* I remember.) The three Kosravi boys all have the same sexy dark hair, dark eyes, and lean athletic bodies. Mitch's hair is the longest and his face the most angular. Will's hair is the shortest and he's the tallest. Raf has the widest smile and is definitely the cutest, if you want my opinion. The three of them look just like their dad, minus the graying at the temples.

Speaking of temples, all the go spelling gave me a nasty headache.

There are already plates of fried wontons, dumplings, and egg rolls in the center of the table. Understandably, they got tired of waiting for me and already ordered. I hope they got General Tso.

"Everything all right?" Kat asks, plucking a grain of rice from my hair.

Excellent. Rice leftovers. "I'm fine," I mutter. "You look great." She's wearing a red sweater dress that shows off her porcelain skin and glossy straight black hair.

"Thanks," she says with a big genuine smile. She's always smiling, which is understandable. Not only is she student council president, but after years of crushing on Will Kosravi, he's finally her one and only. She also isn't living a secret life. As far as I know.

After saying hello to everyone, I sink back into my seat. Since everyone else is already eating, I serve myself an egg roll.

"I ordered you General Tso," Raf whispers to me. "I know it's your favorite."

What a sweetie.

"Kat was just telling us about the Fall Ball she's planning for JFK," Will says.

"I can't wait," I say. "When is it going to be?" For the last year my number one wish has been to go to a school social with Raf, and maybe now it will happen. It won't be the Samsorta, but it'll be something.

"Halloween."

I spit up the water.

"Rachel, are you all right?" Raf asks, rubbing my back.

Cough, cough. I wipe my chin with my napkin. "Went down the wrong pipe." How could that happen to me? How could that happen to me again?

"So you're going to have a Halloween theme?" Raf asks her.

Kat smiles. "Won't that be fun? We'll decorate the gym like a haunted house. And you guys have to dress up."

"We'll be there," Raf says.

I furiously cut into my egg roll. Last year, my dad's wedding was on the same night as the Spring Fling and I had to lie to Raf and then miss the dance. I can't believe I have to go through that again.

Maybe this time I should be a good girlfriend and skip the Samsorta.

No.

I can't miss the Sam. Not because my mother and sister would be mad, but because I don't *want* to miss it. I'm excited about it. About the invites, about the candle spell, about the whole shebang. When did that happen?

No, I'm going to have to lie to Raf.

Again.

Unless, well, if Zach knows the truth . . . why can't Raf?

No. Yes. No.

Maybe?

"Time to get up, girls! Wake up, wake up, wake up!"

It's the next morning, and my mother is standing in the hallway, knocking on both our doors simultaneously.

Is she insane? I peer at my alarm clock. It's five-thirty. I've been asleep for less than five hours! There were mucho Raf-kisses after dinner! I cover my face with my pillow. "Is the apartment on fire?"

"No, dearies! But it's our special day! It's Sunday!"

"Barely Sunday," I grumble.

"Why does our special day have to start so early?" Miri calls out.

"We have a two o'clock appointment!"

"Where?" Miri asks.

"I'll give you a hint . . . it's right next to the Duomo di Milano!" Mom exclaims.

Miri gasps. "Really?"

"DUMBO?" I say, not moving. What is that? Oh, I think it's an area of Brooklyn. "Why do we have to get up so early to go to Brooklyn? It's not *that* far."

"She said the *Duomo,*" Miri calls out. "It's a gothic cathedral in Milan. Fantastic! I can practice my Italian. I heard that if you practice a language while you're under the Babel spell, it might seep in."

"We're going all the way to Italy to see a cathedral?" I yell. "St. Patrick's Cathedral is on Fifth Avenue and we've never been inside that one."

My mom swings my door open. "Let's go, let's go."

"But you don't use the traveling spell!" I remind her.

"You don't know everything about me, missy." She gives me one of her big freakish winks.

She does have two weekends free from us a month. I always assumed Mom spent her spare time watching TV, but now I wonder if she spends it gallivanting around Europe. She is a travel agent. She probably gets great hotel deals.

"What do I need to take?" I ask, throwing off my covers.

"Your camera," she says, and then gives me a sly smile. "And a pair of heels."

"Are we going to a party?" I ask. Maybe the Duomo won't be a total write-off.

"No," she says, "dress shopping. Our appointment is with the world's best Samsorta designer. She made my dress thirty years ago, and now she's going to make yours."

Fantastico!

An hour later, we knock on an ornate door in the Quadrilatero d'Oro, which is the shopping district.

There are tons of people everywhere. Very attractive, well-dressed people. I've always thought that Manhattanites were the most stylish people in the world, but these guys look like they're part of a fashion magazine spread. They are all six feet tall, chiseled, and wearing extremely pointy-toed shoes and humongous sunglasses.

Sigh. Due to the insanely early departure hour, I left my sunglasses somewhere on my floor. (In their case, of course. Hopefully.) Miri offered to do a temporary duplication spell on hers (a permanent one would be stealing, but a temporary one would be more like borrowing), but I shushed her. I'm hoping to get Mom to buy me one of the gorgeous pairs we keep passing in the windows, and she's not going to if I'm already wearing sunglasses, is she? I can use new ones, anyway. Mine have been kind of wobbly ever since I transformed them back from ski goggles. Unfortunately, Mom doesn't seem interested in doing any shopping except Samsorta dress shopping. She won't even let us buy heels here. Too expensive. She wants us to use the ones we brought to figure out the dress length, and said it's cheaper just to buy shoes on Eighth Street in New York.

For some reason, she's carrying a huge shopping bag she brought from home, but she won't show us what's inside it. Returning something she bought during one of her secret trips, perhaps?

"*Ciao!*" says Adriana, the dressmaker, an older woman with thick red lips and heavily lined eyes. Wow. The entire room is swathed with shimmery material. Reams of silk, satin, and lace are draped, making me feel like I've just entered an Arabian tent.

Miri says, "*Ciao,*" which means *hello*.

My mom says, "*Salve,*" which also means *hello*.

I say, "*Buon giorno,*" which means *good day* and also *hello*. Italians sure have a lot of ways of saying hello. They must talk to more people than we do.

Adriana looks my mom over. "You look very familiar," she says in Italian. "Have I dressed you before?"

My mom looks at her blankly. "I didn't take the language potion today and I don't really speak Italian!"

"Of course," she says. She repeats her last comment in English.

My mom nods. "You made my Samsorta dress thirty years ago. My name is—"

"Carolanga Graff! I remember every woman I dress. You haven't been back in a long time. I just saw your sister a few months ago."

My mom clears her throat. "I've been busy."

Adriana nods. "So, what can I do for you today?"

My mom puts her arms around our shoulders. "My daughters are having their Samsortas."

"How wonderful!" Adriana exclaims. "Both of them together? What a blessing! Did you bring your Samsorta dress?"

"I did," she says, opening her shopping bag.

Aha.

"You brought your old dress?" Miri asks. "Does that mean one of us gets to wear it? Can it be me? Can it?"

Adriana laughs. "You will both get to wear it," she says, carefully removing the heliotrope satin dress from the bag, which I recognize from her Sam album.

"Are we going as Siamese twins?" I ask.

"No," my mom says with a shake of her head. "Adriana will split the material into two and then tailor a dress to fit each of you. It's traditional that a mother passes her dress on to her daughter. My mother passed her dress on to me and my sister."

Miri's forehead wrinkles in confusion. "But the material from one dress won't be enough for two."

My mom smiles. "Adriana has her ways."

Adriana examines the dress. "I will expand the material. I will make you both beautiful gowns." She bends her nose into the dress and sniffs. "And I will get rid of that terrible bleach smell. Where did you store this? Under a sink?"

Close enough.

Adriana measures our waists, busts (My sister still has a bigger bust than me. I don't want to talk about it), hips, and hollow-to-hem, which in tailor terms means the length of the dress.

When she's done, Adriana says, "Now you must pick out styles." She claps twice and two pieces of red silk separate like the Red Sea and a catwalk jets out like a plank on a pirate ship. A girl sashays out the door. She's wearing a nude strapless corset. She has wavy brown hair and is about my age, my height . . .

Omigod! "She's me!" I scream.

"A hologram of you," Adriana clarifies. She claps again, and a Miri model prances out, also in a corset.

"Kind of creepy," Miri mutters.

Creepy? Are you kidding me? This is the coolest thing ever. Now that I'm looking more closely, I realize that Model Me is see-through. Too bad. I was thinking that with Model Me by my side, I could finally be in two places at once. Like in Samsorta class and hanging with Raf. Although if I sent Model Me out with Raf and he put the moves on her, he'd end up kissing air.

Adriana calls out, "Model one, capped sleeves, scooped neck, mermaid bodice, empire waist, pearl embroidery.

Model two, strapless ball gown with extra crinoline under the skirt!"

Zap!

The Rachel model is wearing a heliotrope dress with capped sleeves, a scooped neck, a mermaid bodice, and an empire waist. The Miri model is wearing the strapless ball gown, also heliotrope. They both twirl.

Adriana motions to the models. "You tell me what you like, what you don't like, they change. Good?"

Great. "Can I see it in A-line?"

Adriana claps. "Model one, A-line!"

Zap! The top of my dress stays the same, but the bottom expands. I start to feel giddy, like I've eaten too much cotton candy. "Can I see it in a ball gown?"

Zap!

"Can I see mine with less puff?" Miri asks.

Zap!

"Can she come home with me?" I ask.

Adriana laughs.

After we pick out our favorite styles, we let Adriana work her magic while we go to the Duomo and then for gelato. We sit at a tiny round table at an outdoor café right on Via della Spiga across from a ginormous Prada store. I make a big show out of squinting so maybe my mom will want to buy me the pair of big white sunglasses in the window.

"Girls," my mom says, licking her cappuccino-flavored cone, "the invitations are going to be ready today."

"Boy, those magic printers are quick," I say.

"There's one name still missing from the list," she says.

"Dad's," Miri says immediately, taking a bite of her chocolate brownie–flavored ice cream.

"That's exactly who I was wondering about," Mom says.

"Miri wants to tell him," I say. "I don't think we should."

Miri shakes her head. "I don't understand why not. He's our father and he deserves to know! You can't keep lying to everyone, Rachel!"

I flush. "Mom, what do you think? You never told Dad. Should we?"

Mom presses her chin into her hand. "He's your father, and if you want him there, he should be there. Or not. I'll support either decision you make."

"Can't you give us your opinion?" I ask.

She hesitates. "Becoming a Samsorta doesn't just mean you have powers; it means taking responsibility for your powers. That said, what I've learned in life is that it's better to be honest with the people you love."

"Exactly," Miri says triumphantly. "*Mouli*, Rachel, *mouli*. Didn't yesterday teach you anything?"

I take another lick of gelato.

Maybe she's right. He is our father. He has to love us no matter what, doesn't he? I take a deep breath. "If you really think we should tell him, we'll tell him."

Miri cheers. She whips out her cell. "Now?"

"No!" I say, my heart hammering. "Don't be crazy. We'll tell him next weekend. In person."

Mom laughs. "Do you have any idea how much a call from Italy to Long Island would cost?"

Miri raises an eyebrow. "Not as expensive as Rachel's call from China last night."

Mom drops her cone and the gelato spills onto the table. "Excuse me?"

Great. Now I'm *really* not getting new sunglasses.

When we return to Adriana's we stand on low wooden pedestals, modeling our dresses.

"You both look beautiful," Mom says, blinking back tears.

Miri's dress is a sheath with an empire waist and capped sleeves. Mine is a strapless ball gown. Adriana also made us matching light fitted jackets in case it's cold, as well as matching pointy witches' hats.

"Why?" I ask. "Mom, you weren't wearing a hat in your pics."

"You need it for the ceremony," Mom tells us. "Trust me."

"Your boyfriends won't be able to take their eyes off you!" Adriana says, clasping her hand to her heart.

Ouch. I study my purple-pink self in the mirror.

Sure, I want Raf to be unable to take his eyes off me . . . but am I ready to let him see me? The real me? Or do I want to keep padding the truth?

Speaking of padding . . . "Can I get bra inserts built into the dress?"

"Absolutely," Adriana says, snapping her fingers.

Immediately, I have extra cleavage.

"Whoa," Miri says.

"You don't need it, Rachel," Mom says, shaking her head.

I think about her words. Do I need the padding? Not the

boob padding—obviously I need that. I mean the *truth* padding. With Raf.

I want Raf to know the real me. I want him to *love* the real me.

Adam was right. I need to be with someone who knows what I'm going through. But that doesn't mean I have to be with Adam.

It means I have to tell Raf the truth.

21 The Name Game

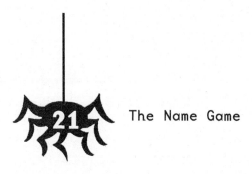

The fashion show list is posted on Monday morning.

Not only is Raf's name on it, but so is Melissa's. And Jewel's. Yippee. I get to spend the next four months imagining Raf dancing and grinding with my ex–best friend and my nemesis.

This would annoy me more if I weren't too busy obsessing over a bigger issue: *I'm going to tell Raf my secret!*

How? I don't know. When? I don't know that, either. But I think I should tell my dad first. Family should know first, right? Also, telling my dad will definitely be less scary than telling Raf. After all, unlike my dad, Raf could always break up with me.

Not that I think he's going to. Definitely not. He's a sweetheart.

But he could.

Anyway, since my Sam is in exactly three weeks and one

day, I figure I have three weeks to spill the magic beans. I should probably give him at least one day's warning. He'll want to get me a corsage.

Of course I'm going to bring him to the Sam. The best part of telling him the truth is that I get to bring him as my date! Hey, if Viv can do it, so can I!

And why should Melissa and Jewel be the only ones who get to dance and grind with him? They should not.

"I wish you had tried out," Raf tells me after school, draping his arm around my shoulders. Raf is off to his first of many after-school fashion show meetings.

"We'll be dancing together soon enough," I say with a secret smile.

"At the Halloween dance, you mean."

"Uh-huh. At the dance." *Dances*. Both of them.

I realized that happy fact when I got back from Italy. Even though it was dark when we left Milan, it was still midday in New York. Which reminded me that, yes, the Samsorta might start at seven p.m., but that's Romanian time. It'll definitely be over by eight p.m. in New York, which is when the school dance starts.

So technically, I could have gotten away with not telling Raf anything.

Too late! I've already decided. It's time for him to know. And now we get to go to two dances! Yay to the power of two!

"Are you going to dress up?" I ask.

"Sure. Why not? We could dress up together if you want."

Aw, that would be so cute! A joint costume with my boyfriend! Talk about publicly declaring your relationship. "Really? You'd want to do that?"

He blushes. "Why not? What could we be? James Bond and a Bond girl?"

"I am so *not* dressing up as a Bond girl."

"You'd make a gorgeous Bond girl," he says, smiling. "Best one yet."

He is *so* sweet. "I love you," I say, kissing him softly.

"I love you too," he says. He loves me! And soon he's going to love the real me!

Maybe I should just tell him. Right now. Everything. No one else is in the hallway.

It's not that big a deal. He won't even care. So I'm a witch. Big whoop. It's a quirk. Lots of people have quirks. He does. He puts mustard on everything. That's a quirk. He talks to the television. Do I like him less because of these things? No, I like him *because* of his quirks.

"Raf, I have to tell you something." I rush the words out of my mouth before I can change my mind.

He leans against the wall. "What?"

"I—I—" Why can't I talk properly? Why is my mouth so dry?

Stick to the plan, my little voice yells. *You had a plan! Dad first, then Raf!*

Right. I had a plan.

"Yes?" Raf says.

"I think," I say slowly, "you should wear all yellow. I'll wear all red, and we'll go as mustard and ketchup."

He responds with another kiss.

A soft, beautiful kiss.

"Raf," I hear. "Are you coming?"

He pulls away, and I see Melissa waiting at the end of the

hallway. She has a smirk on her face, and I can almost hear her saying "*Ha.*"

Just to show her who's boss, I murmur, "One more," and then pull him back in for another fat juicy kiss.

Ha-ha.

On Friday night, after fake getting ready for bed, we wait for my dad and Jennifer to turn in, get dressed in our party outfits for Michael's Sim (I wear another altered version of my prom dress; Miri wears her Bloomie's dress in another color), stuff pillows under our covers, and use the battery spell to go to L.A.

I'm done with the go spell, thank you very much.

When we arrive, we greet everyone in their finery, then stop by the place card table and pick up our names. I see Adam's card is still there. He's at our table—table six. Is it going to be awkward? Is he going to ignore me? I really wish we could be friends. I miss having him as my friend. We follow the group into the auditorium to find a seat for the ceremony. Miri tries to sit with Corey, but he shakes his head.

"All the guys have to sit behind the girls."

"Why?" I wonder.

He shrugs. "Tradition. The foremothers felt men distracted women, so they decided to keep men out of their line of focus. Also, since men are usually taller, this way the women can see better. We're at the same table for dinner, though." He smiles. "I checked."

"Oh good," Miri says, but then she blushes.

We're sitting next to Karin and the rest of our Samsorta girlfriends behind Michael's female relatives. As his date, Glamour Triplet is sitting in the front row.

"I'm so excited to see how it works," Miri whispers to me.

I take a quick peek around to see if I can locate Adam. The lights go off just as I spot him four rows back.

Once the stage lights go on, the ceremony begins. Michael's mother asks him if he wants to join the circle of magic, like in ours. Since there's no actual circle (it's only him), he has to walk around the stage three times. Since this stage is so big—hello, the Oscars are held here—this takes a while. Afterward, Michael's mom cuts off a piece of his hair. It's hard to see how much hair from where I'm sitting, but his was already pretty short, so it couldn't have been that much. I hope she didn't give him a bald patch. I really have to review the hair-cutting bit with Mom. And Este.

Michael's mom carries his hair to the large clay cauldron in the center of the stage. Next, Michael says the light spell in Brixta to set his candle aflame.

He closes his eyes and chants:

"Isy boliy donu
Ritui lock fisu
Coriuty fonu
Corunty promu binty bu

"Um . . ."

I haven't learned the spell yet, but I'm pretty sure "um" is not part of it.

"He's nervous," Miri whispers.

"No kidding." I can see the sweat dripping down his forehead. Poor Michael!

We wait. Miri squeezes my hand.

Michael wipes his brow and then continues.

"Gurty bu
Nomadico veramamu."

He finishes, but his candle does not go on.

A murmur goes through the crowd.

Uh-oh. "What now?" I whisper.

"He has to start over," Miri says.

Michael shakes his head, takes a deep breath, and tries again:

"Isy boliy donu
Ritui lock fisu . . ."

Miri mouths the words along with him.

"How do you know this already?" I ask. "Aren't we learning it in tomorrow's class?" We have three more lessons left, and tomorrow is supposed to be dedicated to learning this very spell.

"I wanted to get a head start," she whispers back. "I don't want this"—she motions to Michael—"to happen to me."

It had better not happen to me, either. My mouth suddenly feels sandpaper dry. Why did Fizguin waste so many classes teaching us about ethics when she should have been teaching us the way to stave off severe public humiliation?

Michael recites the whole spell again, but he messes up the last line and it's a no go.

"He's too nervous," Miri tells me, biting into her pinky nail. "It's only a one-broomer, but you need to say every word *perfectly* for it to work."

He's nervous? I'm nervous! What if this happens to me

in front of the entire witchcraft world? "What happens if you completely forget it?"

"The person next to you can whisper it," Miri says, "but you have to say the whole thing in one fluid motion. That's why the Samsorta ceremony takes so long. Apparently, last year one girl tried thirty-seven times before she got it right. Can you imagine? So embarrassing."

Great. Something else to worry about. I'll forget it so many times I'll miss the JFK Fall Ball.

Miri bites into her thumbnail and I swat her hand. "Don't you want your nails to be nice for your Sam?"

She ignores me.

Thank goodness Michael's wick bursts into flame after his third try. He smiles with relief.

"Here comes the wonderment spell," Miri says, eyes glued to the stage. "Did you hear that Wendaline is the girl they chose to cast the wonderment spell for our Samsorta? She's kind of like our valedictorian."

Witchedictorian? "Really? She didn't mention it. Is that good?"

Miri nods. "It's a huge honor. But it's practically the world's hardest spell. It's six brooms."

"There's no such thing!"

"There is. It's the Samsorta wonderment spell. All your *m*'s have to be working perfectly or it won't work."

I look back at poor Michael. "What if Michael can't do it?"

"If you're just one guy, it's only two brooms. It's six when you're casting the spell for eighty-four young witches. They obviously think Wendaline is really in control of her pillars."

She definitely has self-control. If I were her, I would have blasted Cassandra into dust long ago.

Michael holds his candle on top of the cauldron and chants:

"Julio vamity
Cirella bapretty!"

He sets the cauldron aflame.

The audience bursts into applause.

I'm relieved for him, but I still have butterflies in my stomach.

Probably because I'm excited about telling Dad. Yup. Tomorrow is the big day. We have a plan. Tomorrow night, after Prissy goes to sleep, Miri and I are going to tell Dad we want to watch *Star Wars*. Jennifer will come up with an excuse not to watch and then it will just be the three of us.

We'll tell him then.

And then once he knows, I'm going to tell Raf.

Yay!

I think I'll invite him over. That way I can make sure we have privacy. Or maybe I should tell him at his place? So he feels comfortable? Although what if Will or someone interrupts us?

Maybe I should pick a neutral spot like the park.

We all file out of the auditorium and head into the dining room. Adam is already sitting but plays his cutlery like drumsticks instead of looking at me. I sit next to Karin.

Once everyone has found their seat, the first song comes on and Michael and Glamour Triplet have their first dance. Everyone oohs and aahs. "They're pretty good," I tell Karin.

"They took a lesson," Karin tells me.

"No way! Are we supposed to take lessons for our first Sam dance too?"

"There's no point, since there are so many girls. With eighty couples on the floor, no one is paying attention. But when it's just the two of you . . ." Her eyes trail back to Glamour Triplet and Michael. "Who are you taking, anyway?"

"My boyfriend, Raf," I announce. There, I said it, so it must be true.

"I didn't know you had a boyfriend," she says. She motions across the table, then whispers, "I thought you and Adam were going to be an item."

"I've been dating Raf since the summer," I say. "And I'm going to ask him to be my date next week. First I have to tell him that I'm a witch, though. He's a norlock. Any suggestions?"

She bites her lip. "Yeah. Don't bring him."

My heart drops into my stomach. "Why not?"

She leans in. "It's frowned upon to invite a norlock date."

Now it plummets all the way to my toes.

"Why?" I ask.

"Well," Karin says, "you know that men can't pass the magic gene to their children—it's only passed through the mother—right?"

"Seriously?" I ask. I'm going to kill my mother. If she'd kept us any more in the dark, we'd have been wearing blindfolds.

"Yeah," she says. "If a warlock marries a notch, their kids

don't get powers. It's only passed through the mom. Like baldness."

"But what does that have to do with me?" I ask. "If I marry Raf, my kids are going to get powers anyway."

"True," Karin says, "but that's not fair to the warlocks. If we all marry norlocks, who are they going to marry?"

My head spins. Aren't we a little young to be talking about getting married? I can't even get my license. "But . . . but my mom married a norlock. So did my grandmother. And Viv is bringing her boyfriend and he's a norlock!"

"It happens," she says with a shrug. "But it's not very WC."

I wrinkle my forehead in confusion.

"Witch Correct," Karin explains.

Well, so what? I don't care! I love Raf and I want him to be my date. If Viv can do it, so can I. Can't I? Why does everything have to be so difficult?

If only I liked Adam. My life would be so much easier. If only Adam didn't hate me.

Once the first dance is over, the band invites all the guests onto the dance floor. Our whole table gets up to join them. But I stop Adam before he makes a move.

"Adam, hold on a sec, please?" I move over to the seat beside his. The ice age between us is over.

"Hey." He gives me a sheepish smile.

"We need to talk," I begin. Since we're the only people at the table, I launch right in. "I'm really, really sorry I didn't tell you I had a boyfriend. I should have. I know this sounds lame, but I think you're a great guy, and I really, really want us to be friends. Do you think we could be friends? Or do you hate me?"

He cocks his head. "Yes."

"Yes, you think we could be friends, or yes, you hate me?"

His eyes crinkle. "Both."

I laugh. "Then we're friends."

"Yes. And I'm sorry for mauling you on the chairlift. Do you hate me?"

"Absolutely not."

"Good." He smiles. He picks up the fork and spoon and gently taps them against the edge of the table like they're drumsticks. "So what now, friend?"

Since the song is a fast one, I say, "We can dance."

"Your boyfriend won't mind if we dance?"

"Raf wouldn't mind. He dances with other girls all the time."

Adam raises an eyebrow.

That didn't sound right. "He's in the school dance show," I explain.

"Oh, so that's his name, huh? Raf. What's that short for?"

"Huh?"

"Short for. He wasn't born with the name Raf." He drums his cutlery against the table again.

"Of course he was! Wasn't he?"

He laughs. "How long have you been going out, again?"

I playfully punch him in the arm. "Shut up," I say. "We've been together a long time. He's a great guy. You'd like him."

"He's a great guy, huh? But can he do this?" His eyes twinkle, and he wiggles his fingers and levitates a glass of water.

I laugh. "No, he can't."

"No? What about this?" He raises the fork.

"Nope."

He lifts the fork so that it's gently tapping against the glass.

"No, he can't do that, either. But I'm going to tell him the truth. About me."

"Oh. Well. That is serious."

"Yeah. It is."

"Well, if he doesn't react the way you want him to," he says, putting the glass and the fork gently down on the table, "I'm here for you."

"He will," I say. "But thanks." I push back my chair. "Wanna join them on the dance floor?"

"Absolutely."

This time we stay at the party until the bitter end. By the time we go home, it's four a.m. in Long Island. We use the go spell and arrive in the bathroom.

"Are you getting washed or going straight to bed?" Miri whispers.

"We're wearing makeup," I remind her, lifting my facial cleanser. "Do you want your skin to break out two weeks before your Samsorta?"

"Nooo. And I was thinking about what you said."

"About what? I say a lot of things."

"About my nails. I'm going to try to stop biting."

"Good for you. Let me know if you need encouragement.

I'm happy to swat your hand whenever you want. Or to wrap your fingers in Band-Aids."

Once I get my pj's on, we carefully creak open the bathroom door to go to bed.

The hallway lights are on. My dad's bedroom door is open.

Uh-oh.

"Rachel! Miri!" my dad screams, charging toward us. "Where were you? We were worried sick! I went to check on you and your beds were empty! Do you know what time it is?"

Busted. Well, we were going to tell him tomorrow anyway. . . .

The veins in my dad's neck look like they're about to burst. "Jennifer is on the phone with the police right now!"

Miri and I exchange a look. I nod.

"Dad," she begins, "we have something to tell you."

I square my shoulders and open my mouth. And then I say, "We're witches."

22 The Stinging Truth

As soon as the words leave my mouth, I feel like a weight has been lifted. He knows. No more lying. No more lying!

At least to Dad.

I monitor his veins to see how he's taking the news. They haven't popped. A good sign, right?

"You're witches," he repeats. "You snuck out in the middle of the night because you're witches."

At this point, Jennifer has hung up the phone and is standing by my father's side in her ankle-length silk bathrobe. Guess we're telling her, too.

Miri shakes her head. "No, we snuck out because we were invited to a Simsorta, which is kind of like a bar mitzvah? But for witches? And—"

Jennifer looks up at my dad, eyes wide with fear. "Is it drugs?"

Oh God. Is she kidding me? "It's not drugs," I swear.

"We're *witches*." I give Prissy's room a worried look. "Can we take this into another room?"

The three of them wordlessly follow me into the kitchen. Miri, Jennifer, and I slide into chairs, but my dad just stands by the table with his arms crossed and his veins now bulging.

"As I was saying," I continue, "Miri and I are witches."

"What do you mean?" Jennifer asks, running her hands against the tabletop. "You play on Ouija boards?"

"Not exactly."

Jennifer sits up straight in her chair. "You're not sacrificing animals, are you?"

"Of course not!" Miri retorts.

"Miri once tried to save a herd of cows, actually," I say. "She zapped them into the gym." This might be T.M.I.—Too Much Information.

"I have no idea what you girls are talking about," my dad says. "It's like you're speaking Japanese."

"We can speak Japanese!" Miri exclaims. "We did a language spell."

"That's how come we understood Italian at Al Dente last month," I say hurriedly. "Remember?"

They stare at me blankly.

I turn to Miri. "*Spesso non compire.*" They don't get it. "Dad, Jennifer. We're witches. We can do magic."

The veins in his neck start pulsating again. "There's no such thing as witches!"

Miri puts her hands on her hips. "Yeah, there kind of is."

Jennifer wags her finger at us. "You're being ridiculous."

Miri gives me a look. I don't need to understand a

foreign language to know she's thinking, How do we make them believe us without freaking them out? Mom and Miri made my shoes levitate when they were telling me. That did the trick.

"Dad, Jennifer," Miri begins. "I know this sounds crazy. But do you see that bowl of fake apples in the center of the table? I'm going to lift it. With my mind."

"Oh, come on," my dad scoffs.

I put my hand on Jennifer's but keep my eyes on my dad. "Don't get freaked out, 'kay?"

Jennifer swipes her hands away and places them on her stomach. "You're acting like a child."

It gets cold in the kitchen, Miri purses her lips, and the ceramic bowl of fake fruit levitates toward the ceiling. Then the apples rise beyond the bowl and start juggling.

My dad closes his eyes.

Jennifer screams. "Stop! Stop! I don't want them to break! They were expensive!"

Miri gently rests the bowl and the fruit on the table. "See?" she says softly. "We're witches. We can do cool stuff with our raw will."

"It's like the Force," I tell my dad. Better to use lingo he understands. "And I can do it too. Wanna see?" What can I lift? I look around the room. I spot the fridge. I concentrate. I open it. Then I close it. Then I open it again. "Look what I'm doing! Isn't that fun?" I close the fridge door and look back at my dad. The color has drained from his face, leaving him a pasty white.

"I don't understand," he whispers.

"Dad, are you okay?" I ask. "Do you want to sit down?"

He sinks into a chair.

Miri touches his shoulder. "I know this is shocking for you, but it's true. It was the night of the lobsters at the Abramsons'! Remember? I brought my lobster back to life? I used magic! That's when I knew something was up."

"You brought the lobster back to life," Jennifer says, manically rubbing her stomach as though there were a genie in there.

"Yup," Miri says, giddy. "Unintentionally. It was so cool! I haven't done that since. It's known to be really tough and there are some moral issues about bringing back the dead—"

"I didn't have my powers yet," I interrupt, giving Miri a warning look. Definitely T.M.I. "But I finally got them this summer. Right before camp."

"I don't know what to say," my dad says, looking down at his hands.

"You don't have to say anything," I tell him. But as I say it, I know it's not true. I don't know what I was expecting his reaction to be, but I guess I always hoped that if we did tell him, he'd be impressed. He wouldn't be staring at his hands.

"I don't know what to say," he repeats.

Miri, seemingly oblivious to my dad's moroseness, happily rambles on. Now that the floodgates have opened, it's all pouring out. "Isn't it cool, Dad? Don't you think?"

Jennifer steadies her hands and clasps them together. She looks back and forth between me and Miri. "Have you ever used your powers on . . . me?"

I give Miri a look that is intended to say *I know you want to be truthful, but let's tread carefully, please*. "Before you guys got married," I begin, "we might have tested out a few *tiny* spells."

Miri nods. "There was the ugly spell, the truth serum spell, the love spell that we put on Dad so that he'd fall back in love with Mom—"

"Miri!" I scream. Did *she* ingest some of that truth serum spell? Is she totally incapable of reading the situation here? Don't drown them in info. It's W.T.M.I. (W*ay* Too Much Information).

"What?" She smiles cluelessly. "Mom was really upset about that one, so she undid it."

My dad blinks. And then blinks again. "She undid it? Your mother?"

Miri claps. "Of course! She's a witch too. That's where we got it from. We know she never told you. She didn't want you to know. But it's true, you can ask her."

Thud. My dad passes out and slides out of chair and onto the floor.

"Dad!" I scream and jump over to him. Miri and Jennifer jump right behind me. The three of us grab hold of his arms and heave him back up.

His eyes flutter open. "Let go," he says. "I'm fine. I'm fine."

My Liquid Paper–white dad rubs the back of his head. "Can I have some water?"

Not wanting to let go of him, I focus on the fridge, reopen it, and mind-pull a water bottle across the room.

"The water is flying!" chirps a new voice.

We all look at the door. Prissy. Uh-oh.

I lower the bottle.

"How did you do that?" Prissy asks. "Again! Again! Are you a magician?"

"Um . . ." I wasn't exactly planning on telling Prissy. "Kind of."

She crawls onto my lap. "Can you make me a pony?"

"I don't think so," I tell her.

"I would take really good care of her. Please? Can I have one? Please?"

"No pony," Jennifer says, still rubbing her stomach, her eyes now darting nervously from me to Miri. "Unless you want to. Whatever you guys want. I'm not telling you what to do. The magic isn't bad for the baby, is it? Like radiation?"

"It's not going to hurt the baby," I promise. "Witches use it all the time, even when they're pregnant."

Prissy's eyes widen to fruit bowl size. "You're witches?"

Whoops.

"Yes," Miri says.

"Can you fly?" she squeaks.

"Yes," I say.

She bounces on my knee. "Can I fly?"

"I can take you," I say.

"I don't think so," Jennifer says. She gives us a jittery smile. "That's okay with you, right, Rachel?"

Great, she's weirding out on us.

"I want my pony to fly too," Prissy says. "Can I have a magic pony?"

"No pony!" Miri and I scream.

"What about a dog?"

"I need to lie down," my dad says, still looking at his hands.

"Daddy?" I'm worried. "You don't need to go to the hospital, do you?" Fantabulous. I finally tell someone the truth and it gives him a heart attack.

"I just have a headache. I need to lie down." Without looking at us, he walks out of the kitchen.

"But, Dad . . ." Miri's voice trails off. "I want to tell you everything."

"Not now," my dad says.

"So," Jennifer says, a smile still forced onto her lips, "can I get you girls anything? Another glass of water? Or are you hungry? I can make pancakes! Blueberry pancakes? Banana pancakes? Chocolate pancakes? Chocolate and banana pancakes?"

"We're fine," I say softly. I can't believe Dad just took off.

"Okay, then," Jennifer says, pushing back her chair and avoiding all eye contact. "Prissy, it's time for you to go back to sleep. As long as it's okay with your sisters. Girls, do you mind if I take Prissy back to bed?"

"Of course not," I say.

"You sure?" she asks nervously. "I don't want to upset either of you in any way. . . ."

"Just take her," Miri snaps.

Jennifer grabs Prissy and hurries out of the kitchen, the forced grin still plastered on her face.

Huh.

"That didn't go well," I say, too shocked to move.

A few moments later, Jennifer calls, "Good night, girls! If you need anything, just holler! I'll be there in a flash!"

The door slams shut. I'm sure she wishes she had a lock.

Miri crosses her arms. Her face turns red. She blinks and blinks and then angry tears run down her cheeks. "What a jerk!" She explodes. "We tell him the most important thing in our life, and he doesn't even want to talk about it!"

"It's hard for him to deal with," I say softly.

"It's hard for us, too! I don't care if it's hard for him! He can't just walk away! That was really rude. If my daughter told me she was a witch, I would have a lot of questions. I wouldn't tell her to get lost."

"Miri, you'd be surprised if your daughter told you she *wasn't* a witch."

"If she told me she was something else, then. A vampire. Whatever. My first instinct wouldn't be to go to another room."

"No, it would probably be to put on a turtleneck."

Instead of laughing, she wipes her tears away with the back of her hand.

"Can't we give him a break?" I say.

"Why should we? You didn't freak out when Mom and I told you the truth about us."

"I kind of did."

"No, you had a lot of questions. And that's what I'd expect. Questions." Tears roll down her face. "Who does he think he is? He does whatever he wants, leaves Mom, moves away, gets remarried, has another baby, and we're just supposed to take it. We're supposed to accept him, but he can't even talk to us? Forget it." The words are spewing out of her mouth like daggers. "You know what? I want to go home." Now the veins on *her* neck are close to bursting.

"Miri, it's five in the morning."

"I don't care. I'm mad and I want to go home," she says, sobbing. She stumbles out of the kitchen, throws open the door to our room, and shoves all her stuff into her bag, tornado-style. "Are you coming with me or not?"

"I—I—I guess," I stammer. "Let me just go tell them we're leaving." I say the words, but what I'm really thinking is they won't let us go. If I tell them we're going back to Mom's, they'll try to stop us. They'll say, *Don't be silly! Don't leave us!*

We love you even though you're witches!

"I'm leaving in two minutes with or without you," she blubbers.

I creep back outside. My dad's door is still closed. The house is silent. As though nothing even happened.

I knock. "Dad? Jennifer?"

No answer.

"Guys?"

I turn the handle. My dad and Jennifer are sitting up in bed, side by side. When she sees me, Jennifer protectively puts her hands back over her stomach.

"Miri wants to go back to Mom's," I say. "I'm trying to stop her but she's really upset."

Jennifer gives me that fake smile again. "Oh! Okay! No problem! Do you need me to drive you? I'm happy to! Whatever you want!"

"We're fine, thanks. We have these magic batteries and a powder concoction. They both work well. Miri prefers the powder, but we sometimes end up in bathrooms. . . ." I let my voice trail off. Now she's going to think we're talking about drugs again.

Dad doesn't say anything. Nothing. Not "Don't go." Not "Stay." Not "I love you."

When my dad finally looks up at me, his eyes are shocked. Shocked and disappointed.

Okay, then. 'Nuff said. "I guess I'll go with her," I say, my voice cracking. I will not cry. I will *not* cry. Must be strong for Miri. Must be strong. I close the door and return to our room.

"Ready?" Miri asks, eyes flashing. "If he can't deal with it, then we don't need him."

The world is spinning around me. As Miri sprinkles the powder into the air, I realize that I knew all along that he would react like this. That's why I didn't want to tell him. Why I didn't want to tell anyone. Which is why I will never, ever tell anyone the truth about me again as long as I live.

Even in the unlikely event that Raf and I stay together for the next five years, or for the next ten years, even if Raf and I get engaged and then get married, I will never tell him that I am a witch, because I never want him to look at me the way my father just did.

Mom was right in the first place: magic should be kept a secret.

I can't believe it's come to this. I couldn't wait for my powers to kick in and now I'm ashamed of them.

The powder falls on my head, and I disappear.

We land in the bathroom with a crash.

"Hello?" It's my mom.

"Great, we woke her up. It's just us!" I call.

"Lex is probably here," Miri whimpers.

Right. Awesome.

"Girls? What's wrong? How come you're home?" Mom sounds panicked as she throws open the bathroom door.

We're both sitting on the bath mat, Miri crying, me rubbing her back.

"We told him," I explain.

She kneels beside us. "Told him what exactly?"

"About us," Miri sobs. "All of us."

Mom's lips tremble. "Me too?"

"Oh, all three of us are outed," I say.

Mom nods. "What did he say?"

My eyes fill up and I burst into tears.

Mom pulls us both into her arms.

23 A Shade of Gray

After a long tearful session (Lex went home so Mom could be with us alone), Miri and I finally go to sleep. The next day, we wake up exhausted for our Samsorta class. Instead of jeans, I slip on my comfiest sweatpants and sweatshirt. I don't really care how I look. I just want to feel comfortable. Raf called, but I didn't pick up. I just can't speak to him right now. I'm too upset, and there's no way he could ever understand.

Right before we go, we spot another package in the living room.

"I think you have another Simsorta invite," Mom says.

"I bet it's Adam's," I say, a smile finally cracking my lips.

Miri, calmer than yesterday, unwraps it. Inside the box is a miniature cable car. It's about the size of my foot. When Miri winds it up, the car bursts to life, spelling out the party info in metallic black on the carpet with its exhaust.

"That better be disappearing ink," Mom says warily.

"I guess we're invited now that you two made up," Miri says.

"I guess so," I say, reading the info. The party is next Friday night at the Golden Gate Bridge. That's probably just what I need to feel better: to be around other witches and warlocks. Because they get me. They know what it's like to have to pretend to be someone you're not. Unlike my dad, they won't treat me like a contagious disease.

All of a sudden, the car spurts back up again. "Sorry this is so late but I was waiting for us to be friends again," it says.

"At least someone wants us around," Miri says with a sigh.

"So, what are we doing tonight?" Karin asks.

In class we finally learned the light spell. And then we practiced. And practiced again. And again. I'm not screwing it up in front of everyone. No way. Now we're sitting in the cafeteria eating ice cream. For the first time in a long time, I have nowhere to be. It's my dad's weekend, but we're in exile. I guess I could go home and call Raf or Tammy, but then I'd have to come up with an explanation for not being in Long Island, and frankly, I don't have the energy to lie right now. The confrontation with my dad took too much out of me. Raf called me again, but I haven't listened to his message. I just don't know what I'm going to say to him. Everything's changed. I can't tell him the truth. The only thing I can do is lie, and lie and lie again.

"Let's go see Robert Crowne," Adam says. "He's playing Madison Square Garden."

"Seriously?" I ask. I love Robert Crowne. I saw him in concert on my first date with Raf. First quasi date. "How would we get in?" I ask. "Can you get tickets?"

Preppy Triplet laughs. "Since when do we need tickets? We'll just zap ourselves backstage."

"The opening band comes on at eight and then Crowne takes the stage at nine eastern time." Adam glances at his watch. "I wouldn't mind popping home to change. Do you guys want to meet backstage in an hour?"

The triplets murmur their agreement.

"Let me call Michael," Karin says. "I know he'll want to come." Michael and Fitch no longer spend Saturdays with us now that their Sims are done.

Corey clears his throat and looks at my sister. "Miri, why don't I pick you up and we can go together?"

Could it be? I think it is! My sister's official first date!

"Are you almost ready?" I ask. I'm lying diagonally across Miri's bed. "He's going to be here any second."

"Oh, no, I need more time!" She does up her jeans and spins toward me. "I don't know what top to wear. You're not changing?"

I'm kind of still liking my sweats. "Nope."

"But you're not wearing makeup!"

"Also nope."

"You are meeting us, though, right?"

"Well . . ." I say. Sure, I love Robert Crowne, but now that I'm back home, I'm not exactly in the "going out" mood.

She frowns. "You have to come! I don't want you staying home and moping."

"Just because you seem to have bounced back from yesterday, it doesn't mean I have," I say. I hug her covers to my chest.

"So don't change. Just come with Corey and me. Hurry, though. He's going to buzz any minute."

"I'm not tagging along on your date."

"Yes, you are. I insist." She crosses her arms. "I'm not going unless you come too."

"Miri! It's your first real date! You have to go."

She sits down on the edge of her bed. "I'm kind of scared to be a couple. Come with me? Please?"

I laugh. "*Fiiiine*."

We hear a loud bang inside the bathroom.

"Oh, no!" Miri cries.

"I guess he's not buzzing," I say.

"Go get him!" Miri orders. "I'm borrowing a shirt!" She scurries to my room and slams the door.

I go to the bathroom door. "Um . . . Corey?"

"Hi," he says, laughing. "Sorry, y'all. I hate this spell." He opens the door and is holding a bouquet of tulips.

"Aw," I purr. "Miri! Guess who's here! And he has flowers! Corey, hope you don't mind, but I might be hitching a ride with . . . y'all." Tee hee.

"No problem," he says, flashing a big relieved smile. I think he might be nervous too. No wonder it's taking them so long to have their first kiss.

Aw. He's so cute. *They're* so cute.

My mom rushes over. "Corey, hello!"

Corey blushes and says, "Hello, ma'am."

"Oh, please call me Carol. It's so wonderful to meet you. I've heard so much about you."

Miri opens my door just in time to hear my mom's proclamation. She muffles a groan.

"Mom," I say in a low warning voice.

"Oh! I don't mean to imply that Miri talks about you. Because she doesn't." Her hands flutter in the air. "Except, well . . ." Her voice trails off. "Oh dear."

Er. I point to Corey's flowers. "Miri, look at the bouquet!"

Miri shuffles her feet. "Thanks, Corey. That's really sweet."

Awkward pause.

"Mom," I say, "would you mind putting Miri's flowers in water so we can get going?"

"Right," she says, sounding grateful. "Of course. Have fun!"

Honestly, if it weren't for me, I don't know how my family would survive.

I mean . . . what's left of it.

"The feeling never fades
My sixteen shades . . ."

Robert Crowne is crooning onstage, and for the first

time in forever, I'm able to block out everything else—my dad, Jennifer, not having a date for the Sam—and just be. My phone vibrates a few times but I just let it go. I let myself get lost in the songs.

It helps that we've somehow wormed our way into VIP seats on the side of the stage. At first the manager was kind of wondering who we were, but Michael must have done some kind of Jedi mind trick, 'cause now the guy keeps winking at us.

Of course I can't help repeatedly peeking at Miri and Corey, who are right behind us.

No kissing action yet, but they're holding hands.

How lucky is Miri? Falling for a guy who gets her. Who knows what it's like to have magic powers. Who never has to be lied to.

I wish I were holding someone's hand. Sure, Adam wouldn't mind if I took his, but that would so be leading him on. It would be easy to do, though.

But my heart belongs to Raf.

Instead, I lift my hands in the air and dance to the music.

"That was amazing," I tell the group as we file out of the auditorium. It would be much easier to skip the line and zap ourselves right from our seats, but we're trying not to be so obvious.

"It was off the hook," Viv says. "Rockin' idea, Adam."

"Rachel!"

Did someone just call my name? I look around at my group but no one seems to be speaking to me. My ears are still ringing, so maybe I imagined it?

"Rachel!" I hear again.

"That guy over there is calling you," Viv says, pointing.

Pointing to Raf.

Omigod. He's with his friend Justin and a few other guys. And they're all staring at me.

I see him wave in the distance. He's wearing a new leather jacket. One he designed? He looks amazing in it. And he's wearing that brown shirt that brings out his eyes. The one we bought together. My heart feels like someone's squeezing it.

What am I supposed to tell him to explain why I'm here? That my dad had an emergency? That he surprised us with tickets? That I had my weekends confused?

"Excuse me," I say to my friends, and maneuver my way to where Raf is waiting. The dread in my mouth tastes like vinegar. What am I going to say? What lie am I going to make up this time? When I reach him, I open my mouth to say hi, to say something, but nothing comes out.

"I can't believe you're here!" His eyes look confused, but he's smiling. "I've been calling you all day to tell you I got tickets. Hey, aren't you supposed to be at your dad's?"

I open my mouth, but still nothing comes out.

"If you were in town, why didn't you call me?"

I try to say something. Anything. But I'm so tired of making up excuses. Of padding the truth.

His smile wanes. "Rachel, is something wrong?"

Everything's wrong. We're wrong. How can I be with you and lie to you for the rest of my life? I can never tell you the truth. You will never know who I really am.

Tears well up in my eyes. "Raf," I choke out. "I'm sorry."

"About what? What's wrong?" He puts his arm around me.

Don't cry, I tell myself. Do not cry. I can't believe what I'm about to do. I never thought I would do what I'm about to do. But I have to do it. "I can't be your girlfriend anymore," I say slowly.

He looks stung, like I've slapped him in the face. "What are you talking about? Why?"

How can I possibly explain? Should I say that it's better for both of us if we just break up now? I can't tell him the truth. If my own dad wants nothing to do with me, why would Raf? And what's my other choice? Lie for the rest of my life? Get married and keep lying? Have two kids but never fully show my husband who I am? End up divorced? He deserves more than that. I deserve more than that. Adam's right. Karin's right. A witch and a norlock can't work.

But what can I possibly say that will make sense to him? I look around the room for answers. I look at my witch friends, who are watching me. Waiting. Miri. Corey. Karin. Viv. Adam.

And then I say it—the only thing I know he'll understand. "I'm here with someone else."

He follows my gaze to Adam. "Oh," he says. He takes a step back. Pulls away his arm. His face hardens. "I get it." His voice cracks.

"I'm sorry," I whisper again, and then, before the tears overflow, I turn my back to him and run to my friends.

24 Breaking Up Is Hard to Do, but It's Easier with a Few Choice Spells

Miri immediately whisks me back home.

Raf and I are broken up.

Raf and I are broken up.

My father hates me, and Raf and I have broken up. And to add salt to my wound, when I listen to my messages, there are three from Raf, from *before*. The first two are him telling me he's going to the concert and asking me if I can come back into the city to go too. Justin had two extra last-minute tickets. The last one is Raf at the concert. It's a full minute of "Sixteen Shades of Love," because Raf knows it's one of my favorite songs.

Miri and I climb into my mom's bed, and I sob and I sob until I am empty of tears. I can't believe I just broke up with the sweetest guy in the world. I can't believe I'm never going to kiss Raf again. One hundred and thirty-one kisses. That's how many we've had. That's all we'll ever have. Yes, I kept count. What, you thought I came up with a whole formula for calculating kiss amounts and I wasn't going to try to prove it right? Please.

But I had to break up with him. What other choice did I have?

"My," my mom says, "you guys have certainly cleaned me out of Kleenex this weekend."

I start laughing and crying at the same time.

"I'm hungry," Miri says. "If I make popcorn, will you have some?"

"Yes," my mom and I say.

I turn to my mom and sniff. "Do you think I made a mistake?"

She pats my head. "I think not wanting to be in a relationship based on lies is a very mature decision. I think you could have told him the truth. But I know that's not an easy thing to do. Especially after your father's reaction."

My eyes tear up again. "You were right to begin with. You would have been better off marrying Jefferson Tyler."

She hugs me. "Then I wouldn't have had you guys."

Miri returns to the room with our white popcorn bowl, the one that also doubles as a cauldron. "Don't worry. You practically have a new boyfriend already. A warlock boyfriend. Adam already Mywitchbooked me."

"My life is falling apart and you checked Mywitchbook?"

She pops a kernel into her mouth. "I just peeked. Don't you want to know what he said?"

"No," I say quickly. "Okay, maybe."

"He asked me if you and Raf broke up."

"Don't tell him! I don't want everyone to know already!" If everyone knows, then it must be true.

"I didn't say anything to him, I swear. I told you, I just peeked!" She licks the salt off her fingers. "Do you want me to write him back?"

"No. Yes." Is that what I want? Adam to be my new boyfriend? I know I like him as a friend, but do I like him *like that*? The thought of being with someone else, anyone else, even someone as cute as Adam, just makes me feel . . . blah.

I fall asleep with a hole in my heart, dreaming of Raf.

I mope around most of Sunday. I alternate between lying facedown on my bed and lying facedown on the couch. At least in the living room I can listen to (and watch with the one eye not smushed into the pillow) the TV. The Travel Channel is running an all-day marathon of *The World's Bests*. By four o'clock I've seen *The World's Best Hotels*, *The World's Best Bathrooms* (Yes! People actually rank bathrooms! It must have been a witch, 'cause who else zaps herself into so many of them?), *The World's Best Restaurants*, and *The World's Best Beaches*. The world's best beach is in Greece, in case you're interested.

At five Miri tells me we're going out.

I lift my head up from the couch. "To where? Greece?"

"No. Lozacea."

"But it's Sunday," I say.

"It's a community center. It's open. Karin and Viv are there studying and hanging out."

I sigh. "I don't feel like it."

"Just for an hour. That's an order."

I stand up. "When did you get so bossy?"

We use the go spell and get zapped into the bathroom.

Miri takes the opportunity to pee, and I study my reflection. My eyes are puffy. Do I care? Not really. I feel the tears well up again, and I splash water on my face. I'm going to be fine. Absolutely fine. I did what I had to do.

My cell phone vibrates.

Raf?

I glance at the name. Adam. I pick up. "Hello?"

"What's going on, friend?" he asks.

I let out a low laugh. "Not much."

"You left last night in a bit of a hurry."

"No kidding."

"Wanna talk about it?"

I look away from the mirror. "Not so much. Hey, how did you get my number? I don't remember giving it to you."

"I'm a warlock. I can get anything," he says. "So, where are you now? At home?"

"Actually, I'm at Lozacea."

"Seriously? Me too. I'm in the game room. Viv and Karin just left me to practice their candle spells. Come be my pool partner?"

"Where is the game room?" How many rooms does this place have?

"Make a left after the caf and then walk until you see a red door. Knock three times and say, '*Balio.*' "

"Okay. We'll be there in two." Hopefully. If I find it. I hang up as Miri flushes and then joins me in front of the mirror. I wag my finger disapprovingly. "You did not tell me Adam was here."

She feigns innocence. "I didn't? Fine, you got me. Viv may have mentioned he was here studying. Or pretending to study."

He *is* cute. And sweet. And funny. And a warlock. Could I like him as more than a friend?

Miri goes to find the girls, and I search for, and then find, the game room.

"Welcome," Adam says.

I look around. Ping-Pong. Foosball. Checkers. Monopoly. Adam, looking kind of cute, racking up a pool table. I clear my throat and say, "These games seem kind of ordinary."

"What did you expect?" Adam asks. "Quidditch?"

I force myself to laugh. "You'd think witches would have *some* sort of magical sport."

His eyes crinkle. "Wanna race brooms?"

I lean against the table. "Brooms are so last year."

"Chicken?"

The word *chicken* makes me think of General Tso chicken, which makes me think of Raf, and my heart stops. Great. Now I'll never be able to eat my favorite dish ever again. "No," I say. "Definitely not." I push the thought of Raf away and pick up a pool cue. "What would you want to race for? Broom ownership?"

"Ha. How about these terms. If I win . . ." He pauses.

"If you win what? The race or the game of pool?"

"Either," he says. "If I win either one, you be my date for my Simsorta next weekend."

I almost drop my cue. "Oh. But—"

"Don't 'but' me. Just as a friend. I promise I won't try to make out with you again. Unless you want me to." He gives me an exaggerated wink. "But honestly, my parents keep bugging me about why I'm not bringing a date, and if I don't bring somebody, I'm going to have to dance with my mom for the first dance. You can't make me do that. Please. Save me." He looks up at me. "Unless your boyfriend doesn't want you to."

I shake my head. Guess Miri really didn't tell him. "Raf and I broke up."

He cocks his head. "I wondered what was up last night. . . ." He raises an eyebrow. "How are you?"

Must not cry. Must not cry. I force myself to shrug. "I'm fine. It was the right decision." I think. I hope. "It's too hard to be with someone I can't be honest with, you know?"

"Yeah," he says. "I do."

For a second, neither of us speaks. We hear laughter from outside.

"So does that mean you'll be my date? As a friend?" He gives me a hopeful smile.

I have an idea. "I'll tell you what. Forget the race and the pool game. Let's make a deal. I'll be your friend-date this week—"

"Deal!"

"If next week you'll be mine."

He smiles. "Now, those are my kind of terms."

I don't see Raf all day on Monday.

Some would call it luck, but I would call it the avoiding spell, which I found on page 376 of the spell book. It casts an orange hue fifty feet around him that only I can see. Best way to keep tabs on an ex *ever*. Or someone you're stalking. Not that I'm advocating stalking. 'Cause everyone knows that's bad. But no matter what it's used for, I'm going to have to find out which witch made that one up and give her some serious kudos.

I tell Tammy the breakup news that morning in homeroom.

"But I don't understand!" Tammy cries after her jaw literally hit the desk in shock. Fine, not literally, but her mouth really did fall open at the news. "How could you break up? You guys were crazy about each other!"

Now what am I supposed to say? Because I'm a witch and he isn't? Because it'll never work? "We were just in different places," I say.

"What are you talking about? What different places? You two are in the same place! Here!"

"It's complicated," I say, my head starting to pound.

"This isn't about the fashion show, is it?" she asks, forehead wrinkled in confusion.

"No, it's just . . ." What am I supposed to tell her? I can give her the same untrue explanation that I gave Raf—that it's because of Adam. But Tammy would wonder why I've never mentioned Adam. She'd ask how I met this Adam. She'd want to meet this Adam. "You know what? I don't really want to talk about it."

I feel her eyes boring into me. "But I'm your best friend! You have to talk about it."

"Tammy, I can't." My throat closes up. There are so many things I wish I could tell her. About Raf, about the Sam, about Adam, about my dad. My dad, who we still haven't heard from. Two days and no phone call.

Tammy would understand. Her parents are divorced too, and she would know just what to say. She always does. But how can I trust her? Sure, she's my best friend today, but what about tomorrow? She broke up with Bosh. What's stopping her from breaking up with me? What if I had confided in Jewel? She might have told the whole school by now. I can't tell Tammy. I just can't. The tears threaten to spill onto my cheeks, so I turn away from her to wipe them.

I feel her arms around my back, hugging me. "I'm so sorry. You talk to me whenever you're ready to. I'm always here for you, you got it? Always."

I nod and blink my tears away.

My cell phone rings in the middle of lunch.

"Excuse me," I say when I see Adam's number on the caller ID.

I hurry over to the window and away from my curious

friends before answering it. "Hello?" I'll tell them it was Miri calling with some sister emergency.

"What are you doing?" Adam asks.

"What do you think I'm doing?" I say. "I'm in school. I'm about to have mac and cheese." My eyes did tear up at the sight of the mustard, but then I said to myself, Mustard? What kind of crazy person puts mustard on mac and cheese? Seriously.

"Yum. It's meatball day over here. Trade you?"

"What's up?" I ask.

"Promise not to laugh when I ask you this," he says.

"I can't make promises like that. What if what you tell me is really funny?"

"It kind of is."

"Lay it on me."

"How would you feel about taking a dance lesson for my Sim?"

Laugh? More like groan. "Seriously?"

"Do you care? It would just be one hour tomorrow night. Does that idea make you miserable?"

"Is this because I told you the fashion show story? You're worried I'm going to make a complete fool of you?"

"No!" he says quickly. "That's not it at all. I swear. I'm the one who can't dance. And I just thought it might be fun."

Yeah, right. I spot Melissa and Jewel in the lunch line and think of the fashion show. "We're not going to have to do a routine, are we?"

"No routine. Maybe learn the waltz, or the surky."

"Er, what exactly is the surky?"

"The witch dance that you will be learning tomorrow at five Lozacea time?"

I sigh. Surky-shmurky. This date thing is sounding like a lot of worky.

It's the next day, and we've been practicing the dance for three hours. We're in yet another one of Lozacea's secret rooms. This place is like a labyrinth. I would not want to be here by myself at night. I would never find my way out.

Anyway, we've been practicing this "surky" for the last hour and a half. It involves a few dips, a couple of turns, and a whole bunch of coordinated steps. Matilda, the woman who tested my magic, is also the dance teacher. She zapped me into heels, a leotard, and a matching skirt when I got here, not approving of my school uniform of jeans and sneakers. I reached for my heart necklace straightaway to make sure it was still there, but then remembered I had replaced it with the broom charm from Wendy.

Yeah, it was a pretty sad thing to do.

At least Wendy was happy to see me finally wearing it.

Raf didn't see the switch, since the avoiding spell is still in full use. It's pure genius. I could avoid him all day. I could avoid him all year if I wanted. What I could not avoid was the buzzing about the breakup.

I overheard my girlfriends asking Tammy for details, and her telling them it was none of their business.

I saw the glint in Melissa's eye. I'm sure she can't wait to sink her claws into him.

I heard the pity in Kat's voice when I told her I wouldn't be able to make the Halloween dance.

"Just come on your own!" she told me, assuming I wasn't coming 'cause I didn't have a date. Puh-lease. Skipping an event because of datelessness? That's so last year. All my friends are planning on going stag. But not me. I have enough Halloween stress, thank you very much. And anyway, the gym is barely fifty feet, and Raf will definitely be there, since his brother's girlfriend is planning it.

"Rachel, you have to focus!" Matilda yells, snapping me back to the dance. "One, two, three, your turn is coming up."

"Isn't there a potion we can take to learn this?" I whisper to Adam. My feet are starting to hurt.

"Yeah," he says, smiling and tightening his arms around my waist. "But isn't this better than a potion?"

Huh. He's enjoying himself. He really does think this is fun.

And I wish I were at home watching TV.

When I was with Raf, I would enjoy anything we did together. Fashion show rehearsals. Poster hanging. Anything.

If only I were here with Raf . . . No, no, no!

I squeeze my eyes shut and try to make thoughts of him disappear.

"Six, seven, right! Turn, Rachel, turn, no, no, no turn!"

I keep my eyes closed and turn. I had to break up with Raf! I just had to! What else was I supposed to do?

"No, no, no, Rachel, you turned the wrong way! Again," she grumbles.

The wrong way, maybe. But the right decision, definitely.

That Friday, along with five hundred of his closest friends, I watch Adam perform his Sim. Yup, five hundred witches on the Golden Gate Bridge. It's witchapalooza.

Unlike Michael, Adam aces it in one shot. No repeats necessary. No uncomfy audience squirming. All his pillars are unblocked and working just perfectly.

Unfortunately, as his date, I'm forced to sit with his family during the ceremony. "You and my nephew make the cutest couple," his aunt whispers to me, giving me a major case of the squirmies.

The words *we're not a couple* want to pop out, but I give them a solid swallow and smile politely instead. I mean, she's not wrong. We do make a pretty cute couple. And I should be dating a warlock eventually anyway, right?

After the ceremony, a tall woman named Jenny (Sim planner to the best witch families, according to Glamour Triplet) ushers us to a slide that takes us under the bridge. They've frozen the bay so it looks and feels like we're walking on water. They also placed an avoiding spell on the entire area, so passersby and tourists are rerouted.

Before I sit down, it's time for the first dance.

Adam takes my hand.

I take a deep breath. I can do this. It's just one song. The music starts, and I get the moves (er, most of them) right, and the gazillion guests applaud.

"Are you having fun?" he asks me.

"Definitely," I say, and I mean it. Kind of. What's not to like? It's Friday night, we're dancing under the stars, the lights of San Francisco are sparkling in the distance, my friends are here, the waiters are passing along mini egg rolls.

Life is good. Isn't it?

When the song finishes, Miri, Corey, Viv, Karin, Michael, Fitch, the triplets, and even Wendy join us on the dance floor. I kick off my shoes and let the music take over. When you dance, you don't have to think. At least, I don't. Which might be partly why I'm not the world's best dancer, but whatever.

"You okay?" Miri asks me a few songs later.

"Fine! Great! Why?"

"You seem . . . possessed."

I flick her on the arm. "*Thanks*. It's not like I'm already self-conscious enough about my dancing."

"I don't mean it like that. I just—"

"I'm fine! It's all good!"

The music is thumping, and we're dancing and I'm having a ball. I am.

This is my world. The witch world.

When another slow song comes on, Adam beelines for me. He takes my hand and pulls me into him. "I really like you," he murmurs in my ear.

"Oh. Yeah. Um. I like you too," I say. I do like him. I do. Adam and I make sense.

His smiles and closes his eyes.

I sway back and forth and watch the city lights flicker like candles, making me homesick for New York.

After the party, we land with a thud in the bathroom.

My ears are ringing, and my feet are hurting, but it was a good night. It was.

"You seem weird. Are you upset about Raf?" Miri asks me.

"Yes! Stop bugging me! I had a great time."

She shakes her head. "Mom? We're home!"

"Miri, shush, it's four in the morning here."

She covers her mouth with her hand. "Whoops. I forgot. Then why are all the lights on?"

"Girls?" my mom says. "Can you come into the living room, please? You have a visitor."

We slowly make our way into the other room.

On the couch beside our mother is our dad.

25 A Family Affair

I take a step back, tasting the lump in my throat. What's *he* doing here?

Miri crosses her arms. "I don't want to talk to him."

"Girls," he begins.

"I said I don't want to talk to him," my sister repeats, eyes steely.

"Miri," my mother begins, "I know you're upset. But you need to listen to what your father has to say."

She snorts. "Why? He didn't want to listen to us."

"I'm sorry," my dad says, hanging his head. "I'm sorry I reacted the way I did."

"That's it?" Miri says. "You're sorry. Big deal."

When did Miri get so tough?

"You have every right to be mad at me," he says. "I should have reacted better. I should have listened to you. But can you try to put yourself in my situation for a second?

I had no idea"—he waves his hand in the air—"about any of this. It was a hell of a shock. I found out that my two daughters are witches, and that the woman I had been married to for over ten years is one too. And I had no idea. I was overwhelmed."

I guess that could be a bit of a whammy. "But that was a week ago," I say. "You could have called."

"I know." He looks up at me and meets my eyes. His are rimmed with red. "I'm sorry."

No one says anything.

"I'm sorry too," my mom says. "I know you girls are angry with your dad, but this is mostly my fault. I should have told your dad years ago. It might have saved us all a lot of pain."

"And a lot of money in couple counseling," my dad quips.

My mom laughs. "That too. But more recently, I shouldn't have let you keep such a big secret from your father. Parenting is a shared responsibility, and I should have insisted you tell him about what was happening to you."

"I wish you had told me about you," Dad says to her. "I might have been surprised at first, but I would have gotten over it." He closes his eyes and then turns back to us.

"Does that mean—" A sob escapes my lips before I can stop it. "Does that mean you still love us?"

"Oh, girls, of course I still love you. I will *always* love you." He opens his arms. "Come here. Do you still love me?"

Without thinking, I run to my dad. The tears are flowing and I'm sobbing and nodding and he's patting my hair, telling me that it's all going to be okay. Yeah, he screwed up, but he's here now. He needed some time to get used to the idea.

Unlike me, Miri is still standing apart. "Are you gonna come to our Samsorta?" She picks at her fingers. I almost yell at her not to ruin her nails now (after a week of no biting, they're just starting to heal), but it hardly seems like the right time.

"If you want me," my dad says, "I'll be there. What's a Sumorsta?"

"It's like a group bat mitzvah for witches," I say. "And I want you there." He smells good. Like home. Like Dad. I wipe my fresh tears away with the back of my hand.

"Do you want me there?" he asks Miri.

"I want you to *want* to be there," she replies, clasping her hands behind her back.

"Then there is nothing I want more than to come to your Sumorsta," he says.

I giggle. "*Samsorta.*"

"*Samsorta,*" he repeats. "I guess I'm going to have a lot to learn. And maybe next weekend you can show me what you can do with these powers."

"A little Jedi action?" I say.

"Exactly."

I hug him tighter.

Today is the dress rehearsal, except without the dresses. Also, we're at Lozacea because apparently, witches are allowed in Zandalusha only once a year, which is fine by me. It still sounds creepy.

The other difference about today's class is that our alimities, aka our moms, are here too.

Mom recognizes Karin's mom from the old days, and then Karin's mom introduces her to Viv's mom. Hey, maybe the two of them can be New York witch friends.

Once we're all in the auditorium and on the stage, we run through the whole ceremony from start to finish. Well, as much as we can without any of the other schools.

First up, we practice the opening march.

Next we practice the alimity bit. There's lots of giggling, and lots of listening to our moms tell us how "It feels like just yesterday when I was on the other side of the circle," which is kind of funny. Our moms! Having their Samsortas! Seems impossible, but I've seen the pics, so I know it happened.

Next our moms take turns asking us if we are willing to join the circle of magic. This part starts with the oldest Samsorta, which I kind of assumed was me. But Fizguin announces that the oldest woman is a twenty-four-year-old Australian from the Kanjary school.

I'll admit it. I'm kind of disappointed.

Anyway, after our moms ask us, we practice agreeing, and then they pretend to remove a lock of our hair with the golden knife.

Miri and I both have hair appointments with Este on Monday morning (Mom's letting us both take the entire day off school), and in addition to getting our hair done, we're going to get her opinion on what Mom can cut without ruining our do's.

Next our moms all practice walking toward the central cauldron and pretend to drop the piece of hair in the center. Once they're done, it's time for the Chain of Lights service. We go around the circle, saying the light spell, setting the candle aflame one final time.

I'm about halfway into the circle, and I clear my throat before beginning.

"*Isy boliy donu*
Ritui lock fisu . . ."

I do the whole thing, no problem. Once my candle is lit, I listen as Miri does hers and then wink when she's done.

The warmth of the flame feels nice against my cheeks. I think about how even though my dad said he was coming, Miri still wouldn't hug him. My dad seemed to understand. "Take your time," he told her. "I'm not going anywhere."

He didn't mean that literally, obviously, since he wasn't moving back in with us. But you know. We decided that he and Jennifer would come to the Sam, but that they'd get a babysitter for Prissy. My dad thought it was best for everyone if Prissy was kept in the dark about our magic until she was older. They'd told her that the scene she had witnessed the other day was a dream. My heart feels full that my dad came around.

But as the wax drips down my fingers, I can't help wondering if Raf would have come around too.

We're done early, around three Lozacea time.

"Get a good night's sleep Monday night!" Fizguin orders. "And I'll see you at six Romanian time, which is nine Arizona time, or noon on the East Coast. Don't be late!"

The moms all go home, and we head to the atrium to decide what to do now. After all, it's Saturday.

"What are you doing here?" I ask when I spot Adam and the rest of the guys in the atrium.

"Waiting for you," he says. "We thought we should celebrate your last day."

"Are you guys hungry?" Karin asks.

"Starving," Michael says.

"I'm in the mood for pizza," Preppy Triplet says.

"I know the best new place," Miri says. "It's called T's Pies."

"Yo, I've heard of it," Viv says. "I've been wanting to try it."

What? T's? That's what she wants to eat? I shoot Miri a dirty look, but she won't catch my eye. She's looking at Corey instead.

"We can conjure it up in the caf," I say.

"But conjuring up food is kind of like delivery, and T's Pies is best straight out of the oven," Miri says. "Why don't we all go to New York?"

"Sounds good," Adam says, putting his arm around me.

My shoulders inadvertently tense, but I quickly unclench them. So we're going to T's Pies? No big deal. So he has his arm around me? Also no big deal. He likes me. I like him. We all like pizza. This is the plan.

"Go spell?" Karin asks.

"Batteries," I say. "The bathroom in that place is kind of cramped."

We zap ourselves into the alley behind the restaurant and then head inside. As we get closer, my heart starts beating faster. Miri is still avoiding my gaze.

We grab a table for eight. I sit facing the door, and Adam slides into the seat beside me.

When I pick up a menu, I realize that my hands are all sweaty. I've been reading the same pizza description over and over again.

"Rachel? That okay with you? Two pies for the table, one cheese, one with everything?"

I nod, squirming in my seat. What's wrong with me? So what if this is Raf's place? It's over with him. I'm better off without him. He's better off without me.

When I'm a few bites into my pizza, it happens. The door swings open.

Dark hair. Brown shirt. Leather jacket. My stomach swoops. Raf. He's here! Except . . .

Same hair. Same shirt. Same jacket. But not Raf. My heart sinks.

My eyes fill. I put down my slice. Why did Miri bring me here?

"What's wrong?" Adam asks me. "You're hardly eating."

I look back at the door. That guy looked nothing like Raf. Not his eyes, not his smile . . . I look down at my mostly untouched slice. "It's nothing," I say. Why am I still thinking about Raf? Raf is history! Adam is my future. He's funny. He's cute. He's a warlock. He gets me. I force my eyes up to meet Adam's and smile, then look back down at my plate.

The conversation swirls around me until we're done. Eventually, we pay the bill and spill back onto the street.

"Yo, what now?" Viv says.

"Let's go to the Empire State Building!" Preppy Triplet says. "I've never been. If I was a guy, I totally would have my Sim there."

The gang agrees to check it out. We return to the alley and then begin disappearing. Adam puts his hand on my arm before I can go. "Wait, Rachel, hold on a sec."

"Sure."

Miri looks at me questioningly.

I nod for her to go ahead.

"You sure?" she asks. " 'Cause we can just go home. And hang out."

"Go," I say, turning my back, still annoyed with her for bringing me here.

I hear her and Corey disappear.

I look at Adam. "What's up?"

He takes a step closer to me. Lifts his hand. Runs his fingers through my hair.

My heart stops.

He's going to kiss me. Adam is going to kiss me. This is it. Adam is going to kiss me and we're going to be the perfect witch couple and live happily ever after. And it's really going to be over between me and Raf.

It's going to feel over. Finally.

He leans in closer. And closer. And presses his lips against mine.

And—

I wait. For the charge. For the fireworks. For the magic.

But there's nothing. His lips are cold. Thin. Kissing Adam feels like kissing my pillow.

I pull back and touch his shoulder.

He blinks, confused.

"I can't," I say.

He looks at the ground. Neither of us speaks. In the distance, we hear a succession of honking.

Eventually, he says, "You're not over him yet, are you?"

I want to tell him I am. I really do. But I can't. I can't lie to him. But worse, I can't lie to myself. I shake my head.

He cocks his head and gives me a half smile. "Do you think you'll be over him soon?"

I swallow hard. "I'm so sorry, Adam." And I am sorry. So sorry. Sorry this didn't work, sorry I don't feel the way he does, sorry he's hurting.

He closes his eyes for a second and then opens them. "I'm sorry too."

"Don't hate me," I say sadly.

"I could never," he tells me, then sighs again. "Friends?"

I nod. "Nothing would make me happier."

He shuffles his feet. "But would you hate me if I wasn't your date on Tuesday? I think it might be too weird for me."

I squeeze his shoulder. "I totally understand. But you're still going to be there, right?"

"Yeah. The triplets have a seat for me."

We're both silent.

"Should we go meet up with them?" he asks finally.

"You go ahead," I say. "There's someone I need to talk to."

"Raf?" he asks, with a hint of bitterness.

"No," I say, shaking my head. "But someone just as important."

"Brace yourself," I tell Tammy.

"Okay," she says. "I'm braced. What's going on?"

I called her from the alley and told her I really needed to talk. She was at Annie's but came over to my house immediately, no questions asked. Of course I beat her here, since zapping is faster than the subway. Anyway, as soon as she got here, I brought her to my room and closed the door. When she sat on my bed, I sat on my computer chair. I want to give her some space in case she freaks. And she might. But I'm hoping she won't. I'm hoping she'll be willing to listen—because she's my best friend and best friends should be able to talk about anything. And I need to talk.

But first things first.

I take a deep breath, close my eyes, then let it pour out. "I'm a witch."

No answer. Nothing. Has she passed out? I open one eye and see that Tammy is sporting the biggest smile I've ever seen.

I open both eyes. "Huh?"

"I knew it!" she exclaims, punching an arm into the air.

"What do you mean? Wait. Don't tell me." How could she possibly know? Unless . . . "You're a witch too?"

She laughs. "I wish. But no. I figured it out. See, I've

been keeping an eye on Wendaline—sorry, Wendy, I keep forgetting she wants us to call her that—and last week she kind of disappeared. Literally. Cassandra was coming her way and she ducked into a classroom and she just—*vamoosh*—disappeared. One second I was watching her and the next she was gone. She didn't know I was watching, but I remember her saying that she was a witch on the first day of school. I didn't take her that seriously then, but when I saw her disappear, I thought maybe she hadn't been lying." She takes a quick breath. "It seemed crazy to me, but I thought, you never know, right? Who am I to say what's real and what's not? So when I found her later, I asked her if she really was a witch. She got all nervous and started mumbling that you were going to be mad. But then she admitted it. That she was a witch! So I asked if you knew, and she got all freaked out and said no, but then she made me promise not to say anything to anyone, especially you. And you've been acting weird lately. And there was the fashion show last year, and that weird other language thing this year, and the cupcake and I don't know. I just wondered. And it's true! You're a witch too!"

I push my chair a few inches closer to the bed. "So you're not afraid of me?"

Her eyes dance. "No! Not at all!"

A few inches closer. "And you don't think it's weird?"

"No! I think it's the coolest thing ever."

"Really?"

"Really. I'm so happy you told me. I'm honored that you told me. That you feel you can confide in me."

Aw. I throw my arms around her.

"I have so many questions," she says as soon as I let go. "Did you always know you were a witch? How do spells feel? Did you—"

"I'll tell you everything," I say, "but first I have to ask you something."

"Anything."

Well. "There's this debutante-slash-bat-mitzvah-slash-quinceañera witch party thing on Monday. It's during the day on an island off of Romania. I should add that it's in a cemetery, totally top-secret, and formal. Wanna be my plus one?"

"I'm so there," she says, and gives me a thumbs-up. "Now, start at the beginning."

26 The Big Day

Happy Halloween!

After our very early hair appointment, I drag Miri for her first-ever manicure. But while we're waiting for our turn, she's totally ignoring me, yammering on the phone.

"Miri," I whine. "I'm bored. Talk to me."

"One sec," she says. "Cor? I have to go. My sister's complaining. I'll see you soon? Yeah . . . okay, hang up. . . . No, you hang up! . . . No you! . . . No you hang up!"

"Who speaks to her boyfriend with a baby voice?" I say in a baby voice of my own. "Who does? Is it you? I liked it better when you just squeaked."

She turns bright red. "I gotta go," she tells him, and hangs up.

Hilarious.

Obviously, I speak to her in a baby voice for the rest of the appointment.

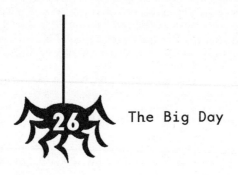

At least by the time we're done her fingers look somewhat normal. I even treat. I kind of owe her for forcing me to go to T's Pies and confront my feelings for Raf. Sisters sure are sneaky. Clever, but sneaky.

After our manicure, we head over to Bloomie's for a little makeup application.

Of course I buy the new products. Hello, it's rude not to.

Back home, we change into our outfits and get ready for everyone to arrive.

The plan is to meet at our apartment, take some pictures (maybe to show our daughters one day?), and then head over to Zandalusha.

When I say everyone, I don't mean our entire guest list, I just mean those of the nonmagical variety, i.e., Dad, Tammy, and Lex. Oh, and Corey.

Not Raf.

I thought about inviting him. Of course I did. My dad got over it, and Tammy is super-excited. So maybe Raf would be cool with it too? Maybe I'd apologize, tell him the truth—and then invite him to be my date.

But I talked it over with Tammy and here was her advice: "Telling Raf is a big decision. A really big decision. And it shouldn't be rushed by a dance. Tell him if you want him to know, but don't tell him just because you want him to be your date."

So mature, that Tammy. Telling *her* was my best decision yet. And she's right. I might want to tell Raf. But I need a clear head—and heart—first. Let me finish with this Samsorta business first and then decide what to do.

When I get dressed, I add the heart he bought me for my birthday back to the chain. For luck.

Anyway, Tammy squeals when she sees Miri and me all dressed up in our heliotrope finery. She looks very pretty in the black dress she wore to prom.

"Do you want to try it in another color?" I ask her. "Not that yours doesn't look great, but I can zap it for you."

"Seriously?" she asks, eyes wide.

"Absolutely."

"Sure."

"Green would look wonderful on you," I say. "It would bring out your eyes."

"Go for it."

I use the color-changing spell and zap her.

"That," says Tammy, looking down at her new gown, "was the coolest thing ever."

When my dad arrives, his eyes get teary at the sight of Miri and me. "You both look so beautiful and grown-up."

He looks pretty handsome himself in his tux and black bow tie. I'm about to offer to zap his bow tie into another color, but decide not to push it. He'll be witnessing more than enough magic tonight.

Despite the fact that Jennifer's still smiling her please-don't-zap-me smile, and she has my dad's hand in a death grip, she's looking pretty stunning in a floor-length black ball gown. I'm hoping it doesn't take her too long to get over her fear that we're going to use her for spell-casting practice.

Dad shakes hands with Lex, gives Tammy and my mom a hello hug, and meets Corey for the first time. Corey calls him sir, which is pretty adorable. My dad laughs and tells him to call him by his first name.

Corey is already in my good book. Not only did he bring Miri a corsage, he brought me one too.

He's a keeper.

After about a hundred pictures ("Oh, come on, just a few with the hats. Please?" Mom begs), Mom asks us if we're all ready. "Let me just put a bowl of candy out for the trick-or-treaters in the building, and we're off."

"I guess we'll use the batteries?" I say. I don't know who's going to take who, but I know I don't want to ruin my hair with the go spell. It'll go through enough trauma today with the upcoming trim.

"I brought my passport!" Tammy exclaims. "Just in case."

"Not necessary," I tell her.

"Er, how does this work?" my dad asks nervously.

Corey pats his back. "Just climb on and close your eyes, sir."

Jennifer grabs hold of my father and looks like she might hyperventilate.

Mom pulls a long braided gold rope out of the cleaning closet. "Actually, I have an easier way. I hold the batteries and you all hold on to this. It'll be like the kids at day care walking down Fifth Avenue."

"Adorable," I say.

It's happening. Finally.

They've handed out the candles.

The cemetery isn't as creepy as I'd imagined. It's actually

pretty gorgeous in a hauntingly beautiful sort of way. It looks like the Grand Canyon, with cliffs and tons of space. The auditorium is built right into the stone and reminds me of the Pantheon. The stone seats are in fact gravestones, and while you'd think this would be supremely spooky, it isn't. It makes me feel like we're somehow being protected by all the women who came before us. Fizguin explains that once the ceremony is over, the seats will sink into the ground and the whole area will morph into a ballroom under the stars.

But now it's time for the ceremony. Our friends, relatives, and extended family we've never met are in their seats, hushed and waiting. My whole family made it over here intact. Jennifer screamed for most of it, but at least my dad didn't pass out. In fact, he whistled when we landed, and called the experience "wild."

Now our school is in line behind the girls from Charm School and in front of the Asian girls from Shi. I wave to Wendy, who's up front. She looks pretty in her long, gauzy heliotrope dress. Pretty but nervous. She has a big job to do today, since she's the one in charge of the wonderment spell.

"Let's go, girls," says a tall woman in a long black robe.

Miri squeezes my hand. And it begins.

The ceremony starts off just as it did in rehearsal.

Except instead of just our mothers here to watch, there are more than a thousand pairs of eyes on us.

The other things on us are the ridiculous hats. Yes, apparently Mom was right. Everyone's wearing a matching witch hat. I hope no one loses an eye. These things are pointy!

After we're all in our spots, we start the alimity bit. It takes a while for the golden knife to get to Mom, but when it does, she asks in a voice that carries though the night, "Are you ready to join the circle of magic?"

"Yes," Miri says, lowering her head so Mom can easily cut off a piece of her hair. When she's done, she moves over to me.

"Are you ready to join the circle of magic?" she asks me.

"Yes," I answer, and show her exactly which piece of hair to cut. No reason to take unnecessary risks, right?

Next up is the candle lighting. We slowly go around the circle, each saying our spell.

I thought I'd be nervous, but I'm not. I know this spell and I'm in control of my pillars. I've been honest with myself, I trust my family and friends, I had the courage to confide in my friend, I feel loved and am loved, and I have decent karma. I hope. I've learned a lot since June and I'm ready.

When it's my turn, I chant the spell loud and clear.

"Isy boliy donu
Ritui lock fisu
Coriuty fonu
Corunty promu binty bu
Gurty bu
Nomadico veramamu."

My candle's wick bursts into flame. Wahoo!

Miri goes next and she says the spell, just as loudly and as clearly. Her flame zings just as high.

I bump my hip against hers and we give each other a big smile. We did it. "Yay," I mouth.

"Yay," she mouths back.

We continue around the circle. Glamour Triplet struggles once, twice, and then three times, but her sisters squeeze her shoulders and then she gets it right. Sister power!

Finally, we complete the circle with Wendy.

She lights her candle, no problem, and then slowly walks to the central cauldron.

Here it is. The last step. After this it's party time!

Wendy holds her candle over the cauldron. She has to hold it strong while all of us repeat the wonderment spell after her.

"*Julio vamity*," she begins.

"*Julio vamity*," we repeat. It means *on the pillars*.

"*Cirella bapretty!*" she finishes.

"*Cirella bapretty!*" we repeat. That means *blooms something wonderful*. That's it! Short and sweet.

We all wait for the cauldron to catch fire.

And wait.

And still wait.

Uh-oh.

After a few seconds, Wendy tries again. "*Julio vamity*," she says, her voice shaking.

"*Julio vamity*," we repeat. What's going on? Wendy

shouldn't be having any problems with this. She's one of the best witches I've ever seen. She can do anything!

"*Cirella bapretty!*" she says again.

"*Cirella bapretty!*" we repeat.

And then wait.

Still nothing. Her hands begin to shake as she starts the spell over again.

"Poor Wendaline," Miri whispers to me.

Wendaline.

Oh, no. I almost drop my candle, but I steady my hand.

I changed her name. I changed her clothes. I changed her hair. I changed her makeup. I made her lie to her friends. I think back to the time my go spell wouldn't work and to what Miri told me. When I disguised my true self, my magic got funky. My pillars got blocked.

Wendy—no, *Wendaline*—needs everything to be perfect or our wonderment spell will never work.

It's up to me to make it right.

27 You Never Know

I need to do something, but what? I need to return her to the way she was before I messed her up.

She needs to be Wendaline again.

I close my eyes, focus on her, and think with all my might:

All the changes I've made,
Please undo.
Wendy become Wendaline again.
I miss the real you.

As I say it, I realize it's the truth. I miss her long hair. I miss calling her Wendaline. I miss her crazy outfits. She is who she is, and she should be proud. I'm the one who should be ashamed.

A rush of cold flows through me, and I cover my flame so it stays lit.

It works. In front of the entire witch world, Wendaline's

hair grows all the way down to her waist. Her nails go from pink to black, and her makeup gets darker. The colors of her dress get richer, her train gets longer, and her whole being seems to sparkle.

All thousand people in the audience gasp.

She seems as startled as everyone else, and looks around for an explanation. I wink.

"Thank you," she mouths.

"I'm sorry, Wendaline," I mouth back.

"*Julio vamity*," she says again, loud and clear.

"*Julio vamity*," we repeat, the excitement building.

"*Cirella bapretty!*" she finishes, smiling. She knows this is it. We know it is too.

"*Cirella bapretty!*" we call out, our voices united.

Abrakazam! The cauldron bursts into flame.

We all whoop and cheer.

I toss my hat into the air, and everyone follows.

I ask my dad to dance the first song with me, and he happily accepts. I try to teach him the surky. We get all the moves wrong, but it doesn't matter. "I'm so proud of you," he tells me, and my spirit soars.

The singer is Robert Crowne. Twice in two weeks! How lucky am I? Not that luck has much to do with it. It's all about magic. He must be enchanted. Or maybe he's a warlock!

There's a huge meal, but who can eat at a time like this? Instead, all of us witch kids (and friends of witch kids) dance our butts off and have a blast.

The only thorn in my side is that I have to talk to my cousin Liana. When I return to my table for a quick water break, she slinks up beside me.

"You've become quite the witch socialite, haven't you?" she asks, flicking her long glossy hair off her shoulder.

"Not exactly," I say.

"Where's your boyfriend? He couldn't make it?"

"We broke up," I tell her.

"Really?" she asks. "He dumped you?"

"No!"

"You dumped him? I thought you really liked him."

"I do."

"Then why did you break up?"

An excellent question, brought to you by Liana. One I don't have a ready answer for. "Well—" I begin.

"Hey," she interrupts in typical Liana fashion, "are you friends with Adam Morren?"

"Yeah," I say warily.

"Will you introduce me? He's hot."

"Um . . ." He might not be the guy for me, but that doesn't mean I'm fixing him up with my evil cousin. No way. "I don't think so." Without waiting for a reply, I spin around and head back to the dance floor.

Now where did everyone go? My dad and Jennifer are dancing and my mom and Lex are talking with a couple. Old friends? The guy looks familiar. Do I know his son?

No! It's the guy from the album! Jefferson Tyler! Ha! Small witch world, I guess.

Smiling, I head off to find everyone else. I push through the dance floor and spot Miri and Corey. Miri's arms are wrapped around his neck, and they're looking at each other very seriously. And then—

"Omigod, he's going to kiss her!" I practically scream, and then clamp my hand over my mouth. Not that they can hear over the music.

I watch transfixed as Corey presses his lips against hers. Oh. My. God. It's happening! It's happening! I want to rush over to congratulate her, but I restrain myself. 'Cause that would be weird. I'm feeling a bit creepy for watching but I can't turn away! But her mouth is open! They're French kissing!

She seems to be remembering everything I taught her. Okay. I'll stop watching now.

Look away. Look. Away.

I turn around in search of someone else to talk to. And that's when I see something equally shocking. No, more shocking. The most shocking thing I've ever seen. The red hair. The turned-up nose.

Could it be?

No.

But it is. "Melissa?" I ask unbelievingly.

My archnemesis turns to face me. She's looking stunning in a long black ball gown. "I thought it was you up there," she grumbles.

"What . . . what are you doing here?" She's a witch? My intuition rocks. Didn't I ask Miri if she was a witch? I knew it! Kind of.

"Not having my Sam, obviously." She crosses her arms. "This sucks. Why do you get everything?"

"Me? What are you talking about?" This is the girl who

stole my best friend and repeatedly tries to steal my boyfriend. I mean, my ex-boyfriend.

"What . . . who . . . why are you here?" I can't wrap my brain around seeing her.

"The triplets are my cousins," she says.

"Are you a witch too?" I ask.

"No," she snaps. "Not yet. My mom's a witch. My dad's a warlock. My two older sisters are witches. But me? Not a magical bone in my body, apparently. Even my boyfriend, Jona, is a warlock."

Boyfriend? "I didn't know you had a boyfriend. I thought . . ." My voice trails off.

"That I was still after Raf? No way. Raf was just a fling. Jona is the real thing. We met this summer. He's the cutest. He's here." She stands on her tiptoes and looks around. "Somewhere."

"I can't believe it," I say, still stunned.

"You can't believe what?"

"Everything," I say with a laugh.

"Yeah, well, believe it. Here I am. A wannabe witch."

After a whole year of hating her, I suddenly feel bad. "You never know," I say. "I bet your powers will kick in soon."

"I've been saying that for the last three years. I even signed up for Samsorta lessons this year in case, but I didn't qualify. . . . I'm going to be the oldest witch to get her powers in the history of the world."

So she's the one who tried to fake it! I surprise myself by putting my arm on her shoulder. "You won't be. I know you won't be." Now I know why she's always scowling.

"You do?" she asks eagerly. "How?"

"Call it intuition." Sure, I'm usually wrong, but whatev.

For the first time ever, she smiles at me. "Thanks, Rachel. You have no idea how much it sucks waiting for your powers to kick in."

Hee hee.

She makes a move to leave but I hold on to her arm. "Wait, Melissa? Quick question?"

"What?"

"Did you ever tell Jewel?"

"Tell Jewel what?"

"About your powers. Or lack of powers. About all this," I clarify.

"No way," she calls out, and disappears into the crowd.

Ironic. Jewel dumped me for Melissa, yet she doesn't even know who Melissa really is.

And now Jewel is at home by herself, while Tammy, my *new* best friend, is here with me, having the time of her life. Now, that's karma.

Smiling to myself, I make my way back to my friends. I spot the triplets; Viv and her cute but kind of greasy-looking norlock boyfriend, Zach; Karin and her also super-handsome boyfriend, Harvey; Fitch; Rodge; Adam; and Tammy. Except for Zach, who's in a seersucker suit, the group are all looking handsome in black tuxes.

Wait. Adam is dancing with Tammy. How did that happen?

"Hi!" Tammy exclaims when she sees me. "I was looking for you, but I found Viv and Zach." I had introduced Viv and Tammy earlier in the night and they'd hit it off. Then she leans into me and whispers, "And this guy is *so* cute. I've been dancing with him for like ten minutes. Do you know him?"

"That's Adam," I say, and wiggle my eyebrows.

"Oh God! I'm sorry. I had no idea," she squeals. "I won't dance with him again, I promise!"

"No, don't worry at all," I tell her, fully meaning it. "Dance with him as much as you want. He's a great guy. Just not for me."

She shakes her head.

"Dance with him!" I order. "I insist. My cousin is after him, and I'd much, much, much rather see him with you than with her."

She shakes her head again.

"Adam," I holler.

He turns. "Rachel," he says with a smile. "Congrats."

"Thank you," I say. "I want you to meet my very good friend Tammy, and I want you guys to keep dancing. Because you're two of my favorite people, and I think you guys would make a great couple."

They both turn bright red.

All right, maybe that was T.M.I. "Just enjoy yourselves, kids!" I say.

"Okay," he says, and gives me a mock salute.

I feel a tug on my arm, and it's Miri and Corey, finally up for air, both smiling.

"We did it!" I holler, giving her a high five. Then I add in a low voice, "And I saw you kissing."

"Finally," she tells me. She gives me a hug. "Thanks."

"For what?"

"For everything. For doing the Samsorta for me. For being the best big sister ever."

"No, you're the best sister ever," I say in the baby voice.

"No, you!" she says in hers.

Then Crowne launches into the Police's "Every Little Thing She Does Is Magic" and the crowd goes wild.

28 Trick or Treat

The party lasts until two. All the old people (my dad, Jennifer, Mom, Lex—basically everyone over thirty) have called it a night, and now it's just the kids. ("Are you sure you don't mind if we go?" Jennifer asked before she left. "Are you positive? Whatever you want, girls, tell me! I'll do it!") But when the gravestones start shifting back to their original positions, we know it's time.

"Where to now?" Karin asks. "We need an after-party."

"How about the Halloween parade in the East Village?" Miri says. "That should be starting around now."

"Oh, fun!" everyone cheers.

So we zap ourselves back to New York and find ourselves a spot on Sixth Avenue. With our hats back on, we fit right in. We cheer for all the people in costume as they pass us by: the devils, angels, hamburgers, buildings, cartoon characters. All these people, coming out in honor of our Samsorta, without even realizing it!

"Having fun?" I ask Tammy, slinging my arm through hers.

"The best time ever," she says and gives me the scuba okay sign with her fingers. Her nose is bright red from the cold.

"And Adam?" I say. I've been noticing the way he looks at her. Like he's bewitched.

"He *is* cute," she says. "But I will never speak to him again if you care about him even in the slightest."

"Tammy, nothing would make me happier than seeing you two together," I tell her. "If only Raf and I were still together, we could witch-double!"

"Do you miss him?" Tammy asks me.

"More than anything," I say.

She turns away from the parade and faces me. "Then let's go," she says.

"Where?"

"You know," she says.

"I do?" I ask. But then I realize. I do.

"Whip out that battery," she orders. "It's time to get Raf back."

I nod. It *is* time to get Raf back. "I think we can walk. School is only a few blocks away."

"Oh, come on," she says with a glint in her eye. "The batteries are fun!"

Frankenstein parades by us. "I hope I haven't created a monster," I say.

The school gym is decorated like a haunted house. There are skeleton cutouts pasted to the door, and the fog machine is on full blast inside.

When we pay the entrance ticket, Kat throws her arms around us. "I'm so glad you made it! I thought you weren't coming! Wow, you guys look gorgeous! And you brought so many people! You're the best!"

I hadn't been planning on dragging along the whole gang, but it's harder to shake a group of witches and warlocks than you'd think.

I sniff something familiar. "You smell great! Like . . . what is that?"

"My new perfume! I just picked it up a few hours ago! What do you think? It's supposed to smell like Paris!"

Interesting. Could that be our Sam *giftoro*? It's no Grand Canyon, but it sure is fun. "It's magical," I say. I look around. "Is Raf here?"

"He left," she says, and gives me a knowing look. "He didn't seem to be having too much fun."

"He left?" I repeat.

"Just two seconds ago," she says. "He's probably just around the corner."

I take off. I have to find him. I have to tell him. Tonight.

I run down the street and spot him about to turn the corner. I know it's him because I can still see the avoiding spell. "Raf!" I scream. He's wearing another new leather jacket, this one with funky green stitching. A Raf original, I'm guessing.

He turns around and sees me.

I'm too far away to read the expression on his face, but I don't stop running until I reach him. "Raf," I say, out of breath.

"Hey," he says, but I can't read his eyes.

Up close I see that under his funky new jacket, he's wearing all yellow. He's mustard. Mustard without his ketchup.

"I need to talk to you," I say.

He looks at the ground. "About the other guy?"

"There's no other guy," I say, shaking my head. "There never was. I mean, he exists. I just never had feelings for him."

"But then why did you break up with me?" His eyes are filled with confusion. His beautiful brown eyes.

Here it is. The real moment of truth. But I need him to know. Sure, he might get freaked out. He might get scared. But I have to try. I have to give him a chance to *get* me. I take both his hands. He looks back up at me. And I jump right in. "I know what I'm about to say sounds crazy. But just listen. I'm a witch. My mother is a witch. My sister is a witch. And I don't mean dressed like a witch, which I am. Kind of. I mean an actual witch with magical powers." The words are pouring out fast, but I want—no, I need—to get them all out. "And at first I was going to tell you. But then, see, I told my dad, and he freaked out. Didn't talk to me for a week. So then I decided that I wasn't going to tell you. Ever. But then I decided that you deserve more than that. We deserved more than that. So I broke up with you. And told you I was with Adam. When it had nothing to do with Adam. He's just a warlock friend—a friend who might be hooking up with Tammy as we speak, actually. But anyway."

I stop to judge his expression, but he's still just staring. He hasn't let go of my hands, though. That's a good sign, right? Of course, he could be frozen in shock. I take a breath and continue. "See, my dad got over it, and I hope you can too. Because I love you. I really truly do. See?" I point to my necklace. "I'm still wearing your heart. I'm also wearing a broom charm that I got, because my magic is also important to me. You both are. But anyway. I love you. And I hope that you still love me. I know you probably need proof, so here's what I'm going to do. I'm going to turn your outfit red." I take a breath. "Are you ready?"

He still hasn't let go of my hands. He nods.

I chant:

"Like new becomes old,
Like live becomes dead,
Raf's Halloween costume,
Please become red!"

Okay, I know that mentioning death might freak him out, but the only other option was "Like single becomes wed," and that definitely would have sent him running. Hello, he's a teenage boy.

(And no matter what happens, I'm adding my color spells to the spell book tonight. It's only fair that I share my spell brilliance with the world, no?)

A rush of cold, and zap!

His pants and shirt quiver and then darken to red. His jaw drops.

"Crazy, huh?"

He nods. Closes his mouth. He still hasn't let go of my hands.

"Raf? You still with me?"

He nods again, looking dazed.

"And I just want to tell you again how much I love you," I add. " 'Cause I do."

He opens his mouth again.

"Yes?" I say, my heart thumping.

"I think I might be in shock," he says, "and I know I need time to absorb everything you just said. But all I keep thinking is, *She loves me!*"

My heart soars. "Really?"

"Yeah." He looks back down at his outfit. "Although I might have some questions for you tomorrow."

But he doesn't have any questions for me now. And that's good, because it's time to kiss and make up.

"Wait," I say suddenly. "I have a question for *you*. What is Raf short for?"

"Raphael," he says.

"Raphael," I repeat. "I like it."

I lean in for my kiss. Kiss 132.

Instead of standing in the middle of the street, we decide to pop in at the dance. And by *pop*, I mean open the door. I can show him spells tomorrow. I can give him more info then too. Tonight we should just enjoy. (I'm assuming he doesn't need to know the whole "I once put a spell on your brother because I thought it was you" part right away, right?)

When we walk in, I see that my whole gang is still here. Dancing.

"More witches?" he asks, taking in the other heliotrope dresses and hats.

I nod.

"Cool," he says.

Cool! He said *cool*! That's another good sign, right?

Ribbit.

What was that? I look around.

Ribbit.

Wendaline grabs me by the arm. "Rachel," she murmurs. "I may have done something bad."

"What?" I ask, turning to her.

Ribbit.

"Well, Cassandra was here, and as soon as she saw us, she started in again. You know, chanting my name. And you're not going to believe what she was dressed as! The evil witch from *The Wizard of Oz*! With a big fake nose and a black hat and a black cloak! I tried to ignore her but then I saw her bugging Tammy! And I know you wanted me to keep magic out of school, but—"

"Wendaline, forget what I said. Honestly. You be you. Do magic, don't do magic, Appear, disappear . . . do whatever you want."

"I'm glad you feel that way." She raises her hand and shows me a frog on it. A frog in an all-black mini witch's outfit.

Ribbit.

" 'Cause I kind of snapped. I'll turn her back after the

dance. It's all good. And I'm keeping her in my hand so she doesn't get stepped on."

I laugh. I can't help it. I think back to the frog Cassandra put in Wendaline's locker. "If anyone deserved to be turned into a frog, it was Cassandra."

She smiles. "I'm glad you feel that way. But I should warn you—I think she knows I'm a witch now."

"I wouldn't worry about her," I say. "I can't imagine she's going to give you any more problems."

The frog hops out of her hand, and Wendaline chases through the room after it.

So Cassandra knows. And Tammy knows. And Raf knows. Will other people find out too? What will they think? Will they be afraid of me? Shun me? Or think it's cool?

"I'm guessing Wendaline is a witch too?" Raf asks, putting his arm around me.

"You'd have to ask her," I say. Witch honor and all that.

"But she's chasing after a frog. Did that frog used to be a person?"

"It's all good," I tell him, leading him to the dance floor. "I'll explain everything tomorrow. Tonight, we dance."

He pulls me against him. And we're swaying, back and forth. We're dancing. *We're dancing*. Wahoo! It took almost a year, but my number one wish—to dance with Raf at a school social—has finally come true. And I didn't even need to use a spell.

I just needed to be my charming self.

Halfway through the song, Raf asks, "Can you just tell me *who* Wendaline turned into a frog?"

"I think it was her boyfriend," I joke. "So you better be nice to me."

He laughs. "You're kidding, right?"

"Of course I'm kidding!" I plant kiss number 133 on his lips. "I'm one hundred percent kidding."

Er, maybe ninety-nine percent.

You never know, right?

Rachel Weinstein's Mywitchbook.com Profile

Hometown: Manhattan

Magicality: Pink! No, make that sparkly pink . . . hot sparkly pink

Favorite Activities: Math (yes, I know I'm a dork), making up my own spells, riding my bike (fine, not yet, but it's going to be)

Hero: Miri, my little sis

Relationship Status: Truly, madly in love with my Raf/Raphael/shmoopie!

If you had the chance to give your younger self advice on how to live her—well, *your*—life, would you do it?

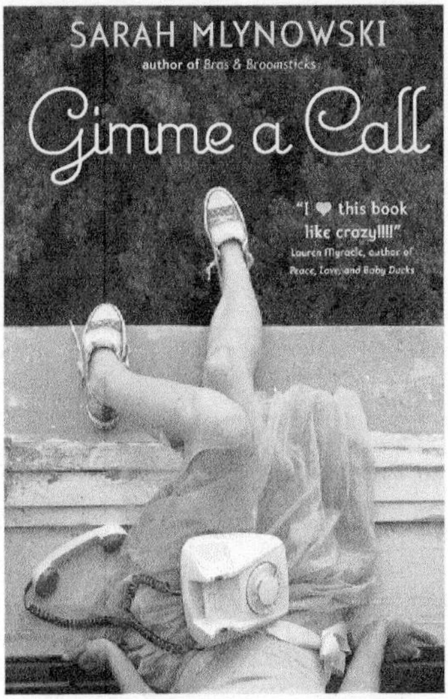

Turn the page for a preview. . . .

CHAPTER ONE

Friday, May 23 • • • Senior Year

I should just return Bryan's watch to Nordstrom and go home. Instead, I'm sitting by the circular fountain in the Stonybrook Mall. Staring and staring at the window of the Sunrise Skin Spa, which features a poster of a wrinkle-free woman and the slogan *Go Back in Time*.

Sounds good to me. If I could go back in time, there's lots I'd tell my younger self. Including:

In third grade, do not let Karin Ferris cut your bangs. Your best friend is no stylist. She's going to accidentally cut them too short. And uneven.

In fifth grade, do not put marshmallows in the toaster oven, even though it seems like a good idea. Toasty! Gooey! Yummy! No. When they expand, the tip of one of the marshmallows kisses the burner, and the toaster catches fire, and your entire family will forever bring up the story about how you almost burnt the house down.

Sophomore year: don't leave your retainer in a napkin in the cafeteria—unless you want to wade through three spaghetti-and-meatball-filled garbage bins to find it.

This December: do not buy the Dolly jeans you like in a size 4 because you believe they will stretch. They don't.

May twenty-first: do not buy Him a silver watch for a surprise graduation present, because then you will spend senior skip day at the mall returning it. Which brings me to the most important point.

Bryan.

If I could go back in time, the most important thing I would tell myself would be this: never *ever* fall for Bryan. I would warn fourteen-year-old me never even to go out with him in the first place. Or even better—the party where we officially met when I was a freshman never would have happened. Okay, the party could have happened, but when he called me later and asked me out, I would have said no. Nice of you to ask but I am just not interested. Thanks but no thanks. Have a nice life. Maybe I'd tell myself to stay home instead and organize my closet.

Imagine that. Talking to my fourteen-year-old self. I wish.

I spot Veronica at Bella Boutique, right beside the Sunrise Skin Spa. She waves. I wave back. "Devi! Come see my new stock!" she calls. "It's so hot!" As if I'd listen to her. She's the one who swore up and down that my jeans would stretch. "I'll give you the employee discount!" she offers, even though I haven't worked a shift since the winter holidays.

"I'll come look in a minute," I call back to her. I rummage through my purse, find my phone, and dial for my messages. I want to hear the one he left this morning. Again. I've only listened to it once. Fine, seven times. I know: pathetic. But I keep hoping each time that it'll be different.

"Hi, Devi. It's me." Bryan's voice is low and raspy, like a smoker's. We tried cigarettes once, together, at the Morgan Lookout on Mount Woodrove when we were sophomores. But when we kissed, he tasted like a dirty sock, so that was the end of our smoking.

Everything goes up in smoke.

"I wish you'd answer," his voice continues. "You always answer." A pause as though he's waiting for me to answer. "I'm sorry. I mean, I'm really, really sorry. I never meant to hurt you."

The message is still playing in my ear, but I can barely hear, because now I'm crying, and my cheeks are all wet and my hand is all wet and how could he have told me he loves me when he obviously doesn't and—

Splash!

Like a bar of soap in the shower, my cell phone has slipped through my fingers and landed in the fountain.

Superb. One more thing to tell my younger (by two seconds) self: don't drop your cell phone into a house-size saucer of green chlorine. I peer into the water. A flash of silver twinkles up at me. Is that it? Nope. It's a nickel. The pond is filled with coins in addition to my phone. Are there really people out there who believe that throwing a nickel into the water can make a wish come true?

Aha! I see it, I see it! I stretch out to reach it, but it's a bit too far away. I lie down on my stomach and reach again. A little more . . . almost there . . .

The cell phone gets pulled farther out of my reach by the swirling water jets within the fountain. Ah, crapola—I'm going to need to get in there.

Luckily, I'm wearing flip-flops. I look around to make sure no security people are watching, then stand on the bench, roll up the bottoms of my oxygen-depriving jeans, and step in.

Cold. Slimy. When I look down, my toes are bloated and tinted green. Maybe the water is radioactive and I'm turning into the Hulk.

Out of the corner of my eye, I spot Harry Travis and Kellerman marching through the mall like they own the place. Harry—definitely one of the best-looking guys in our class—has dark hair, a muscular build, a blinding smile, and the rosiest skin. He also has this sexy stubble going on—very rugged and hot.

And Kellerman—everyone just calls him Kellerman—looks like he's already part of a frat. He's always wearing his older brother's Pi Lambda Phi hat, and I don't think I've ever seen him out of sweatpants.

I duck down so that the coolio senior duo won't see me. That would just make today perfect, wouldn't it? The water soaks through the knees of my jeans. Crap, crap, crap! When the guys turn into the food court, I find my footing and try to relocate my phone. And there it is again! Yahoo! Balanced on top of a pyramid of nickels. Got it. Yes!

Now all I have to do is safely make it back to the side. . . .

Splat. The swirls of water push me over, and the next thing I know, I'm flat on my butt. Great. Just great. My eyes start to prickle.

I heave myself up and back to the safety of the fountain's edge, leaving a trail of shiny green droplets. I ignore my sopping wet jeans—maybe the chemicals will help them stretch?—and wipe my phone against my shirt, as if that's gonna help. Please don't be broken, please, please, please. I press the power button.

No sound. No connection. No nothing.

I spot Veronica staring at me. "You okay?" she hollers.

Um, no? "I'm fine!" I wave, then turn back to the phone. I press power again. Still nothing. I press the one button. Nothing. The two. Nothing. Three, four, five, all nothing. Six, seven, eight, nine, the pound button, the volume button. Nothing, nothing, *nothing*. I kick the floor. My flip-flop makes a squishy sound.

I hit the power button. Again. Nothing.

I hit the nine, the eight, the seven, the six, the five, four, three, two, one, the pound button, the volume button. All nothing.

I press the send button.

There we go. I have no idea who I called, but it's ringing.

CHAPTER TWO

Friday, September 9 • • • Freshman Year

The first time she calls, I'm sitting beside Karin and across from Joelle Caldwell and Tash Havens at our table in the cafeteria, the one in the back next to the garbage. Not ideal, since the location has a definite decaying-meat scent, but as far as I can tell, we're lucky to get any table. Some freshmen are actually sitting on the floor.

My two-week-old cell phone vibrates next to my half-eaten burnt grilled cheese and undercooked fries. Last week at orientation we were told that all us Florence West High School students—I'm finally a high school student! Crazy!—have to keep our cell phones on mute. There's so much vibrating going on in here, you'd think the cafeteria was built over a subway. It isn't, obviously. There is no underground transit in Florence, New York.

"Is that your sis?" Karin asks while slurping down a chocolate milk. "Tell her I say hi."

I get a quick glance at the Banks name on the caller ID and hit send.

"Hey, Maya!" I say, trying not to open my mouth too wide when I talk, as I suspect that a wedge of cheddar might be lodged between my two front braces. I hate these things. Yes, I have clear brackets, so it's not like I have a mouthful of metal, just a metal wire, but ever since I got them on last week, I've been constantly getting food stuck in there. Cereal, grilled cheese, undercooked fries—if it's on a plate, it's most definitely in my braces. "Hi!"

"Hello?"

"Finally! I've left you two messages this week! I know UCLA has a three-hour time difference, but I'm sure a smarty-pants like you can figure out how to get in touch," I tell her.

"Excuse me?" a girl says. A girl who isn't Maya. Huh? I look again at the caller ID but now it's blank.

Hmm. I have no clue who I'm talking to. But her voice sounds familiar, so maybe I should. It's like I'm watching a game show and I know the answer, I do, but it's on the tip of my tongue and I can't get it out. "Who is this?"

"Sorry, I think I called the wrong number," the girl says.

"No problem," I say, and hang up. I return to my grilled cheese.

"So what are you guys doing this weekend?" Karin asks.

"Nothing," Joelle says with a sigh. She uncrosses her über-funky bright green leggings and then adjusts her denim mini and off-the-shoulder blouse. "There is nothing to do. Maybe we should take a shopping road trip."

"To where? Buffalo?" Tash asks.

"Noooo, Buffalo is so lame. Let's go to Manhattan."

"Shall we take our flying bicycles?" Tash asks, rolling her big green eyes behind her glasses. I don't know why she doesn't get contacts. She has the most stunning eyes ever. She hunches over when she sits too. I'd tell her to sit up straight and show off her awesome height and looks-like-a-supermodel's body, but I don't know her well enough yet.

"I wish we didn't live in the middle of nowhere," Joelle whines.

"You can't be bored two weeks into high school," Karin tells her.

"I can and I am," she says. "I'm thinking of joining yearbook. Anyone want to do it with me?"

None of us respond.

"You all suck. I'm going to find out if there are any parties this weekend. See where my future husband, Mr. Jerome Cohen, will be." She wiggles her pierced eyebrow.

I would definitely not mind going to a party with cute boys. I've barely met any since school started.

There are a few hotties in my classes. There's Harry Travis, who has the most amazing smile I've ever seen. His hair is dark, and he has the clearest, rosiest skin. He looks like he could play a TV heartthrob. And there's Joelle's Jerome Cohen, who's obviously off-limits, being Joelle's future husband, but still adorable in his low jeans and nineties band T-shirts. And there's this one guy I've noticed in the halls a few times, whose name I don't know. He doesn't usually stay in school for lunch, and I have no classes with him, but he has cute spiky hair and a big smile. I've never been on the receiving end of the smile, but I'm working on it.

My phone vibrates again. Another wrong number?

Joelle picks it up and squints at the caller ID. "You're calling yourself," she says.

I'm not sure what she means until I glance at the screen and see that it says my number. And my name. Now, that's just weird. "Hello?" I say again.

"Oh, hi," the same girl as before says. "That's weird. I was trying to call my voice mail. I don't know why I keep getting you."

"Don't know why either," I say. I hang up again and take another bite of my sandwich.

The phone vibrates again.

Joelle leans over the table. "Who *is* it?"

I take another look at the caller ID. Still says my number. "Me again," I say. I take a quick sip of my apple juice, trying but failing to unstick the piece of cheddar in my teeth.

"There's something wrong with my phone," the familiar-yet-still-unidentified voice says. "I dialed my mom at work and I still got you. Can you tell me who I called?"

"Devorah Banks," I answer in my polite voice, the one I use with teachers, new people, and dogs. I don't know why I use it with dogs. It might be because the very sight of their big mouths and sharp vampire teeth makes me break out in hives and I hope they'll interpret my courteous tone as a peace offering.

"Oh, good, you know me," she says.

"I do?" I ask.

"Well . . . you just said my name."

I press the phone hard against my ear to try to block out the chaotic noise of the caf. Am I missing something? "What are you talking about?"

"Who is this?" she asks again.

"This is Devorah Ban—" I stop in midname. Why am I giving out personal info to a stranger on the phone? "Sorry, but who is *this*?"

"Look," she barks. "My jeans are sopping in green goo and I'm having a really bad day. Can you please just tell me who I'm talking to?"

"Um . . . ," I say, and then giggle.

I giggle a lot. When I'm nervous, when I'm happy, when I'm around boys, when I'm sitting in class. Seriously. On Monday, I was at Karin's house and I pressed play on her tape recorder. She tapes all her classes, including American history (one of the two classes I have with her)—she's kind of a perfectionist that way—and the next thing I heard was my giggling reverberating around her bedroom. Like a hyena. He-he-he-he-he-he. So awful. Giggling, in American history! There's nothing funny about Ms. Fungas's history class. Except her name, which is downright hilarious. Fungas! Ha!

"Obviously you know me. You just said my name," the girl on the phone snaps. "Are you going to tell me who you are?"

Er. Is this some kind of scam? A telemarketer trying to get my information so she can steal my identity and charge a Thanksgiving trip to Panama on a fake credit card? I wish I had a credit card. Can I steal my own identity? "Would you like to tell me what number you're trying to call?"

"I tried to call my mom's number at work! And before that I tried to call my voice mail! And before that I just hit the send button!" she says, her pitch rising. "But each time, the display just has these weird symbols on it!"

"Well, you called me," I say, starting to get annoyed.

Joelle waves at me from across the table. "Do you know who it is yet?"

I shrug. "No idea."

"Then hang up," she orders. "You're wasting your minutes."

"I think it's a prank," I whisper back. I take another sip of juice to clear my braces.

"Want me to tell him to get lost?" Joelle asks.

"Her," I say, correcting her, and reach across the table to hand her the phone. If someone wants to take control of the situation, I'm happy to let 'em.

"Watch the fries," Tash warns, but her voice is too soft and I hardly hear her.

"What?"

"I said watch the . . . fries."

Too late. I've just dragged my beige sleeve directly through the ketchup.

I jerk my arm and the phone back toward me . . . and right into my Snapple bottle. The bottle teeters—don't spill, don't spill!—but then decides, Why not? tips over, and gushes down the table.

"Whoops!" Fantastic. Must not try to do multiple things at once. Talking on the phone while checking e-mail? I end up typing my conversation. That game in which you try to pat your head with one hand, rub your stomach with the other, click your tongue, and make the *whhh* sound at the same time? If I tried it, I'd probably end up in the emergency room.

"Sorry! I gotta go," I tell the stranger.

I hang up and sprint toward the lunch line in search of napkins.

The phone vibrates inside my backpack when I'm leaving school for the day. I dig around, but my cell has somehow ended up at the bottom of the bag, buried under seven hundred loose pieces of paper, my French conjugation book, *Jane Eyre*, and my American history binder.

"Ready?" Karin asks me. She's waiting for me at the front door.

The phone vibrates again. I scrape my hand on a pencil but finally find it. Maya? I glance at the caller ID.

It says my number. My number is calling me *again*. What is going on? I click the send button. "Hello?"

"It's you," the girl from before says. "Good. I must have misunderstood you earlier. When you said, 'This is Devorah Banks,' you meant *me*, right? As in I'm Devorah Banks? You recognized my voice?"

What is she talking about? "This is Devorah," I say slowly. "Me. *I'm* Devorah. Who are you?"

"This is Devorah Banks!" she screams. "I am Devorah Banks! Just tell me who this is!"

Hotness erupts at the base of my neck and spreads to my cheeks like a bad rash. "I'm. Devorah. Banks."

"You can't be," she says. "That's impossible! I'm hanging

up!" The phone goes dead. A second later, it vibrates. Again, my number.

"Still me," I sing.

"You're crazy!" she screams.

"Alrighty then." I press end, turn off the power, and toss the phone back into my bag. What, am I going to stay on the phone with some nut job who calls me names? I don't think so. There's a tingling on the back of my neck, and I try to scratch it away. I hurry to catch up with Karin. "Sorry."

The mid-September air cools me down like a glass of ice water. Or like wet cotton, which is what I've been wearing since lunch, when I tried, unsuccessfully, to rinse the ketchup out of my shirt.

We spot a pack of students playing softball on the baseball diamond and pause outside the wire fence to watch.

"Tryouts," Karin says, pointing to the scoreboard. "Baseball, basketball, and soccer today; cheerleading, swim, and gymnastics on Monday. I'm so nervous."

"Don't be. You're definitely going to make the gymnastics team."

"Maybe. Maybe not." She twirls a blond ringlet between her fingers.

"Oh, please. You're a shoo-in. You've been doing gymnastics since you were six. You're gonna make it."

"You should try out for something too," she tells me.

"Sure," I say. "Maybe cheerleading."

"I can see that," she says seriously.

I burst out laughing. "Oh, shut up, you cannot. I'm the most inflexible person in the history of the world. Plus I'm too short. Those girls are all gazelles. You be the athlete. I'll be the . . ." My voice trails off. I don't know what I'll be. "Why don't *you* try out for cheerleading?"

"Yeah, right," she says.

"Why not?" I ask.

"First of all, I don't think you can be on both the gymnastics team and the squad. Travel conflicts. And second, I'm not pretty enough to be a cheerleader."

I flick her on the arm. "You are so!"

"Am not." She shakes her ringlets.

Karin will never admit she's pretty—even though she is. She'll say, "My nose is too wide and crooked," or "My eyes are too far apart," or "I have no boobs," even though her nose is fine, her eyes are normally spaced, and a 34B is *not* nothing. I'm a 34B, thank you very much. "Are so."

"You're pretty enough," she says.

"Of course I am," I say with a toss of my hair. Then I giggle. It's not that I think I'm gorgeous or anything, but I'm not insecure about it. Sure, I break out on my nose and forehead, but whatever. Who doesn't? I'm fine with my looks. Or I will be after I get my braces off. I point to the fence. "Wanna watch?" Maybe watching cute boys will cheer her up. It usually cheers me up.

"For a sec. But then my mom's taking me to the mall. I need some new sneakers. Wanna come? I'll treat you to a Cinnabon."

It's not like I'm going to hang out here by myself. "Sure."

Karin points to Celia King, who's sitting on the bleachers. "Joelle got us all invited to her party tonight."

"Seriously?" I ask, impressed.

"Yup."

"Celia's so sparkly," I say. "It's like she bathes in glitter."

"Switch it up!" the referee on the field screams, and everyone on the outfield runs in. A crew of new guys take their places.

Karin holds on to the fence and leans back. "So do you want to go to the party?"

"Obviously," I say. "It's a good thing your parents are friends with Joelle's parents. 'Cause she's certainly connected."

"I know she can be a bit bossy, but she means well."

"I like her," I say. "I like Tash too. I thought she was snobby at first, but I think she's just shy."

"I know. It's because she's so gorgeous. With a little styling—"

"I should warn her not to let you cut her hair. Unless she wants bangs that look like an accordion."

Karin grins. "I'll keep my hands to myself. Promise. You know, Tash is a supposedly a science genius."

"Seriously? I have chemistry with her. She hasn't said much yet."

"I'd pick her as my lab partner if I were you. Joelle told me that her mom died of leukemia back in elementary school and now her goal is to be an oncologist when she grows up so she can cure cancer."

"That's . . . wow," I say. Better than my goal, which is to meet cute boys and avoid getting bacon bits stuck in my braces.

"So tonight," Karin continues, "we're meeting at Tash's at eight and then we'll walk over. Celia lives in Mount Woodrove."

"Fancy." Mount Woodrove is one of the most expensive areas in town.

We watch as a goateed, giant junior at bat whacks the ball and sends it flying into the outfield. And wait! The cute, spiky-haired guy with the fabo smile who I've noticed in the hallways chases after it. Now he's wearing a black and red baseball jersey and running backward to catch the ball, his glove above his head.

He's got it, he's got it, he's got it—he jumps and tries to catch it—he don't got it.

The ball sails way over his spiky hair. Miles over. Like me, he's on the wrong side of five foot five, and when he jumps, he somehow falls backward and lands on his butt. Ow. Spiky immediately springs to his feet, takes off after the ball, grabs it, and shoots it to second base, but it's way too late.

"Safe!" the referee yells.

Spiky shakes his head in defeat, but he's smiling. A big, broad, two-dimpled liquefy-my-heart kind of smile.

"You okay?" Jerome Cohen, the third baseman, asks him. Instead of a jersey, he's wearing an old Foo Fighters T-shirt and ripped jeans.

Spiky salutes him. "I've been working on that move all week."

Cohen laughs.

"Do you know who that is?" I ask Karin. His track pants are covered with dirt, his jersey completely disheveled, but his cheeks are red and he's laughing.

"Jerome Cohen," she says. "That's the guy Joelle has a crush on."

"No, I know *that* guy. He's in my algebra class. I mean the guy who dropped the ball."

"Ryan. He went to Carter. No—sorry, it's Bryan. Bryan Sanderson."

Hello, Bryan Sanderson.

Published by Delacorte Press,
an imprint of Random House Children's Books,
a division of Random House, Inc., New York.